The Ghost Engine

THERESA FULLER

Published by Bare Bear Media
ISBN: 978-1-925748-03-1

Cover by Ravven Kitsune
Interior Photo Credits:
Part of 'Difference Engine No 1' designed by Charles Babbage. From Collection: Museum of Applied Arts and Sciences. Photo: Ryan Hernandez
One of the late Allan Bromley's slide rules. From author's private collection
Interior formatting by Author E.M.S.

Praise for The Ghost Engine

"Theresa Fuller primes *The Ghost Engine* with vivid description to transport readers on a steam punk journey into a dangerous world with her defiant heroine in this audacious challenge to Victorian oppression laced with historical insight."

— Gregory Lamberson, author of
Johnny Gruesome and *Black Creek*

"*The Ghost Engine* is a non-stop thrill ride fueled by adventure and suspense. Readers will find themselves captured by a magical world where the concepts of humanity and AI become blurred and reality loses its meaning. This one will have you turning the pages faster and faster to keep up."

— JG Faherty, author of *The Cure*,
Ghosts of Coronado Bay, and *The Burning Time*

"*The Ghost Engine* is a sharp and intriguing re-imagining of the Ada Lovelace/Charles Babbage Analytical Engine. The writer takes us on a fantastical journey into the heart of the Engine, and the societal struggles of women at that time."

— Amanda J Spedding, two-time
Australian Shadows Award winner
(*short fiction; graphic novel*)

Dedicated to my family, in particular my son, Tim.

Sincere thanks and deepest appreciation to my mentors:
Jess Granger
JG Faherty
Jennifer Fallon

Acknowledgments

Special thanks to Kylie Griffin, Gregory Lamberson, Kate MacEachern, Katie Marciniak, Amanda J Spedding, Alicia Styles, and Timothy Travaglini.

Part of 'Difference Engine No 1', designed by Charles Babbage, with parts made by Joseph Clements.

After Charles Babbage died, his son Henry Provost Babbage, used the parts of the incomplete 'engine 1' to build a number of models. One of these models was acquired by the Museum of Applied Arts and Sciences, Sydney, at the instigation of Associate Professor Allan Bromley of the University of Sydney. It was Professor Bromley who led the research into Charles Babbage's papers and lobbied the Science Museum in London to build Difference Engine 2 from Babbage's plans.

Collection: Museum of Applied Arts and Sciences, Sydney, Australia. Photo: Ryan Hernandez

Chapter 1

London 1880

THERE WERE TIMES Berd wished she could speak with the dead. Today was one of them.

Light from the ormolu chandelier set in the domed ceiling of the auction house foyer fell upon the sign 'Auction: Deceased Estate' written in black type that crouched like spider's legs.

Berd blinked. The letters gleamed straight back at her, bold and black and outlined in gold. Ordinary calligraphy. Certainly not like spiders.

This is no time for second thoughts.

She tightened her grip on her silk reticule and quickened her pace, inhaling the odour of pipe weed and newsprint, as she crossed the foyer's wide expanse of black and white tiles. Her maid followed.

It was a fallacy, Berd knew, for the world to believe that if one chose to work on machines one also knew everything about them. Grandmother was a good case in point; while she was proficient at instructing a machine to carry out a set of orders — programming, she called it — she had not the slightest notion as to how to assemble such a device. Thank goodness for the late Mr Babbage and his Difference Engine; he had compensated for her deficiencies.

If only Berd had a Mr Babbage.

If only Berd still had her grandmother.

The old woman had been a member of the nobility. She was the sole offspring of that wastrel prodigy known as Byron, and a brilliant mathematician, but none of that had made any difference to the physician who treated her for cancer. When Grandmother inquired about a second opinion, the physician had impressed upon her that if she, *a woman*, proceeded to do so, he would wash his hands of her. Grandmother spent her last months in agony.

Nobody deserved to die like that. Nobody.

Berd stepped up to the registration desk and came under the scrutiny of the black-suited clerk. "We are here to attend the auction."

"My lady." The clerk handed her a form. His gaze lingered on the black netting of her veil.

Let him believe she was hiding eyes red and swollen from weeping. Believing her to be a widow meant, by default, that she must be of age, which would satisfy auction house requirements. Her pen-nib scratched over the papers as she signed a fictitious name in black India ink. She handed back the forms for the clerk to blot, cleared her throat then spoke down to him in the same imperious tone her late mother, the Countess of Lovelace, employed with recalcitrant servants. "Is my registration complete?"

Weak-kneed with relief, Berd knew her disguise worked when the clerk swallowed hard then held up a wooden paddle with a red number painted on the rounded end. "Number Thirteen. The only remaining."

Little wonder no one had taken it. She nodded toward Rose, and he presented the paddle to her.

"Room Two, down the corridor, my lady. Bidding should already have begun," he said.

Begun? Oh blast! That was the reason the auction house appeared so empty. A greater fear settled deep in Berd's stomach: what if it had already been auctioned? "Come, Rose." Forcing herself to appear composed, Berd's heels clicked rapidly against the marble passageway.

"My lady, your catalogue!" the clerk called out.

She waved his words away. "It isn't needed."

She was here for one item only.

A year ago, the owner of that one precious item had declined her written offer. Shortly after, the papers had announced the man's passing. Now his estate was being settled. This was her last chance to obtain the object she believed would have saved Grandmother's life.

Rose trotted behind, her face pale in the gloom of the unlit passageway. Doorways were open either side of the hallway. Which was Room Two? The one to the right brimmed with people, and Berd caught sight of the gold number two on the oak-panelled door just as Rose pointed to it.

Berd's heart sank at the size of the crowd. Two hundred people or more in dark suits and fine hats had their backs to her as they sat in red-velvet chairs that looked up to a podium far to the room's front. More people meant a higher price; maybe more than Berd could afford. Once again, she squeezed the drawstring neck of her reticule, the contents of which seemed strangely lighter.

The men standing at the doorway in the House's livery led her down the main aisle to two seats in the back section, not more than three rows into the room. Yet even from this distance Berd smelt the paraffin. Her knees softened, as there, at the front of the auction room, was the object of her desire. Around her, voices whispered, "Let the lady sit. Please, let the lady sit."

They were ushered to two red padded chairs. Rose leaned close. Whether it was out of fear or to provide comfort, Berd could not tell; she was too busy staring across the crowd at the massive structure of copper and brass enthroned upon the entire dais.

Through the hazy pipe smoke, the structure resembled a miniature mechanical city, and just fitted against the length of the wall. Deadly carriage spires pierced the air. Her arms tingled.

The Ghost Engine.

Grandmother was right in her description. It made Berd feel as if God Almighty was in the room Himself. Grandmother referred to the giant calculating machine as a *computer* in her writings, but the term *engine* seemed so much more appropriate.

Berd's mind raced as she attempted to determine the purpose of each polished cog, wheel, and cam. What function did those small copper platters serve? Input? No, no, storage! And where was the punch-card reader? Row after row of vacuum tubes glistened under the yellow glare of gas lamps. What an elegant method of switching! That brass outlet…was that…? And those dials—

"My lady?"

Someone tugged at her sleeve. Berd started breathing again as she recognised Rose's voice. The buzz of conversation in the room swelled over them both, but then everything was drowned out by the tap of staccato footsteps up the passageway.

All heads turned to the back of the room as a lady, dressed like Berd in the black silk of widow's weeds, proceeded down the centre aisle. Her distinct lack of crepe denoted she was coming out of mourning, yet no jet jewellery adorned her garments. And the black was unrelieved by other colours, which should not be the case, not in this late stage. That meant she deliberately wished to remain in mourning. She, too, was also followed by a lady's maid.

All in the room sat straighter, Berd included.

The black-suited auctioneer bowed. His thinning red hair combed to one side, threatened to slide back to the middle. "Her Grace, the Duchess herself…" He pressed one finger against his mouth, as if to prevent the secret of her identity escaping. "I realised you were missing and held the auction for you."

"Proceed, Barnaby." Without pausing, the duchess made her way up to the front of the room where several preeminent seats had been left unoccupied.

So that explained why the auction had not yet commenced. Beneath her veil, Berd licked her dry lips. How could her measly allowance compete against the wealth of a duchess?

She squeezed her reticule, but neither the feel of her favourite pomander, the orange studded with cloves, nor the bundle of pound notes she had packed with such enthusiasm this morning, brought any comfort.

The auctioneer bowed first to the duchess and then to the audience. "Ladies and gentlemen, it is my sincerest pleasure to welcome you to Bingley's, where quality takes precedence over price. We are most sad to have to inform you of the passing of the late Mr Robert Fotheringay, Esquire, of Marylebone, one of the great inventors of our Industrial Age. But we are also proud to have been selected to handle the auctioning of his estate. There are many items of great interest in the catalogue today, but we have decided to start the show with the most storied—and some say the most cursed—of all Mr Fotheringay's possessions: The Ghost Engine.

"The history behind this Engine is mysterious. A rare item. Mr Fotheringay spent the last ten years bringing it to life. As you can see, it is a contraption composed of cogs and wheels, a miniature city of brass and oak. Did it ever work?" He cocked his head at the crowd like an experienced showman. "The Devil himself only knows."

An expectant hush settled upon the room.

"Apparently, the inventor was great friends with the illustrious Charles Babbage. Both men tried to foster life into their creations. In the case of Mr Fotheringay, however, it was taken one step further."

The crowd leaned forward, as if by doing so they could come closer to its secrets.

Through half-lidded eyes, the auctioneer continued, "Mr Fotheringay made a pact with Lucifer himself. He sacrificed the life of his only son. Just as the Bible tells Abraham did of Isaac."

The silence in the room was so deep, Berd could not move. She could only stare at the white face of the auctioneer. His words had infected his movements, making them more graceful than a bird's as if he, too, was coming under his own spell.

"It is said the heart of the young man beats within the engine. And when the engine speaks, it speaks with his voice."

The crowd gasped. The temperature in the room fell noticeably as he said the words. One woman fainted and had to be carried out. Berd rubbed her lace-covered arms, trying to warm the chill as Rose clutched her elbow. Rose's grip was strong, but that was to be expected: she always fell for stories. Any story. Yet Berd felt herself trembling, too. Normally she never succumbed to such nonsense.

Over the heads of the crowd, the shining Engine gleamed through the smokers' haze. When the crowd settled, the auctioneer took a moment of silence at the podium to collect their attention then spoke in a deeper voice, "Ladies and gentlemen, this diabolical Engine cost a man his only son. Murder, it was said, though they could never prove it. And in a father's grief and sorrow and regret, Mr Fotheringay met his demise a year later."

The auctioneer gazed at the silent faces. "We cannot, therefore, start the auction at anything less than the sum of a hundred pounds. And throw in an extra hundred, for the ghostly tale!"

Laughter tittered around the room.

Then one man flung his hand up, paddle raised. "Two hundred!"

"Two hundred and fifty!"

"Two hundred, sixty!"

If only there was a method to determine if these

were genuine bidders or fakes. Berd had heard of auction houses planting their own people in the crowd to deliberately increase the final price.

She took a deep breath, but before she could open her mouth, a female voice cut through the noise.

"Three hundred."

The duchess had started to bid.

A heavy silence descended upon the room as the bidding abruptly halted.

Nobody spoke. None moved. And if nobody did anything, the Engine would be in the possession of the duchess within the hour.

As if this was the cue the auctioneer waited, he raised his hammer. "Three hundred going once! Three hundred go—"

"And one." Berd lifted her right hand, realised there was no numbered paddle in it, turned in a panic to Rose, seized the paddle Rose held out to her and waved it.

All stared, all except the duchess, who sat stiff-backed, still facing front.

No doubt the woman was annoyed at her. Or maybe she was just waiting? Either way, Berd did not like to think what the repercussions would be should she thwart the duchess.

Startled, the auctioneer snapped his mouth shut and then cocked his head at Berd. "Another bid, from the back," he said, his words clipped. He rolled the hammer in lazy circles like a toy, as he appraised her.

He was probably trying to ascertain if she could afford the Engine.

Berd gave one stiff nod, her hand held high.

"Very well then, three hundred and..." he prompted.

"*One*," she said, afraid her voice sounded far too childish. The less she spoke the better, in case someone recognised her. Three hundred and one she could manage. Pray it didn't go much higher.

"Four hundred." The duchess bid once more.

Berd swallowed.

"Four hundred will do nicely, Your Grace." The auctioneer bowed. "Four hundred going once! Four hundred going twice! S—"

"And one," Berd squeaked.

This time the gasp around the room was audible. Worse, the duchess turned to see who was attempting to outbid her. She scanned the room, finally fixing her eyes on Berd.

"A protégée of yours?" the auctioneer asked.

They must have seemed strikingly similar, Berd realised, both being all in black silk. Both accompanied by a lady's maid.

The duchess shook her head. "I would not wish such a fate on anyone. But come, my dear, let me see your face."

Berd froze. If she unveiled herself, the gossip would spread around the *ton*, and her brother would eventually find out. So, she stood her ground and sat still. It was perfectly allowed to have secret bidders and proxy bidders at an auction, after all.

To her horror, the duchess rose. The entire crowd was motionless as the woman glided, wraithlike, toward the back of the room. As the duchess reached the row, Rose, poor Rose, bless her heart gave up her seat to the duchess.

But the duchess remained standing at the edge like a ghost.

Through the black gauze of her veil, Berd saw the woman's watery blue eyes.

"I bid because I would contact the spirit of my late husband. You are young. Are you sure you want the company of the dead in your home?"

The temperature in the room dropped again, and all the hair on Berd's body prickled. Spectral fingers seemed to lace her throat, and once again she could not speak.

But the macabre words burned in Berd's mind like brown paper cut-out dolls, lifting as they danced above orange flames.

The company of the dead.

Would Berd wish to speak to her grandmother if she could?

Something of that pain, that longing, must have shadowed Berd's face through her own veil, because the duchess laughed then faltered. "Let her have it if she dares." And without another word, the duchess and her maid swept from the room.

The auctioneer stared in disbelief at the duchess's back then at Berd, his eyes wide. "Four hundred and one, my lady?" he asked, his voice cracking.

Four hundred and one pounds, Berd cringed. Much more than she'd expected to spend; an amount she'd never be able to hide.

But she had to have it.

"Four hundred and one," she breathed out. It was everything she had, everything for the future.

It struck her then that perchance the duchess was a kindred spirit. Perchance she herself recognised some of that longing in Berd, for the more highborn the woman, the lonelier her upbringing.

"Four hundred and one going once! Four hundred and one going twice! Sold to the young lady at the back. Number thirteen. Lucky for some. Unlucky for others."

Chapter 2

"**WHY WON'T YOU** work!"

Alone in her stable—now converted into a workshop—Berd scowled at the Engine as she wiped her greasy fingers on her leather apron. "I've cleaned you, oiled you, and filled up your blasted generator. So why won't you work? And why can't I find that blasted punch-card reader!" It was as if the machine wanted to turn over, but simply couldn't manage it.

The auctioneer was right, though. It was a miniature city of spiralling brass and copper, and she could imagine tiny autocars motoring around on the pitch macadam. For the third time that morning Berd cranked the Engine's handle for a good ten minutes before flicking on a switch.

The hum began immediately. It ran along the wooden base of the Engine, shuddering each metal component as it reached upwards. At the same time, the hum spread out, shaking the floor and travelling up against her legs like static. She gritted her teeth as her knees knocked against the insides of her woollen pants. The rumble vibrated up the walls, roaring in her ears. Cogs clicked and turned. Wheels spun. Pins popped in and out. The needles on dials twitched as the Engine came to life.

Before her eyes, vacuum tubes glowed. The gas lamp on the stable wall grew in brightness. Like the dawning of the sun, Apollo rising to set off on his chariot, the luminescence deepened.

Heat bathed her face. The oily fumes of paraffin swirled around, clinging to everything they touched. The generator woke with a bang. As usual, her eyes teared from the smoke, but she rubbed the irritation away.

And then, as it did every single time before anything got started, the Engine began winding down. It coughed tragically. Cams slowed. Black smoke plumed the air.

Berd slammed her fist against the heated metal. "No!" she choked out through the fumes. "No. Not again." She searched for something, anything that would prolong the life of the Engine. In desperation, she reached for a lever, pushing it all the way to maximum, beyond the sign that said 'Danger. Do not go beyond.' She had never attempted this before. But hang the consequences, she could think of nothing else.

The Engine sputtered bravely on.

It had to make it!

Her heart was in her mouth. Her chest squeezed tight in desperate hope as she whispered, "You can do it. You can do it. Come on."

It had been going a whole five minutes longer than it ever had when a force smacked Berd in the face. She reeled backwards. Her throat was burning. Smoke filled the air.

What on earth was that? Oh heavens! Something's on fire. Oh please, not the Engine!

Instead of finding herself surging forward to save the Engine, she found herself falling. The black cloud of smoke overcame her and noxious fumes were all she could taste. On her hands and knees, strength ebbed from her body until she lay flat on the ground, sinking fast into unconsciousness. Even as she stared at the ceiling blinking, she saw a figure…no, two figures, bending over her.

Angels…

But there was no heavenly choir. Instead, the first figure gazed at her, his outline shimmering blue. It was the ghostly image of a young man clothed in what appeared to be shadows. He had hair of coal black and soot smudged his cheeks. Then, the other young man, identical to the first, came closer.

She remembered Nanny telling her that everyone had a guardian angel, someone to tell them right from wrong, and a little demon, to try to push them off the path of righteousness. These must be hers. It was her time to go…

The force must have killed her, but her spirit didn't know it yet. *So cold… Can't…move.* All she heard was her own laboured breathing. In and out; in and out. The bitterness of paraffin flooded her mouth, and she was about to spit when the first young man leaned closer.

His figure sharpened slightly; *blue eyes.* Brilliant blue eyes like his twin beside him.

They must be the ghosts of the Engine.

But Robert Fotheringay only had one son…

A tremor shook her body.

As the world faded fast, the first man vanished leaving the second man crouched over her. Ice-cold fingers touched her neck.

He's feeling for a pulse. I am really dying...

As the black closed in, those ice-cold fingers slid across her throat.

And tightened.

Banging on the stable door roused Berd; Rose calling for her. "My lady, are you all right?"

Berd's ears were ringing, but worse, she smelled smoke. As she struggled to her feet, the room seemed to sway. Strange light flickered ahead of her — orange and yellow and red.

A section of the Engine was on fire.

Berd grabbed a rag from the pile and sprang towards the Engine. Thank goodness the door was shut and Rose under strict orders not to enter. "I am perfectly fine," she shouted, desperate to keep the edge of panic out of her voice as she smacked at the fire. *Blast! Blast! Blast!* No doubt Rose could hear her mad dance and wonder what was going on.

The hammering on the door stopped. "My lady, we heard an explosion!"

"Everything's fine. Now please, I need peace and quiet." With one final whack, the fire was extinguished. Thankfully each glass vacuum tube was off, and the only radiance inside the stables came from the gas lamp on the wall. Berd collapsed against a chest. And as she pressed a palm against her throat, she shivered at the memory of the ghostly hands that had gripped her. All she felt now was a layer of ash. As if on cue, she sneezed. Rose would have heard that.

"Yes, my lady, I mean, no, my lady, I mean, oh!" Rose had been muttering all the while through the door.

There were times when Berd could happily have strangled her maid. "Rose, I need to work," she said.

"Yes, my lady, but I mean, I mean…it's the Earl of Lovelace."

Even as Berd frowned, she heard those oh-so-familiar footsteps of her brother approach.

James.

The last person she needed to see. He was here, at Aunt Agatha's house, when he was supposed to be at the estate. What wretched, wretched timing. But already the thick, wooden door was swinging open. Berd jumped to her feet, bent over the Engine and began furiously wiping.

She heard James's shoes click like knives on the wooden floors as he entered. "What in God's name happened here?"

Berd continued to clean, studiously ignoring her sibling. She was sure James was scowling, irritated by the fact she had not greeted him. As if in confirmation, one foot tapped. He was five years her senior, her guardian, and an earl. Had he ever stopped to think the price of his rank was their father?

Tap. Tap. Tap.

"Berd?"

Berd straightened, an annoyed expression on her face. "Oh. What are *you* doing here, James? How nice to see you."

"Don't give me that. What the devil happened to Aunt Agatha's fine stable?" He looked her up and down, frowning at her hair that cascaded around her shoulders. "And to *you*." He sniffed. His frown deepened at the sight of her apron.

"You mean my new workshop," she said, waving the rag around, hoping to distract him. She was proud of the place, truth be told. She and Rose had spent many hours transforming the stables into a workshop.

"Work—" James choked and had to thump his chest with one fist. "Aunt Agatha allowed you to do *what* to this stable? And what foible have you got there?"

"Why, it's my new autocar!"

James grimaced at the Engine behind her. "And I'm the Prince of Egypt. What sort of idiot do you take me for? The bleeding thing hasn't even got wheels! How could Aunt Agatha allow you to destroy a perfectly decent stable? I turn my back on you for a moment and look what happens."

The foible in question consumed a bob's worth of paraffin each time she turned it on and burnt out vacuum tubes at the rate of one per hour. Better not let James know she paid the workmen extra for their troubles when they delivered it. Or what it had cost in the first place. Or that the Engine was supposedly haunted.

Imagining the copper platter that she was cleaning was her brother's face, she rubbed it so hard it squeaked. "This little thing?"

James narrowed his gaze, as if he knew what she had been thinking. "Out with it, Elizabeth."

Elizabeth? Now she was in trouble. "First, all I spent was my allowance. I cannot spend my inheritance even if I wanted to; everything is locked up until I am twenty-one."

"For your own protection." He pointed in the direction of the Engine with his latest silver-tipped walking cane as though it were evidence.

Berd snorted. "Would you prefer I spend three times as much on a new wardrobe for the season?"

"I want to know what that contraption is doing in the stables, while your autocar, one of six in the entire country, is *sitting* out in the street. With pigeons all over it! And you could *use* a new wardrobe. In fact, what are you wear—" His eyes widened with sudden recognition. "Oh heavens! Those are my brand-new riding pants, aren't they! You—you chopped the hems off? Bloody hell, Berd!"

Too late did Berd remember she was not wearing a skirt! And how else was she to learn about engines unless she had one to tinker with? At least she had had a month of driving around in it. Berd looked James in the eye as she spoke each word, "Well, I wasn't about to be seen getting fitted for trousers, as I knew you'd explode. And I'm sure you'll agree it's better than to be seen in your nightwear! Precautions must be taken as you always say. This contraption is an engine."

James swore under his breath. "It looks like no engine I've ever seen."

Berd flicked a glance heavenward. "You say that like you've seen many engines! That, dear brother, is the future. It is what our late dear Grandmother Bird would call," she paused. Surely James would not have forgotten the stories their father told about grandmother's dream. "A computer."

James crossed his arms and glared at her. "And what, pray tell, *is* a compute-er?"

Berd felt a pang of grief. He *had* forgotten. Still she answered in all seriousness: "It is a machine that can think."

A flicker of doubt glinted in his hazel eyes, and hope surged inside her. Then he frowned. "Why would anyone want a machine that can think? We have enough problems with the peasants believing they can think! We don't need some worthless device adding its opinions to the mix."

She forced a smile. "It doesn't work that way."

"How much did you pay for that—that—thing?"

Berd tensed. He would find out anyway. "Four hundred and one," she said, trying not to sound defeated.

"Four hundred and one—what? Pence?"

"Uh…pounds," she said. Even as she spoke, a section of the Engine collapsed into ash. Blast!

"Four hundred and what! Good lord, Berd. Can't I leave you alone without you wasting your funds on another frivolous hobby?"

"Hobbies are all I have, brother. You've seen to that. Besides," she said, changing the subject as she wrapped her rag around the first tube and started twisting to remove it. "It hasn't kept me from my duties. Speaking of which, what brings you here today?"

"I was going to come down tomorrow, but I thought, being the devoted brother that I am, I'd come a day early."

"To add unexpected visiting to your expected visiting! How thoughtful of you, brother."

He wouldn't meet her gaze, instead he cleared his throat. "Heavens, that looks dangerous. Tinkering with bits of junk. You're supposed to be visiting. Have you returned all your calls?"

With a yank, the first vacuum tube came off, and with that came accomplishment, relief. But it was short-lived. "Cousin Cuthbert complained, didn't he? That's the real reason you're here. Oh, hand me that other rag."

"I beg your, pardon? That slimy thing?"

If Berd wasn't so furious, she'd have laughed at the sight of James wincing. She gave her brother a withering look as she strode over and picked up said slimy thing.

James glowered back. "And what's wrong with Cuthbert? Have you anything against a viscount? You are seventeen. You're supposed to be meeting people. Enjoying your season."

And getting married. Just not to Cuthbert. She wrapped the rag around the second vacuum tube. "I am out. Ask Aunt Agatha. Remember the big ball months ago, where I was paraded like a prize sow in front of everyone in that atrocious pink silk?"

"You have done nothing since."

"Nothing? What do you call this? Don't you understand, there's no way I'm ending up like Aunt Agatha."

"What are you on about? She *eloped*," he answered, as if he were dealing with a slow-witted child. "Had she not, she'd have had a marriage contract to protect her when her husband died. Oh, dear God! Where'd we go so wrong?"

"Contract? The *only* reason women need one..."

With another hard twist the second vacuum tube popped out. "Is because the law favours people like you."

"People like me?" Then his brows shot up in shock as understanding hit. "You mean men?"

"Finally, he gets it," said Berd.

"I did not come here to be insulted. And I'll have you know that Rohan gives her an allowance. Not all brothers-in-law are that considerate!"

"I can't believe you said that, James. I really can't. A hundredth of what's hers, while he legally stole the rest! But that's not the point," she said as she eyed him, grim-faced.

"It's not?" James frowned. He lifted his top hat and ran one hand through his blond hair a few times. When he was done, he set his black top hat back down upon his head.

"Why can't we women support ourselves? Yes, you heard me. Why can't we be equals?"

"You're not serious."

To stop herself from throwing the tube at her idiotic brother's head, Berd started unscrewing a cog. Having melted in the heat it wouldn't come off easily. "Hand me that wrench." If only everything wasn't going wrong all at once!

"What?"

She gritted her teeth. "Wrench. That thing."

James groaned, but went over and picked up the tool. With two fingers, he passed it to her. Then he pulled out his handkerchief and made a show of wiping his fingers. "So, all this time you've been hiding in the stable. Working on this Engine."

"And what if I have?" The cog was proving harder

to remove than she thought, just like some people she knew. She put her leg on the machine's platform, to get leverage for the manoeuvre.

"Wait a moment. A thinking machine — Now I remember! That was what Grandmother Bird —" James shot her a peeved expression before continuing to wipe his hand. "Was working on." His eyes lit. "That's it. Programming. To teach the computer to carry out a set of instructions. That was what she was trying to accomplish, wasn't it?" He smiled, pleased with himself.

Berd halted mid-turn as she gave her brother a curious look. If he was at last beginning to hear her then maybe he'd understand why she wanted to work with engines. She spoke eagerly, "This is an improved version. The one Grandmother was working on…"

But James was staring at her, with her one leg balanced in a precarious position. To her dismay, he waved away the rest of her explanation, and any hope he might see her side of things.

"Foolishness. Thank goodness Grandmother passed away, or she'd have scandalised the whole family. Traipsing around at all hours of the day and night with that Cabbage fellow. He lost his entire inheritance, and serves him right, though I wouldn't wish it on Grandmother, of course. Then they'd had that madcap idea of going to the races to try to win money — of all things."

Thank *goodness* Grandmother had passed away? "Babbage," Berd said in a tight voice. With a final effort the cog came off. It made a loud clatter on the floor.

"Pardon?" James blinked.

"His name was Babbage, Charles Babbage, and he was the inventor of the Difference and the Analytical Engines," she spat the words out between clenched teeth, as she walked over and picked up the cog.

James groaned, as if this was all too much for him. "So, this is an improvement on that? How delightful. What does one use a thinking machine for?"

Would he ever listen! "Originally, Babbage wanted a device to calculate logarithms, but then he devised a more general-purpose engine. He called it The Analytical Engine. Think, James. Remember when you purchased your autocar? Remember the fifteen reasons the salesman said why an autocar is better than a horse-drawn vehicle? No stable. No daily grooming. No manure heap to poison the air? Well, a computer will be able to work twenty-four hours a day and it'll never get tired. Or sick. No pay increases."

Berd flourished one hand over the Engine, but what with bits of it already disintegrated and the blackened vacuum tubes, the Engine was a sorry sight. It took every ounce of strength to stand tall before her brother.

James looked dour as he held up one grey gloved hand. "If you please. I'm having a dinner at our townhouse in a month's time. Do me the honour of planning it — that's what girls are *supposed* to do. Ones that behave, anyway. I imagine Aunt Agatha would be delighted. Why, between the two of you, you could decide the guest list."

More like a ploy to meet Cuthbert or any other number of dandies. "Or what? You'll disinherit me?" But James wasn't even listening as he twirled his cane and bowed right through her words.

"Dear, sweet, *obedient* Berd — make sure that

monstrosity is removed the next time I visit. Indulge me."

Berd had had enough. "Maybe it won't be so bad if I'm disinherited. I could always be the first Lovelace to set up my own workshop. Repairing engines, hooray!" She waved the rag gaily, as if it were a flag.

James's face darkened.

"Wouldn't the *ton* love that?"

"Don't tempt me," he warned as he threw open the door.

"I think I am the one being tempted." Her rag hit the door just as it closed. Beast. He hadn't even tried to understand. And the things he'd said! Their grandmother had died before her time, and not even the promise of money-to-be-made could make him care about her dreams.

Berd strode over to the door, picked up the rag, and then flung it at the door once more. "Even a possession can have feelings!"

Her chest heaved as she retrieved the rag again. She glowered at the Engine. If she could just get it working, she could program it, furthering the research on her grandmother's mysterious illness. Faster than humanly possible.

Most importantly it would vindicate you, Grandmother, prove your predictions correct.

Berd grimaced as she dusted herself down, annoyed and disappointed at today's outcome. She'd tried her best, but her best didn't seem to be good enough.

She studied the Engine, running her fingers along a bit of charred wood. Thank goodness, she'd extinguished the fire, but as her fingers brushed the wood, it disintegrated further.

"Oh…oh," Berd whistled, frustration replaced by curiosity as the wood crumbled, revealing what looked suspiciously like a metal drawer. The fire had revealed a secret compartment. Her hands shook as she slid the drawer open. A thin book bound in green leather. She picked it up.

The log book of Charles Babbage Fotheringay the cover read. A chill slid down her back.

Robert Fotheringay had named his son after his good friend Charles Babbage. That'd make this the journal of the missing man — the ghost said to inhabit the Engine.

She sank onto an old trunk, remembering the phantom figure of the young man. It made perfect sense. Robert Fotheringay was co-inventor. His son, doubling as his assistant, had kept a journal, a log book of their experiments. Only when the invention was working would they be able to patent it. This logbook was, for the time being, the sole proof this Engine was theirs.

And now it was hers.

Maybe she'd find the answer she needed in here. She flipped the journal open.

"A computer is a simple device."

The words were scrawled in tight, black loops — some careful and clear while others were slanted more strongly. Both reflective of entries written with careful deliberateness, while others, almost illegible, were entries scribbled in great haste. She turned the page.

"The ability to insert data is through what we call the INPUT Section."

If she just knew which page held the answer she needed. She flipped through the pages until she came to the last entry.

"No matter what Father and I have tried, we cannot surmount the power threshold. The obstacles seem too great, and I feel Father has given up. Last night I'd had an idea. Now we need to wait for an Act of God."

Berd lowered the book, shaking her head. Maybe this would all make sense tomorrow. She had a little time; James would no doubt be at his club this moment, or at least on his way to it. The earliest he'd be back would be in a week's time. She rubbed the bridge of her nose, only to cover it with soot. She sighed and stood; she'd done all she could do for one day. Rest was needed now. Perhaps tomorrow she'd have answers.

An Act of God…

The only way to discover what they did was if she spoke with Charles Fotheringay.

She had to speak with a ghost.

Chapter 3

OW DID ONE speak to a ghost?

Especially if one didn't believe in séances. It was another reason Berd understood why she never fitted into society. Almost everyone she knew believed. But thanks to what she'd witnessed during the explosion yesterday, she was actually contemplating such foolishness.

She rubbed a finger against her lips as she stared at the old leather journal in her lap. The rays from her lamp stained the pages yellow. Normally she enjoyed reading by the flickering light, but today the shadows they created in the stables made her skin crawl. And no matter how hard she'd tried, she couldn't keep from thinking about what she'd experienced.

Explosions. Ghosts. Murder.

She tried not to look too hard at the shadows that stole along the floor, or the ones seeping from the corners of the stable. Light, however, appeared to be working in tandem with the dark, for each time the light quivered, the shadows trembled. Berd jumped each time it occurred.

She'd never noticed the shadows in such a way before. It wasn't the darkness alone that bothered her but the Engine to her left. Of course it wasn't watching her! It was just a collection of cogs and wheels assembled for functional, rather than aesthetic, purposes. But then eyes with which to view something was a functional feature, too.

She cleared her throat and read again. "A computer is a simple device made up of four sections. The first is called the INPUT SECTION. This section enables data to be fed into the computer, hence its name. Data is different to information because data by itself is meaningless."

She slammed the book shut. Yes, she knew all that, but what she still didn't know was how to get the blasted computer working, and this was her second reading.

According to the book, Mr Fotheringay and his son, Charles, had attempted to use an Act of God to start the Engine…

There were no more entries after Charles's suggestion, as this was when he'd disappeared. Berd had no idea if it worked, or if they had been able to input data and to process it or to store the data and then output it. Or whether his father had murdered him, perhaps arguing over how to start the Engine, sacrificing him to the Engine like savages to a heathen god…

The young man who'd bent over her yesterday had looked in fine condition. Vitally alive. She'd not noticed any strangulation marks about his neck. Or maybe he'd been knifed…there was that heart to think about.

She stole another glance at the Engine, sitting idly without its cover. In the gaslight, shadows flickered amongst its tubes, as if they really were the buildings of cities, and tiny people were walking around them. She jerked her head back to the book in her lap. *Stop it.*

The young man's face had been smudged with soot, and his strange black sleeves rolled up, as if he'd been in the middle of something and interrupted. But she couldn't comprehend what a ghost could be engaged in. That was the afterlife. They should all be playing harps and singing!

Unless he wasn't Upstairs…

Berd shook her head, wishing she'd paid more attention in church; then she'd know whether one proceeded straight to heaven or whether there was a half-way stage before either. Or even if Hell was mechanised. The only non-risky way to find out was if she engaged the Reverend Waid in a discussion, but then she'd be stuck for hours. His mother would assume she was interested in him, and she'd affront all the other unattached women in the parish. Let them have him. She found nothing attractive in a sallow-faced young man who was always clasping and unclasping his hands.

Charles Fotheringay, on the other hand, if that was in fact him…

Intelligence had shone in his blue eyes. He looked to be someone she could commune with, in daily life. Perhaps, even a man to have a conversation with that didn't involve her acting as if she'd her brains removed.

Long hair, dim witted.

That was regarded as man's sole view of woman.

Berd sighed. How ludicrous! She'd gone from disbelieving in séances to trying to contact the ghost of the late Charles Babbage Fotheringay.

But he was the only person who could possibly solve her dilemma: how to get the Engine running so that she could solve the mystery of her grandmother's illness. And vindicate her!

She sat up straight as she stared at the journal in her lap.

A woman *could* be the world's first computer programmer. That'd prove to the world that women were equal to men. Grandmother Bird had started the journey, and Berd was determined to see it through.

She turned to a dog-eared page and reread the contents. It appeared she'd not been the only person who'd had such thoughts. Even the late Mr Fotheringay had attempted to contact the spirit of his old friend, Charles Babbage. The Fotheringays must have succeeded as the Ghost Engine had come a long way from the Difference Engine. And though there were no clues in the logbook, maybe ole Sir Alphabet Function himself, as the late Charles Babbage used to address himself, had indeed been giving his friend hints from the Great Beyond.

But contacting a spirit was entering the Devil's Domain.

A sin…

All she wanted was an answer, not some diabolical contract whereby she'd lose her immortal soul. Sliding her hand to her throat, she remembered the ghost's fingers, tightening, like a threat…

Berd's heart raced; she struggled to breathe. Even the hand she currently pressed over her dry lips was noticeably cold. She set the book aside, rose from the chair and faced the Engine.

"If you could just speak, and tell me what I'm doing wrong. I need power."

The Engine remained silent.

Berd gave a little laugh. "Here I am communing with an engine. And if you'd responded I'd have run out the door screaming like a lunatic and they'd cart me off to Bedlam."

She sighed, looked down at her black boots and then at the Engine. She sucked in a breath.

The Engine looked different. Copper platters gleamed, a fiendish light arcing off edges that flashed, knife-sharpened. Every inch of its metallic surface flamed, protruding as if backlit by some mysterious inner light she could not place. In contrast, the wooden panels darkened as if the wood sweated.

It *was* different.

She knew it.

Berd could not explain the manner of the change. It was as if, before, the Engine had been an inanimate object, and now, as if something had entered it, possessed it, and controlled it, she felt it was listening to her. Nervous, she fingered the little gold cross around her throat.

"Mr Charles Fotheringay?" she whispered, feeling foolish. "If you're in there…" She rolled and unrolled the logbook. "Please, if you're in there. I know you're dead, and I'm very sorry for that. But could you help me, please? I just need to…"

Find out how you got the Engine working. And you're

the only person who can help me.

The words stuck in her throat; she squeezed her eyes shut. Somehow, being without sight made talking to a ghost easier. "I can't believe I'm even doing this. But I saw you. I know I saw you. So if you're in there, please give me a sign. Please."

Her throat tightened. She opened her eyes. And screamed.

The brick walls were blurring as they leaned over her; the ceiling had shrunk away. And the Engine — the macabre Engine — was rolling forward like a juggernaut. The floor rumbled as if pistons were going off beneath the soles of her feet, and a dull humming filled her ears.

Berd wanted to run. But she couldn't. She wanted to call out to stop what was happening, but her lips wouldn't form the words. She could not move. It was as though she'd passed through a gateway into some unknown dimension; a giant eye had opened and now stared at her.

She finally shrieked and jumped backward, her mobility returning to her all at once. The lamp light trembled, its rays shimmered; the shadows quivered.

Then the room returned to normal. Everything was as it had been — quiet, still, and in normal unwavering proportions. Even the Engine now sat in its regular position — dull and innocuous.

But her heart was still racing.

Lord, she couldn't go through with this! She'd never attempt to contact the dead again. Ever!

Frantic to escape the stables, she flung the logbook down and ran towards the door. A wisp of wind fluted through the bottom, as if enticing her back to the world.

To life. She shoved the door open, but all around her was darkness.

The light was gone.

It was supposed to be morning, but there was no blue sky to reassure her all was right. This had to be hell.

Berd stood still in the doorway, unable to understand what was happening. The sun had disappeared.

The skies were black.

Black shapes roiled like oil within the infernal canvas overhead.

Black.

That's it!

It was about to rain. Rain! The wavering wraiths across the sky were storm clouds. Thunder rumbled in the distance. Thunder… She clapped her hands. Of course!

Lightning.

Lightning was an Act of God!

That must have been what Charles and his father had done.

She flung her hands to the sky. "Thank you, Lord! Thank you." She dashed back to the brick townhouse.

"You!" She stabbed a finger at a footman coming down the steps. He was one of the new help. "Peter, was it?"

He doffed his cap. "Henry, if it please, my lady."

"Henry! I need for you to get me a chimney sweep!"

The footman frowned. "A chimney sweep, Miss? In the middle of a storm?"

"Half a crown if you can get him within the hour."

"Straight away, Miss!" Henry grinned, bowed, and ran down the front stairs.

Within the hour, the lightning conductor at the top of Aunt Agatha's townhouse was taller by at least six feet, but there was no time to celebrate. Berd was too busy struggling to attach a length of telegraph wire from the Ghost Engine in the stables to the end of the lightning conductor. She'd just finished and was stepping off the ladder when Rose hurried up to her with an umbrella.

"My lady, it's raining," Rose said, trying to shield Berd from the rain.

"I know, Rose. It's glorious!"

"Come inside, my lady, please."

Berd allowed Rose to guide her towards the front door as lightning split the skies. A second later, thunder crashed in her ears. At her doorstep, Berd dreamily lifted her gaze to the sky as rain pelted her body, drenching her mauve silk blouse and running down her upturned nose. If she could but see lightning strike the conductor and race to the Engine…

The Engine! Oh no! It wasn't even on. She'd forgotten entirely.

"Wait! I've got to do something."

She broke away from Rose and ran for the stables. Overhead the storm's front line was beginning to pass. *Hurry, hurry!* She'd have to turn the Engine on fast.

The door swung open with a bang, and Berd hurried inside. Thank goodness the lamp was still on. Her fingers felt for the Engine's handle. Hurry! Hurry!

Berd cranked the handle furiously. Brilliant light flashed in her eyes.

Everything seemed to be outlined in gold. The after-effect burned in her brain. Berd was aware she was standing, and that she saw the lamp clearly hanging from the wall. She reached for the switch.

Flicked it.

And the world disappeared.

Chapter 4

ORRIFIC SCREAMING WAS echoing through Berd's head when she awoke. Blue light wavered all around her, fishtailing and bubbling, giving her the impression of being underwater. But that was impossible. She would not be able to breathe if that were the case.

But she was, undeniably, floating in a world of blue radiance.

Her skin tingled, even as water pushed in from all sides. Berd lifted her hands in scrutiny, expecting to find a gaping hole in one of them. She had dreamed it. The black dirt under her fingernails was gone, and every torn nail had regrown.

Baffled, she continued her examination, pressing the skin of her face and running fingers down the delicate curves of her ears. Jagged bursts of intermittent pain erupted in various parts of her person. The stink of charred flesh made her wonder if she had been set alight, but soon all was replaced by overwhelming bliss.

This had to be the afterlife…

She was beginning to revel in the peacefulness when a subtle sound filled her ears.

Water that sounds like bees humming…

She looked up and saw a blue radiance wrinkling in sheets before her. Then intense yellow light flashed. Blinding. A searing dread rose from deep within as she squeezed her eyes shut.

I must get out.

Berd moved her hands back to raise herself, only she could find no purchase…

There was nothing beneath her.

Her chest constricted and her heart thundered above the sound of the supernatural water. She opened her mouth to scream just as a voice spoke.

"Please, relax." A melodic voice burred. Male and young, it had a firm guiding tone like a doctor's.

Of course! She had to be at a retreat. James must have sent her to take the waters after the explosion. With that in mind, she closed her mouth and unclenched her fists.

The voice came again. "It's far safer to keep your eyes closed while you're under. At least you're whole again."

Whole again? What kind of spa was this?

Confusion seeped into her consciousness, and her muscles tightened. She squinted against a halo of sulphurous yellow light.

"What has happened to me? Where am I?"

To her annoyance, the speaker ignored her questions. "Excuse me, my lady, while I carry you out of the river."

A shadow passed over her. Pain re-entered her

body. Her muscles tensed. It was all she could do just to clench her teeth and hold back her scream.

"I'm sorry it hurts. Being one with the energy of the river causes you to feel pain as you're removed, but it'll pass." As he spoke the light dimmed, and as he placed her on her feet the pain subsided. Finally, she was able to see.

Only what she saw did not make sense. She had expected to find herself indoors, instead she was outdoors and the ground she was standing on, if it was indeed ground, was composed of bright green enamel that reflected the frail light like polished glass.

She tapped her foot, and heard the resulting echo. Whatever it was, it seemed solid enough. She appeared to be on the bank of a river, but this was like no river she'd ever encountered. It rippled with translucent blue silk skeins, its surface undulating and shimmering as if worked by a million looms beneath. And she had been in there. Inside. She lifted her gaze. The heavy odours of metal shavings, paraffin, and engine oil wafted over her face.

A city was spread to the horizon. A city composed of blocks. Huge blocks. *Gigantic* blocks. So titanic that even as she stared, she felt herself shrinking into the landscape. Copper, brass, silver, and polished steel took the place of brick and painted wood. The cubes, arches, pyramids, and rectangular prisms closest to her were the size of the workmen's cottages back on the estate, but others in the distance rivalled the Great Pyramid at Giza.

This was no spa.

Except for a slight humming, it was silent. No one and nothing moved in this alien landscape.

Berd's throat was dry as she stared.

Models of geometric figures… Wasn't that what Grandmother Bird had required in order to help her understand mathematics?

Berd wrapped her arms around herself and turned to the stranger who stood nearby, one hand resting on his hip, as he observed her.

The yellow grail-like halo that obscured him earlier had vanished. He looked not much older than she. Jet hair, finger-raked off his high forehead, fell straight to his shoulders in the style of the knights of old, but there was a sense of wildness about him she doubted any knight ever possessed. This was evidenced by the rakish curve of his brows over deep-set eyes, narrowed in grim contemplation. But he did not look at her as a damsel in distress. More like a dragon to be despatched.

Berd frowned back at him. He wore no hat, not even a commoner's one, and what appeared at first like shadows wrapped around him, was on closer examination more akin to black leather. Whatever it was, it was certainly no morning coat.

He took two almost predatory strides towards her, completing his aura of danger. This was not someone who *played* by the rules. This was someone who *made* the rules.

He was neither Sir Gawain nor even Sir Galahad. Naught but the Black Knight himself.

For a moment neither spoke. The only sound was the dull hum that seeped through the soles of her feet and fluttered the tendrils of her hair from her shoulders. She smoothed down her blouse, rubbing a fold between her fingers. The mauve silk crackled, proving what was happening was real.

If she'd appraised his outfit, he was now doing the same to her. With a start, Berd remembered she was still clad in James's pants. After that latest encounter, it'd been a point of honour to continue to wear them.

Let the stranger think they were bloomers or whatever. On her they were baggy enough that her form was not revealed. She owed him no explanation.

"Who are you, my lady, and where's my father?" Steel edged his tone.

"I…" She glanced up, only to be caught by his eyes. They were the intense blue of the sky at twilight.

This was the young man from the Engine the day before. The ghost.

The realisation stole her breath away, but at the same time a part of her rejoiced. Jubilant. She'd succeeded. She'd wanted to speak to Charles Babbage Fotheringay, to find out how to get the Engine working, and now she was. Not that she'd ever have imagined this. For not only was she speaking to him, she was actually in here with him. And the only place 'here' could be… She shook her head, trying to deny what her eyes and mind told her was truth. Her heart raced, and fear gripped her in tight hands. She was within the Engine itself.

Trapped.

Absolute panic flooded through her. Berd jerked her head up, desperate to see the comforting inside of her stables, but all that greeted her was an alien gold sky.

I wanted to teach the Engine. Not end up within it.

"My lady?"

The anger she sensed in him earlier was gone. His behaviour now appeared geared to pacify, as he reached one hand, palm-up, towards her.

The faint blue veins across his wrist, the bluntness of his grease-stained fingernails, even the stink of paraffin...

She inhaled sharply as all her senses screamed: this was not the hand of a ghost. Her voice was raw when she spoke, "Mr Charles Babbage Fotheringay, I presume?"

She thought she caught the glimmer of a smile.

"And you are?"

"Lady Elizabeth Ada Lovelace. My brother, James William—"

"Is the Earl of Lovelace." His face darkened. "You wrote my father over a year ago, indicating your desire to purchase our Engine. I was overseas at the time but Father informed me of your attempt when I returned." He gave a bitter laugh. "Well, it appears you have succeeded."

So he knew about her letter. But all she'd done was make an innocent offer, which his father had declined. She'd not pursued the matter further until she heard of the Engine being auctioned. "Sir, you mistake me. I've done nothing wrong."

However, the way Charles Fotheringay was regarding her, she had no doubt that if she told him his father was deceased he'd think she had a hand in it.

This was certainly not the time to inform him of his father's passing.

"Congratulations. You wanted the Engine. You're now in it. Enjoy yourself." He bowed, and without further ado, strode towards a golden trapezoidal prism balancing at a dangerous angle a hundred yards away.

Berd bristled. Though the last thing she desired was to come under any man's protection, by now the silence and immensity of the place was creeping in.

Eager for shelter, she took a step towards the city and was about to take another when one of the distant brass cubes shimmered oddly. Its faces had turned liquid. A movement arose from within, as though something inside was trying to escape.

I must be losing my mind!

In the distance, Fotheringay hadn't even slowed. His black form was growing smaller by the second. The hum increased until the ground rumbled. It felt like it was going from the city toward Fotheringay.

Then the trapezoid began to melt. It oozed into the air like water down a glass. Berd cupped her mouth to stop a scream. She had expected him to exhibit the same response as her, but his stride never slowed. *Surely he must see what is happening!*

The ground continued to rumble. He was fifty yards away when, to her left, cracks began opening in the green enamel, as though in an earthquake. At the same time, the trapezoid he was headed for melted completely, exposing a hot-air balloon behind it.

The balloon could be used to escape from the earthquake and maybe the Engine itself! This must be the reason he wasn't worried. He must have known.

And to think the churl wasn't going to take her with him. The nerve! Well, she would rectify the situation!

She raced towards the balloon.

Fotheringay was shaking his fist at the sky as she passed him. "I wondered if I'd have to issue an invitation," he called after her, his voice carrying a note of wry amusement. But even as he spoke, his steps quickened. He caught up easily and to her annoyance then kept pace with her.

The middle of an earthquake was not the time to take offence with the only person who could aid her.

"Are you attempting to escape the Engine?" she puffed, feeling like a bird with ruffled feathers. And she would have been better to be a bird, for how much the ground was shaking.

"That's a good question. A very good question." His mask of ease broke through and contorted with the effort of running. "How did *you* enter the Engine?"

Berd decided that she loathed people who could talk and run at the same time, especially ones who did not answer questions. "Found your logbook. Mentioned an Act of God. Lightning."

The balloon loomed ahead.

"Are we dead?"

Fotheringay burst out laughing. To Berd's annoyance, he laughed so hard he had to wipe his eyes with his sleeve, but it was a genuine laugh, too — all the latent anger was gone.

"If we were dead, we wouldn't be running for our lives. Come, we must make haste!" He held out an arm.

Though she couldn't go any faster, being left behind was not an option. Still, she hesitated to take it. The golden trapezoid, now but a puddle, spread before them.

With a shout that sounded strangely cheerful to her ears, Fotheringay grabbed Berd's arm and pulled her up with him as he leapt onto the edge of the puddle. She'd have crashed onto the surface had he not also seized a handful of her trouser waistline and effortlessly hauled her upright. Embarrassed heat flooded her throat.

With a suddenness that took her already strained breath away, the golden pond transformed again. A series of stairs rose, solid and liquid simultaneously.

Berd screamed, but Fotheringay never hesitated. He pounded up the steps. There seemed to be a hundred of them, extending right to the edge of the balloon's metallic wicker basket.

Each time, her foot connected with the metal surface a ping rang out, further confirming she was really here. She was actually climbing steps that had not existed a moment ago!

As they neared the top, Berd turned to him in breathless disbelief. "What on ea—"

"Come on!" He pushed Berd into the transportation, tumbling in beside her just as the balloon rose. Stunned and dumbfounded by such treatment, she managed to grasp the side of the basket and pull herself up.

Berd had been to France; she'd seen a red-and-yellow Montgolfier lovingly ascend to the heavens. Her nose crinkled at the memory of burning straw. Back then, she'd wished it had been her floating away in the basket. Now that she was, though, she'd never imagined it'd be under such dramatic circumstances.

The ground continued to tremble. Beyond the water, blocks quivered like blancmange. The rumbling became a roar as an obelisk of silver rippled, then exploded beneath their feet. Berd jumped as silver projectiles launched in every direction, some right at them.

The flashing shards, as if pulled by a thousand invisible hands, transformed into an exact miniature of St Paul's cathedral. Over its exterior, a wondrous maze of large, protruding pipes grew; a bird cage of plumbing.

She inched forward just as droplets from the pipes sliced the air, little silver blades hissing as they stabbed the ground, and embedding there like morbid flowers.

Berd reared back, taking refuge in distance. "Danger, magic, beauty and chaos…" she whispered, sure that the electrocution must have affected her.

There had to be a logical explanation, but only one person would have the answer. Pity he was mad.

After his earlier manic behaviour, Fotheringay was a silent figure as he studied the scene. Propped against the basket opposite her, not bothering to even flick his dark hair out of his eyes, he seemed pleased with all the turmoil happening below. In the reflected light, his outfit of sable leather, roped round his body with the thinnest of strings, sparkled as if miniature stars skated upon its surface.

He caught her gaze, pushed his shoulders back, and gave her a half-smile as if he'd just remembered he was not alone.

To Berd's annoyance, her heart fluttered. She tilted her chin away from him, and clasped her hands primly in front of her.

His smile only broadened. "Do you remember the pain? A burning sensation as though your insides were eaten alive? And as for your hand…" He twirled a finger at her right side, at her ungloved hand, pointing with a lazy flourish to her wrist. "There. The entry point."

"I beg your pardon!" she said stiffly, wishing she was anywhere but here, and with anyone else but him.

Fotheringay waved his hand insistently. "Lightning! Lightning always finds the path of least resistance into the ground. Unfortunately, that meant using us. If the

Engine had not sucked us in, it would have been our deaths."

She was sure that if she had not tightened her grip on the gunwale of the gondola, she'd have gone sliding to the ground. Cold metal bit into her hand. So it was true. The images in her head when she awoke weren't from a dream — the emerald green ground stretched out before her, and in the distance sat the city of brass.

For all her anger with him, he was the only one who could answer her questions. "If we are not within our proper bodies, nor are we ghosts, then…what are we?"

Fotheringay laughed, as if he knew all the answers she was dying to ask. He probably did, only she wished she didn't have to be dying in order to ask.

"We're not dead, if that's what you mean. We've been converted into a pattern of energy. Electrical matter. But fear not. All matter is merely a pattern of energy. Ours." He sighed and turned to concentrate on the blocks below. "Ours has merely changed."

Changed? Everything had changed. Right now they were so high she could not bear to look down. And as for her body becoming an energy pattern…

"Why, I feel as solid as ever!"

"Of course, you do. Energy feels solid to other energy."

A hot gust of wind buffeted their balloon and the gondola swung wildly. She grasped the railing, felt the metal grow warm in her grip.

"Wind is normal. Being buffeted by the wind is normal. You are mistaken, Mr Fotheringay."

He stared at her a moment; brooding melancholy filled his face, then he lifted one finger.

The swaying ceased.

Her stomach dropped; she gripped the railing harder. "No, this is not possible. This balloon is solid."

I am solid. Real.

His eyes only grew wider. "Everything you see around you is energy."

Everything. She released her grip on the railing. The taste of metal was strong in her mouth.

"Mr Fotheringay, we were almost burnt to death," she said, trying to steady her voice as well as her feet. "We need to get out of this balloon." Though where they could go, she'd no idea. Not with an earthquake still rumbling below, sending knives of steel and brass flying around.

His eyes locked on hers a moment, curious. "Charles."

"I beg your pardon?" Only children raised together were allowed such intimacy. Not even married couples used such informality — unless of course they were commoners. To acquiesce to this request would breed a familiarity that at this stage, if ever, she was not keen to encourage. And he wasn't answering her question again.

"Charles," he repeated, undeterred.

His eyes glinted in the amber glow from the buildings. His coal-black hair blew devilishly loose across his shoulders, like the pictures she had seen in the papers of savages.

"We are in what you may find to be a 'strange land', and in certain situations that may arise I've no time to waste on niceties."

Certain situations…the churl meant those of life and death. She remembered his desperation to get her on board the hot air balloon before it took off — but he had waited long to do so. She did not like to think as to what might have happened had he not done so accordingly. She met his gaze with what she hoped was a cool, detached expression. "Understood. So long as we have an accord, that you will avoid causing such situations."

He snorted then he turned his back to her and looked out. "We're here." The words were spoken quietly.

"Where pray tell is *here*? Have we reached another city?" Berd looked around.

Fotheringay flung out one arm. As though he had cast a further spell, the smoke cleared. Their balloon bobbed against a building sprouting beside them. The top of the green onyx building disappeared into the sky, far above their heads. Weird brass turrets decorated with red enamel drops jutted around its exterior.

This was like no dream or nightmare she'd ever had. Maybe they had reached another city. "But the earthquake…"

His eyes sparkled mysteriously. "Look below."

Beneath them, the earthquake appeared to have ceased. Roads laced the land, only they didn't wind through the landscape: instead, each sparkling highway gleamed straight and long, thin-stretched wires of gold.

She shook her head. No, not landscape. This was the computerscape. She was in a computer.

Even as she gazed, the constant sensation of falling never left her.

"No matter how many times I've seen it, its beauty always astonishes me."

Awe hung in his words. Fotheringay's eyes were bright as a winter's morn, his gaze transfixed by the view. Though she was angered, she had to admit that his world was stunning. *If he was the inventor of the Engine, he's created all of this. He's truly the Great Enchanter.*

"Majestic," she whispered, herself caught up in the magic. And some of her fear eased.

"Come." He offered his hand.

She took it; the skin on his palm was roughened.

He waved his free hand and from out of the side of the building, like a seedling budding, tendrils twisted out, lengthening and thickening and filigreeing until they formed an arched door that opened into the smallest room she had ever seen, the walls and the roof were of glass, while the floor was rock-like, veined and flaked like mica.

"An elevator?" she muttered, amazed.

Again Fotheringay did not answer. Instead he leaped inside, turned, and then reached down to place his hands around her waist.

"I can manage!" she protested as he lifted her out of the balloon.

He placed her on her feet. Then he waved behind them.

The balloon was gone.

Berd's heart pounded, rising to her ears as she followed him into the elevator. Inside, the hum intensified. The scent of ginger floated around her as the door closed, increasing her sense of unease. She was Alice in Wonderland about to go down the rabbit hole.

Right now she was in a tiny room that had not

existed moments earlier. Just like the balloon now no longer existed. Energy. "How far up did we go?"

Fotheringay smiled. "Almost to heaven." He soothed the glass as if it was a wild stallion. Then he whispered, "Down."

The elevator began to free fall.

Her stomach lifted, as did the rest of her. For a moment, her body felt as if it weighed nothing; that she was going to fly right out the glass top and plummet to her death. A scream tore from her throat. No one knew where she was. If she died, no one would know what had happened to her. She gripped his hand with all her strength, as if that might somehow save her from the crushing effects of gravity. And indeed he stayed still, as if affixed to the bottom of the car, but his arm lifted up with her as if she was a balloon and he were the feather.

But weight returned gradually, not in a grand finale of a single moment. She floated to the floor and rejoined Fotheringay, her hair and clothing tamed once more. The ever-present hum lessened to almost nothing, and then the elevator came to a halt.

The door snapped opened. He released her hand and continued on his way, as if falling elevators were a natural occurrence. The ground no longer rumbled, but Berd could not smooth the shaking inside her. She wiped her damp hand on her pants and peered out.

She stood in the midst of another city of gigantic blocks. No doubt these blocks would also transform or explode into wonderful buildings. And if she stayed in the lift, it would also transform and entomb her in the walls.

Ahead of her, Fotheringay walked out into the street, his movements smooth and unhurried. He was the white rabbit pulling her into this Wonderland, his Wonderland. She hurried after him, her feet clattering across the metallic floor, the taste of metal in her mouth, and the hum buzzing in her ears.

Like Alice, she wanted to be home before the Queen of Hearts said, 'Off with her head.'

Chapter 5

HE CITY PURRED. A monstrous cat that needed to feed…

Berd shivered and pushed the ghastly image from her mind. She scratched her wrists, trying not to look too hard at the shiny surfaces of the computerscape around her in case something stared back.

Ahead, Fotheringay was charging through a dimly lit passageway between two tall copper buildings, hurrying as though determined to leave her behind again. Berd knew she needed to speak, to ask where they were going, and what was happening. Explorers, when in unknown territory, always hired a guide, but then *they* had a choice of guides. Here she was down to a single entity: Fotheringay or no-one.

Thankfully, he spoke the same tongue as her, though she was loath to use his Christian name. Until now, she put it down to the fact that they did not share familiarity, such as that which existed amongst children who had grown up together. But she knew in her case, there was more to her reticence. Opportunities of conversing with members of the opposite sex, especially ones around the same age as her, rarely happened.

"Where exactly are we go—" Before she could finish her question, a distant roar cut across the humming, so unexpected that it felt as if a skeletal finger had scraped across her shoulders. "Another earthquake?" she asked, peeved when her voice hitched.

Fotheringay threw her a glance; light and shadow flickered across his face, making it difficult to read.

"Data train. Our ride after I set up the batteries."

He turned and sped on, and Berd stared after him in disbelief. Perhaps he expected her to understand and was disappointed that she did not. But she had cleaned the Engine twice and hadn't noticed any batteries. Or train. However, batteries meant an energy source and since an energy source meant the possibility of home, it was hard not to get excited.

She sniffed the air, desperate to catch a whiff of the unmistakable odour of smoke created from burning coal which a train would have to have. And though relief filled her at the naming of something so familiar, it didn't last.

Fotheringay may have acted like a god up in the balloon, but back on the ground, he was behaving as if another earthquake was imminent. If he really was the creator of this space, then there would have been no need for him to escape in a hot air balloon. Surely all he need do was say the word or lift a finger like he had done earlier. It struck her that while he might be the inventor, perhaps his creation had gotten away from him…like he was getting away from her. She was forced to half-run after him. He strode into the open and with lithe, powerful steps, crossed a street then passed under a steel archway that led between another set of buildings.

If only he would slow. She pressed her hands deep into her sides, hoping if she squeezed the bottom end of her corset, that the top might open up a little and allow her to take deeper breaths. But after half a block, she had no such luck, though she was gaining a little.

"Mister — I mean, about these batteries." She was so close now. "I would like to know —"

Fotheringay turned towards her so abruptly she almost crashed into him. "What do you *wish* to know about *my* Engine?"

While he had not been particularly friendly now he appeared openly hostile. The change was so swift she could have believed it was a different person standing in front of her. Why, the very way he was looking at her made her think she was a spy about to steal his secrets.

And that must have been what it was. But he had no right to think so ill of her. She was not some patent stealer, and he should know that. But to confront him with this accusation would be poor manners to all parties.

"The Engine is the reason I am here." It should not matter to whom the Engine belonged, she convinced herself. Escape should be their top priority.

"That is the truth. But it is *my* Engine."

Berd pursed her lips as they stared each other down. If she admitted she had purchased his Engine, he, no doubt, would ask her to return it.

She'd refuse, which then opened up the possibility that he might leave her behind. She decided she would not tell him she owned the Engine, not until she knew what was going on.

"I'm afraid your Engine was sold at auction a month ago." That much was true.

"I see." He rubbed his chin carelessly with a finger as he studied her face. "May I ask who was with you when the lightning struck?"

His question caught her so unexpectedly that she muttered, "No one," before she even had time to think.

Annoyed, she realised his fall into decorum was only a ploy to get information out of her. She met his gaze fully…only to look away.

Something is wrong with his eyes.

"Did *you* purchase my Engine?" he asked.

The smile on her face died.

He knew.

But then, how else could she have gotten here, unless she had been fiddling with the Engine. *Her* Engine.

When she pressed her lips into a thin straight line, Fotheringay smiled and stood taller.

"I'm afraid, Lady Elizabeth, there's been a mistake. Rest assured that you will be amply compensated for whatever monies you have expended."

The churl, no doubt, would force her to give it up. But the Engine was in her possession, and from what little she knew of the law, her case was stronger than his. Displaying every ounce of her breeding, she tilted her chin proudly. "I understand your distress, but I do not wish to be compensated."

They were staring each other down when she caught a flash of green in his eyes. Startled, she blinked. She had thought his eyes were blue earlier, but now they were ringed with green. And as she stared they grew greener still. Greenness crept into the centre of his eyes, the colour growing more intense with each moment.

Something is wrong with his eyes.

"My lady, this Engine belongs to me, and to my father. I understand now your reluctance to provide me with information of my father. Simply put, he's ill. Doubtless, he has expended both time and money in his search for me, and you've taken advantage of his ill health to seize our Engine."

The insult could not have been greater than if he had slapped her. She had been mistaken to have thought him a knight. "I—"

"Please don't patronise me, Lady Elizabeth." The muscles tightened around his mouth then he swivelled on his heel and strode away.

She would have willingly forgone her breeding and throttled him. "You mistake my intentions," she called after him.

"I'm in a hurry to see about the batteries. I don't have time to argue."

Blast him, blast him, blast him!

She would teach him to think twice that he could dismiss her so easily. "I can be of assistance."

"A delicate thing like you?"

It sounded like he truly believed that. And for Berd, who stood behind him in her brother's trousers, and who had spent the last six months fiddling with engines, his words stung. He was simply another James. She dug her fists into her hips as she fought to contain her anger. "You left out illogical."

He swung round again, his face creased in furious confusion.

She put on a brave smile. "It's what my brother always called me."

To her relief, one corner of his mouth twitched as if genuinely holding back laughter.

"I can help. I can do anything you set me to. Anything at all," Berd prompted. She could tell him she had dabbled in engines. Well, more accurately *one* other engine. Her autocar. Trouble was, the Ghost Engine was far more complicated than her autocar. And her autocar no longer worked.

Fotheringay scrutinised her, deadly serious. "What we are about to undertake is a matter of life and death. But while the Engine can do many things, one thing it cannot do is heal itself. For this, the Engine needs hands. I am those hands." He flicked a caustic glance at the sky, as if arguing with it. "But two sets of hands mean the work gets done faster."

Berd frowned, convinced she was stuck in the Engine with a mad man. So convinced was she, that when he turned and offered her his arm, she gaped at this unexpected show of manners.

"Suffragette?" he asked, curious. Then his eyes narrowed and he looked at her as though seeing her in a different, though not necessarily complimentary, light.

She scowled at the term. He probably thought she would bite. If she did, he deserved it. She needed no sermonising to know what a man thought a woman's proper place was. Not that she agreed.

"No, though their cause is noble. I have my own method of fighting for equality."

He lowered his arm. "Of course! I should have guessed. But equality for the sexes," he mused as if delighted, then in a louder voice, as if speaking to an equal, he drawled, "Come on then, *princess*. This isn't London, and I have no time to waste in drawing room conversation. If you want to wear those trousers, make me believe you have the stuff to put in them."

Berd clenched her teeth. At those words, she expected him to head off without her, but this time, despite the taunt, he actually waited, behaving for once like a complete gentleman.

She eyed him suspiciously, vigilant for conversational tiger traps. Still, it was an interesting thought: to be a princess or a man.

Berd knew which she would rather be.

She had asked to prove herself and he had accepted her offer to help. The price was tradition, its loss for the gaining of equality. If she really wanted to be treated as an equal then she should expect to be treated like a man. Only she had never before had a chance to put it in practise with anyone. Any man.

As she took one tentative step forward, he nodded amiably. They set off. Together.

She inhaled deeply as she mentally prepared herself for the task ahead.

The Engine was his life.

Whatever task he asked of her, she had to accomplish it.

She had a suspicion, though, from the way he was beaming, that she was not going to like it, whatever it was.

The air tasted of metal.

It buzzed as if stung with electricity, giving Berd the sensation of being out of her body. Perhaps there was some truth in the Theosophists' belief of out-of-body sensations, after all.

She grimaced and the silent steel walls of the buildings, like two mirrors placed opposite, reflected it a thousand times, her images shrinking progressively until they vanished altogether. Almost as if it were foreshadowing that if Berd and Fotheringay could not escape, they would disappear into the Engine eternally.

Become energy.

She quickened her steps.

Berd scratched her neck. She had been scratching different parts of her anatomy for at least an hour, baffled as to why she was itching so much. Maybe she could start by asking him the reason she itched, and if he answered truthfully, she could then ask about the Engine.

This now provided her with another problem. If she was to speak with Fotheringay, she would have to use his first name. He had insisted on it back in the balloon. She supposed it was a fair request, for, if she wanted to change the way society thought in the area of equality, she would have to be prepared to change the way she thought, too, especially if it meant progress. Only why was it hard to speak to a man, especially this man.

She exhaled heavily. After her attempts at conversation, which admittedly could have gone much better, she was determined their next conversation succeed. He had offered to let her work on the Engine.

In that sense, they were partners, and partners did not fear communication.

"Charles?" To her ears, her words sounded as if there was gravel in her mouth.

She was not alone in being uncomfortable.

His jaw worked, and she was convinced she must have upset him when he cleared his throat and gave the most fleeting of glances. "Forgive me, but I have not heard my name for a year."

Berd could have sunk through the ground with mortification, but his explanation made perfect sense. She took this as a good sign to proceed to the next step of her plan and hoped she would not sound foolish as she asked, "Forgive me, but why do I want to ummm, scratch?"

"Scratch?" He frowned, as though momentarily thrown off by the change of subject. Then he grinned. "Ah! It's your new growth. When I placed you in the river of energy, your wounds were healed. Think of scabs."

Scabs? This itch was all over. Surely she hadn't scabs all over. A more direct approach was needed. "What do you do to relieve the itch?"

"Ahh…mmm." He would not meet her gaze as he answered. "I rolled on the ground."

Roll on the ground! Now that was going from being a man to being a child. She swallowed, unsure how to respond.

Fotheringay must have sensed her confusion and abhorrence, because he quickly added, "Perhaps you could try this. The walls of the buildings are fairly cool to the touch. Why not press yourself against them? The cold might relieve the discomfort."

The alternative did not sound much better. She could not imagine how pressing against a wall, even a reflective one, would help.

His face was flushed as though he could mind-read all her objections. He bowed stiffly. "I shall withdraw. Call me when you have finished. Pray do not take long."

And then he was gone, suddenly, round the corner, his footfalls dying in her ears, and she was alone. The thought that he would desert her to retain ownership of his Engine flashed through her mind. She shook her head. Someone with that much pride wouldn't desert her on such ridiculous pretences at the very least. Still in moments, she could not hear him and the narrowness of the alleyway only amplified her anxious breathing.

The intensity of his gaze as he looked out of the glass elevator returned, and she peered uncertainly at the rectangle of bright emptiness beyond the walls of the two buildings.

Maybe he was testing her.

She stepped close to the building and looked up. The sky was a ribbon of gold above her head. Then she pressed herself against the wall's gleaming smoothness. Cold seeped through her clothes, sucking most of the itch straight out of her and replacing it with a sensation of numbness. Her arms sagged by her sides and soon grew weightless. Berd exhaled softly and closed her eyes. Fothering—No, Charles his name was. And Charles was right. This was good; she should have trusted him. If only she could remain like this forever. However, her other side still itched. She opened her eyes and pushed herself from the wall, her pleasure at the relief reflected in the mirror opposite. She grinned.

Her reflection grinned.

She winked.

It winked pleasantly back at her.

She was not alone.

"It was foolish to have been so bothered," she whispered confidentially to her reflection.

It whispered back obligingly. As did the hundreds of diminishing images before her, only they did so one after the other. Taking it in turns as if there was a delay.

Her skin crawled. That was not how mirrors worked. She shook her head. No, this was impossible, she had to be mistaken. The humming had unnerved her.

She was not alone.

"I have got to get out of here," she muttered, but even as she took a step back the hum intensified.

The wall shivered, like a cat twitching, as every image of her faded away, blending into the cold, grey steel. A point in the wall to her left bulged as if an elbow had been pressed into it, and then disappeared.

Her heart hammered against her chest. It had to be fatigue. It was making her see things that weren't there.

She had thought this wall was solid steel, but maybe it was more like the brass cube. Even as she stared, she saw the wall thinning, the centre sagging as if it had gone soft like toffee that had melted in the sun. And then an image pressed itself against the wall.

From the inside!

Berd froze as the image took form.

It pushed itself in frenetic motions against the wall, as if trying to get out. Trying to get to her.

Only the steel wall stood between them. Or what had *been* a steel wall. The features of the figure became clearer as the wall seemed to melt away. She recognised the face. Charles Fotheringay. But that was impossible!

Then the creature's fingers broke through. She screamed, backing away rapidly, remembering how they had tightened round her throat, just as hands grasped her.

They closed.

She twisted, struggling to wrench them off, but the hands were too strong.

"Elizabeth? My lady!"

"No!" she shrieked. There was something wrong about all this. The arms were hard, but warm, not cold as she had imagined they would be.

Berd froze and stared down at her sleeves. These were Charles's arms, not the apparition's. She had mistaken his arms for the arms of the creature. Then she caught the stink of the real Charles Fotheringay's leather outfit, of paraffin and more.

Berd blinked, and blinked again. Everything was returned to normal. She was back. Safe. She glanced round the glittering silver alley before focusing on Charles. Her heart-beat slowed a little and her breathing eased.

He stared at her, puzzled. "What's wrong?"

She closed her eyes, sighed then opened them. When she was steady on her feet, he carefully released her and stepped away.

Charles's hair was pushed back from his face, the

dark circles under his eyes as obvious as the concern on his pale face. "What happened? You screamed."

"I saw it. Something was trying to pull me into the wall."

He frowned. "The wall? What wall? Why would anything want to pull you into the wall, if such a thing is even possible? I said to press against the wall. Not merge with it."

"I am not an idiot. This wall tried to suck me into it." Even as she turned, she knew the wall would be as it was before.

And sure enough it was a blank piece of steel, reflecting only her baffled expression.

He said nothing, but stepped up to the wall, laid his palms against it and pushed powerfully. She could see the effort he was expending, but despite his best attempts, the wall remained impervious.

She massaged one frozen ear vigorously, trying to recall what had happened. "That wall. I pressed half my face into it to relieve the itch, but when I tried to switch sides, a figure appeared."

Charles's frown only deepened as he moved up and down the wall, shoving hard at various spots. Nothing budged. After a while, he stopped and looked at her, worry etching his features.

He would think she had gone mad to say the mysterious figure had his face, but if it hadn't been Charles then there was only one other it could be: the second figure she had seen the time she fainted in the stables, the malevolent one. Her heart skipped a beat.

"Do you have a twin, by chance?" Berd asked, hoping desperately.

"No why?"

The blood drained from her face. So whose ghost was it? To think it had almost succeeded breaking out of the wall…

She couldn't stop shaking as she slipped her cold hands protectively around her throat.

Chapter 6

O N THE ONE hand, Berd felt she had succeeded in her original objective: she had spoken with Charles the ghost.

On the other hand, he wasn't even a ghost. Or dead. He was real and living, and now she was trapped inside the Engine with him.

She had just spent what seemed like an hour trailing behind him as he pushed his way through the depths of the computerscape of the Engine until they reached the vacuum tubes.

Gigantic glass bulbs two-storeys tall, and contained in each the skeleton of a tree of lightning. Blazing light and radiant heat poured out, as if the sun within could not be contained.

Again she was reminded that this was not the world she knew.

The Valley of the Vacuum Tubes was Berd's 'Burning Bush' experience that lingered even with each blink or closure of her eyes. Her cheeks were still hot to the touch.

She felt she understood now, what Moses had undergone. She could empathise.

Charles dimmed the tubes through a series of switches. "Or it would be impossible to work," he said, via way of an explanation.

Then he proposed she help prepare for the chemical reaction that would allow them to return to the real world. She had agreed, thinking it would be an excellent way to learn about the Engine, until he explained that her actual job was to inflate these...

A sigh escaped her as she looked down at the creature she was nursing in her arms. Charles had referred to it and others like it as battery beasts. Which she guessed was as good a name as anything for something that looked part-insect, part-mammal, part-who-knew-what?

The truth was that the creature in her arms resembled a honey-pot ant because of its fat, expandable belly and six segmented legs. Except, the battery beast didn't have a hard shell like an insect, and it was surprisingly warm and furry, like a puppy. A puppy mixed with a sloth, a rather slippery sloth. She had regrettably dropped quite a few of the beasts, and winced guiltily as each had turned an accusing eye up at her.

At a distance, they resembled silvery dashes, cast-off bits of lead solder, stretching horizontally along one brass wall: Morse code.

Every single one of them had just laid there, barely moving, as Charles patiently demonstrated what needed to be done by placing his mouth on a snout and using his own breath to gently inflate the creature like it was a child's balloon.

And every single one of them had those large, silver puppy-dog eyes that bulged with surprise if she blew a touch too much air into them. Her first two attempts at inflation had been disastrous for not only had the battery beast's eyes bulged, but a little silvery something had emptied itself onto her pants in order to make room for the air.

Now she knew better then to inflate each beast beyond ten inches. Her current beast trembled, as she held it in her arms and a bit of saliva dribbled out the side of its snout. It smelt of burnt solder and wet dog. To think she would have to put her mouth on it. Each one seemed only fouler than the last.

Her stomach turned.

"Do you do this often?" she asked.

"Not if I can help it." He sighed and plucked another off the wall.

If only she had a choice, but time was running out. Above, the sky was in afternoon hours. By now the people back home must have noticed she was missing but even if they knew where she was, none would know how to extricate her.

Berd gathered her resolve, bent forward, cupped one hand around the battery beast's muzzle and then blew air into its mouth. The bag that was the beast's abdomen bulged. They must have some sort of valve, because they never deflated. When it was about ten inches in diameter, she placed it down in a pile of others then wiped her mouth on her sleeve — her handkerchief was soaked — and reached for the next battery beast.

She found herself staring hard at it. Wide-eyed and trusting, it gazed back at her from its spot on the wall.

When she plucked it away, it wriggled its six legs. It did look like an adorable, silky-soft puppy, if she could ignore the extra set of limbs, and the segments…

'Beast' was the wrong word for them, though they did have six legs like the ladybirds everyone loved in her garden. 'Birds' also seemed wrong, as they had no beak. What was it the Americans called them?

Not ladybirds, but ladybugs!

Strange how two countries that spoke the same language had different names for the same objects.

Like paraffin was kerosene.

However, ladybugs, yes, that was it!

Bugs. Battery bugs.

She picked up another beast — *battery bug* — and blew once more. Seeing them in a different light, and with a new name, the task didn't seem so irksome. When the bug had inflated to the right volume, she put it next to the others.

A short distance away, Charles was energetically attaching the half-dozen he had taken from her onto a frame he had constructed. He had explained that during their escape attempt, these vacuum tubes would operate at maximum power, and the frame would prevent the creatures from being fried, as the last thing either of them wanted was a short circuit.

But was this the truth?

She chewed a corner of her lower lip as she studied him. As a guide, he appeared trustworthy, but Charles was an enigma. A magnet. And like a magnet, he both attracted and repelled her. She told herself she was drawn to him because he was the sole living thing besides her in a dead world.

He knew the computerscape. He knew how to

manipulate it, too. But he didn't seem to understand the other figures that appeared in it from time to time, and that seemed more worrying than anything.

He had survived long in the Engine, and she was curious as to how close he had come to dying throughout his trials here. To be here all alone for a year would have affected the decisions he had made in order to survive.

When Berd had first met him, he had said something disturbing: something about the Engine pulling them in. If it had not happened to her she would never have believed an engine could pull them in. Unless he meant to say this Engine was alive. But an engine was simply the sum total of its gears and wheels and cogs.

She looked down at the bloated pile of battery bugs. Creatures alive. If the Engine had pulled her in on its own initiative, then the Engine could think. And by that, she didn't mean thinking what it had been programmed to think, but rather thinking freely of its own accord. Exactly as if it was a sentient being.

The Engine was supposed to be a computer, the first ever digital calculating device. Only she was beginning to suspect that what she thought the Engine was, and what it actually was, were two vastly different entities.

I must find out what exactly Charles and his father have created. And whether it is finished —

"Lady Elizabeth?"

She looked up to find Charles striding over. From his stance, she surmised that the reason he approached was, because he did not trust her, a woman, to finish the job.

"I am perfectly fine, Mr Fotheringay. You may continue with what you are doing." She waved at him, trying to shoo him back to his section of the Engine opposite her. Men and their ironclad obstinacy! He was mistaken if he presumed she would allow him to supervise. She would have to explain without insulting him that she would be more comfortable with him at a distance.

In the half-shadows, his eyes appeared grey. "I was thinking that I'd like a competition."

She almost snorted. "As you are attaching these creatures to that frame, after I blow them up, I will be finished before you. Therefore, I win. Do you not agree?"

He wrinkled his nose, amused. "You did say you wanted to prove yourself. I'll take this pile. You have the other." Even before he finished speaking, he had grasped three battery bugs.

Before her astonished gaze, he whipped them up to their perfect sizes and then deposited them in a new pile. He didn't seem to mind their discomfort, let alone his own.

"That's my first three."

She grabbed a couple more bugs.

"Three more." He sounded almost bored.

"Mr Fotheringay! I have not accepted any competition. And I refuse to believe efficiency is the sole measure of a man."

He shrugged lazily, his jet hair falling over his face so that he appeared devil-may-care. "Ah, that's only because you know I'm winning."

She was sure steam was coming out her ears. She dropped the second battery bug, winced as it bounced on the ground like a bladder full of water, secured the first and blew it up. "There!"

"Three!" He eyed her, his brilliant eyes gleaming with unspoken challenge.

Berd longed to punch him, but propriety forbade her. Instead, she did the next best thing. She gritted her teeth, lifted the next bug and lowered her head. If only they tasted better.

"You're doing well, my lady."

She refused to look at him, irritated by the fact he was winning so easily. "A man of skill does not invest in a competition with amateurs and call it fair. That is the domain of a louse and a cheat and I hold you to better than that, Mr Fotheringay!"

"You're just sore because you're losing. But you're doing well for an amateur."

She shoved every bit of effort into inflating the pile before her.

"Three." He spun them expertly onto the ground.

Three? She blew harder and then cringed as once again something warm and wet dribbled onto her boots.

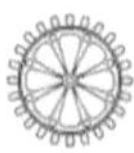

Berd handed Charles the last of the battery bugs. It burped a puff of brown stinking air as it was latched onto the frame.

Yes, definitely solder and wet dog.

"That's it. We're finished." Charles stood back, hands on his hips as he surveyed the line of bugs. "And now with the beasts all end-to-end on the frame, it will enable a full charge of electricity to elevate the platform mechanism I've spent the last six months building."

"Our hope of escape," she breathed, as his plan formulated in her mind.

Berd had to admit, grudgingly, that Charles's competition had enabled them to complete the inflation of the bugs in less than half the time she knew it would have taken her alone. With her help, he had attached them swiftly to the frame. It pleased her that he had seen her as an equal, like her grandmother who had worked with Mr Babbage, though Charles's personality still needed work.

What a shame Babbage had not succeeded. Had he completed the Difference Engine, or even the Analytical Engine then Grandmother could have tested her programs, and the world would have seen that women possessed intelligence and stopped treating them like children. Then she would truly have been the Enchantress of Numbers! The High Priestess and Prophetess of this New Age of Machines. Babbage had tried, oh how he had tried, and when the government grant was depleted, he had used up his own fortune. It was just not to be yet…

Charles was still adjusting a few of the bugs' positions.

Hurry, hurry, please. Mr Fother — I mean Charles. I mean…

Berd quelled her impatience by stroking one of the bugs with a finger. "They are curious little creatures, aren't they?" She glanced at Charles. His hands looked strong from this angle.

He continued to fuss.

Surely he must have heard her. "I did wonder what you meant when you mentioned batteries. I had been working hard to clean up the Engine and had not noticed any batteries." If only she didn't babble when nervous.

He grinned at her. "It would be good to see Father again."

His father...

She struggled to speak before the words strangled her. "Your father had cleaned it up. But the Engine had been left awhile when I got it. It was dusty. A couple of moths had laid eggs within... Charles, I'm sorry, but your father died of grief a year after you disappeared."

The second the words left her mouth, she wished them back. She should have picked a better time, but there was never a good time for such news. She could not delay any longer.

For the longest moment, Charles stood unmoving, pale golden light bathing his face. His eyes widened, then shut.

Her heart twisted. She knew what it was like to lose a parent—both parents. She turned away, intending to leave him to his grief, when she heard tiny pulsing noises.

In the open distance beyond the Valley of the Vacuum Tubes, the air above a silver block quivered. As she watched, a stream of bright white dots rushed round the corner. They shimmered, dazzling like a thousand miniature suns as they streamed in the direction of her and Charles. Beautiful...

So far in her limited experience in the world of the Engine, she had discovered that beautiful things were often dangerous. And these objects resembled suns. Beautiful miniature suns.

In her world, if she came close to a sun she would

be burnt to a crisp. And across the computerscape, thousands were coming at them.

"Mr Fother—Charles."

Charles glanced at her and then at the point where she was staring. "What the devil— Ah, bits." Some unreadable emotion crossed his face and then he stirred, lord of the situation once more. "It looks like we're going to have a *bit* of fun."

"You're making a pun at a time like this?" She grabbed his arm in order to flee only he shrugged out of her grasp.

"My father loved puns," he said.

The suns resembled swarms of glowing bees. And bees stung.

She licked her lips nervously. "Maybe if we stole away, the creatures wouldn't notice us." She stepped back but he was no longer next to her.

Charles's voice rang out in a summons. "Here!"

Her heart skipped several beats and she rounded on him. "Mr Fotheringay, what did you just do!"

His eyes were wild as he answered. "It's Charles."

His father's death must be affecting him. Pray he did nothing foolish. "Charles, please…" She reached out one hand, trying to soothe him.

He took another step away from her. "I commanded them to come to show you they're not dangerous. Look, bits are fun. Little binary digits. Just watch what I do."

Binary digits. They were what she needed in order to start programming. Only these resembled the silver shards that had stabbed the ground. "They look most dangerous."

"Nonsense," he scoffed as he strode towards them. "All one has to do is toggle them. A bit, you see, represents a value. One or zero. On or off. A bit is like a switch. Actually they're exactly like switches. Flags."

Flags! So she was right. They did have something to do with programming.

The swarm was halfway towards them, a silver lightning bolt snaking around the open space. They looked anything but safe.

"I do not think this is such a good idea. Charles, please." Waves of cold bathed her and she touched his elbow again.

"Watch this." He spread his arms wide, as if about to invoke a spell.

Blast! Boys could be so annoyingly stubborn! They should be able to admit when they were wrong!

The glowing silver bits circled him, whorls of liquid mercury. If Charles was a celestial planet, they were his spiralling rings.

Berd hugged her shoulders where she stood a few paces behind him, petrified, not wanting to watch, but unable to tear her gaze away. The demented ringing of a thousand bells rung by lunatics vibrated the air and tickled the tiny inner hairs in her ears as they swarmed Charles. It was madness in a melody, and she was being shaken to death by invisible hands. He must have a death wish.

"Fun," said Charles, as he flourished an arm, full and confident of his power, only his eyes glistened. He turned to check she was watching, and then flicked the nearest bit.

The creature exploded in his hand. His smile

vanished. And his mouth opened in a surprised yell of pain.

No! He was being attacked! That was impossible, surely; he was the lord of this world. The creator himself! But if the creator of this world could be attacked, then no one was safe.

She raced towards him.

Charles was shaking his hand from within the swirling cloud, which had lifted a bit to swirl furiously above his head. "Blast! Blast! Blast! Must have been the lightning, because those blighters have a lot more zap than I expected." Then he calmed. "Look here, old chaps, I simply wanted to show this young lady what you're capable of."

This wasn't the time to have a discussion with one's attackers. Despite her fear and the incessant pain in her head from the noise, she ducked under the circle of bits and grabbed his arm. "Charles, I beg of you. Stop! You will be killed."

"Nonsense, princess. Just one more." He threw her a look of utter self-assurance, extended his hand and swatted another bit.

A brilliant burst of white and yellow light exploded from the tips of his fingers. The smell of singed flesh soured the air.

His countenance creased in agony. "Stop it, you blasted fools! Stop." It was the surprise on his face that convinced her something was seriously wrong.

In a blink, the bits enclosed them in a glittering sphere. Tiny, deadly balls of light burst all around them, each explosion bringing a thousand red-hot embers raining down. Berd screamed each time they came in contact with her flesh. She smelt her clothes burning, her hair singeing, and blood in the air. A large ball of energy, glowing silver, blazed towards her face. There was no avoiding it. This was it. The end.

She was going to die.

Chapter 7

ERD SCREAMED AS the ball of energy flamed towards
her.

Each time a bit's tiny feet clawed at her, a
streak of radiant white light erupted, blinding her even
with her eyes shut. She dropped to her knees to avoid
them but it didn't help. Writhing in agony, she
huddled closer to the ground as Charles covered her
with his body.

As suddenly as it had started, the pinging and the
bangs stopped.

Silence.

She felt weight lift from her, as he rose to his feet.

"Are you all right, my lady? Are you all right?"
Charles's voice echoed in the vacuum. His arms were
around her, protective, helping her stand.

Wary, she lifted her gaze. The space around the
buildings was clear, and the only evidence of the
assault was the lingering taste of blood, smoke, and
metal in the air. But the bits were gone.

A small, nervous cry left her throat. She rounded on

Charles — the cause of it all — but then she saw him…

His face was blackened, his outfit scorched and singed. Blood dripped freely from his fingers and nose, and spattered onto the green-enamelled ground.

The next thing he did surprised her even more. He touched her gently on the shoulder as if she were an injured child, more concerned about her injuries than his. It made no sense for him to act this way, especially after his ill-treatment of her.

"Are you all right?" he repeated.

She pulled away from him. "How could you summon them!"

Guilt flashed over his face before he whipped his hand back and straightened. "Normally, they're fine. I simply wanted to show you something about the Engine. The lightning must have caused the bits to be filled with more electricity than usual. That's all."

This was more like the Charles she was used to. "We. Were. *Attacked*, Mr Fotheringay. Attacked. We could have been killed."

Unexpectedly, his face softened. "Yet you darted inside the circle."

He was staring at her with such intensity that Berd shifted her feet uncomfortably. "Well, someone had to rescue you, Mr Fotheringay."

He arched one brow at the formality of her address, and then his expression grew serious. "I admit I made a mistake. I invited them over, not knowing the consequences. There was a slight delay in their responding to my change of direction, but you covered your face, so it's mostly your hands and arms that were injured. Actually…"

He tapped a finger against his mouth as he flicked a

glance up and down her, an assessment as impartial as if she were an autocar. Despite the clinical nature of his perusal, Berd felt heat rise to her throat.

"Just as I thought! It was *because* your garments were soaked from working with the battery beasts that you suffered a little more than was to be expected."

To her annoyance, he was right. Her garments had taken the brunt of the assault, but that was not the point. By now she was seething. Tired and miserable, the last thing she wanted was to engage in an intellectual debate as to whose fault it was, especially when it was obvious.

"*You* asked to help," he reminded her gently.

Had a battery beast been within grasp, she would have flung it at him. Charles had known the task, and had known she was wet, and yet still, he had commanded the bits over.

He knew the land.

He may not have known the bits were overflowing with electricity, but the point was he knew they were filled with electricity. This latest incident proved she could not trust him. Though she had no idea how, she was determined to make her way out without him.

She glared at him. "Thank you for your assistance, Mr Fotheringay, in ill circumstances *you* created. From here on, I shall be able to manage perfectly."

Charles groaned through gritted teeth as if she had pushed him to his limits. "My lady, just stop your lecture and give me a minute, please."

Berd held no sympathy for him. After what he had made her suffer, if she could push some more, she would, but she waited, readying herself to punch him if he tried anything untoward.

"All right, this is what we'll do." His voice was softer. "You will be fine, do not fear. It was more the shock of minor electrocution you felt. Now if you please, hold out your right hand." From a fold in his suit, he pulled out a small receptacle.

Light brown, round and leathery, it looked like a bladder. It was also ten inches in diameter.

The battery bugs…

She cringed and looked to him, taking for confirmation the fact his face tightened and that he would not meet her eyes.

"Well, princess? Are you too proud to accept a local remedy? This isn't from Harley Street." He untied the bladder as he waited for her decision.

She was a fool to even think he was going to apologise. If it wasn't for the fact her burns were throbbing so violently, she would have ignored him and gone her way. Reluctantly, she held out one hand.

The drop he poured onto the first burn dazzled in its radiance. At first it felt as if he were pouring cool water onto her hand, except it looked like…

Liquid sunlight.

Hissing smoke issued from the wound.

She would have jumped back, had he not grasped her hand and held it steady. Her whole body grew warm and her heart sped up. Then she gasped. Her palm felt as though worms were crawling under her skin! She opened her mouth to protest, but he held up a finger.

"Wait and watch." His eyes, almost silver through the smoke, sparkled with confidence.

When the smoke cleared, she examined her hand. The burn was healed. "I—I—don't believe this."

In answer, he poured a drop each onto the remaining two burns. Hissing, smoke, crawling, and then her hand was healed. With a solemn smile, he indicated for her to hold out her other hand.

An unnatural buzzing throbbed in her veins as if her blood were thicker. Then her skin started itching and she knew what was in the flask.

Energy from the river.

Pure energy. That must have been how he managed to stay alive and how he had gotten his powers. And if she drank it, no doubt she would get them, too. Other creatures had also imbibed of the energy.

The moths.

The moths she had removed from the Engine in the stable.

Each time she turned the Engine on, the vacuum tubes glowed. Insects were attracted to light and the charge *must* have somehow affected them. In turn the eggs the moths laid must have become the battery bugs. She should have noticed that the battery bugs bore slight traces of wingless silver moths.

Silver moths whose fat bellies swirled with energy.

The energy had mutated them.

She grimaced, and linked both hands behind her. "No, thank you. No more energy for me, please, I do not wish to be experimented upon."

Charles, who had been waiting for her to hold up her other hand, took a step back, aghast. "Princess, I have created a device to help mankind. Not injure them. I am not Dr Frankenstein. My Engine is not a monster."

How she wished she could believe him. Instead, an image fanned before her eyes: the battery bugs framed on the wall like a butterfly collection, followed by a hollow-eyed Charles pinned beside them. If he continued to partake of the energy, he would end up like them.

Before she could think further on it, a familiar whistle blew. To her delight, it sounded like that of a train's.

"Hurry! We must catch it." He shoved the bladder into the fold in his suit and then held out his hand.

We must? He had said something similar regarding the bits. And look what happened. She needed proof before she followed blindly.

He could be mad. Or trying to kill her, because he thought she killed his father. She took a step back and placed her hands deliberately on her hips. "No."

His outstretched hand faltered. "What?"

Again Berd debated whether to go with him or not. The train represented either safety or danger, and she needed to test the waters.

"I will come with you if you will refrain from drinking any more energy." She held her breath, hoping he would agree.

He gave a small nervous laugh. "Are you serious?"

His God-like exterior was cracking. She nodded, more confident now she could see his discomfiture, pleased she had some power over him. "We are leaving soon, are we not? You won't need the streams of energy." Her heart pounded and she tried to keep her face impassive as she watched him slowly lower his hand.

The whistle shrilled again, angrily, urging them to hurry.

"Come on!" He pulled the bladder from his suit, tossed it to one side then grabbed her arm.

"Mr—"

"Yes! Yes. Don't you want to go home?" He flicked a glance heavenwards, as if beseeching it for patience.

In answer, she locked fingers with him. This train was the next step, and whether it represented safety or doom, either way, she was going to find out in a hurry.

They dashed down a golden alleyway, turned sharply left, ducked under the doorway of a brass building, and into a long, curving passageway. Though she had seen many of these buildings transform she had yet to enter one.

It was hard to believe this was really a train station. There were no plastered advertisements anywhere, but of course, she reminded herself there was no reason to have advertisements. There was no one for the advertisers to advertise to except her and Charles...

Her and Charles.

They were the sole inhabitants of this land. Human ones, anyway.

Berd swallowed, her throat dry, promising herself if she ever got home safely that she would never, ever, ever find fault with advertising again. Ever.

Around them, the walls were limed in glossy green tiles of various hues; the floors in contrasting buttercup yellow. The passageway rumbled with muted murmurs and comforting rattles, as if a distant train passed above.

She turned in wonder to the youth running beside her, but he merely pressed his lips together more tightly. The passageway split into two, and he took the right passageway. It beckoned them into a vast open space where pillars of iron arched skywards like the ribs of a gargantuan beast. Leadlight from the overhead dome strew the air with jewelled light: ruby, sapphire, topaz and emerald. Silence incensed the place.

If an angel descended from on high, she was sure it would feel at home. On holy ground.

They *were* in an underground train station, but one so lavish she would have believed Charles if he said they had taken the wrong turn and ended up in a cathedral. Or that decadently fabulous new invention: a department store.

I am in love.

And she was partners with the man who had created all of this.

At the moment, however, his priorities were not on the architecture. "Come on!" He tugged.

"It's so beautiful," she whispered, deliberately lagging so she could take in as much of the ethereal atmosphere of the station.

He frowned, clearly irritated with the delay. "Yes. You want to be left behind. There." He pointed to the train waiting like a promise on the tracks.

Golden tracks.

Berd's eyes widened. On those thin wires she had seen from the top of the building…a glorious, fire-breathing dragon of brass and steel crouched: the locomotive. At the end of the platform it waited, a chariot ready to ascend to the clouds, followed by a luxurious passenger carriage. Polished brass trucks curved into the shadowy darkness of the tunnel. Golden fenders gleamed provocatively at her. As they passed the locomotive, her wide-eyed reflection gazed back at her, trapped from within the shining prison of the boiler.

At the sight of her reflection, every nerve stood on end. With a pounding heart, she remembered the blocks, and her fear that the world would explode returned. But, as if the Engine itself were aware of her trepidation, the metal leviathan graciously exhaled, silently enveloping the platform in hot minty clouds that warmed her feet. She could almost believe she was once again catching a train at King's Cross.

"Come on! Mustn't miss it."

Before she could object, Charles lifted her onto the top step of the passenger carriage. The floor felt as solid as his hands had been around her waist.

The train jerked forward, and she had to fling out her hands to avoid colliding against the walls. Cold metal caused a shiver to go through her, but it was reassuringly firm.

"Pick a compartment, my lady!" He scrambled up close behind.

She nodded and moved further in.

Down a slender hallway, there were doors to her left. She grasped the silver latch of the first door, again flinching at its icy coldness, but managed to lift it. It opened into a bare but spacious room, with a bed on her right. Straight ahead was a silver window, the green station walls opposite already sliding past.

He bowed, half-turning away. "Have a good res—"

"Wait! Where is the train taking us?" She couldn't believe that he had expected her to go mildly into a cabin and wait for his instructions. Her suspicions were confirmed when his pale face creased in confusion.

"You're sa—I mean—you want to go home, right?" he asked, his features relaxing slightly when she nodded.

"Well, we are. Going home that is. Rest, you must be exhausted. Rest and I'll come for you when it's time." He dipped his head then moved on, his footsteps swiftly dying away.

She closed the door, slumped against it then replayed his words in her head. 'You're sa—'

What had he been about to reveal?

You're safe?

Chapter 8

ERD STARED INTO the room, collecting her thoughts. Her control over the situation seemed to be slipping away just as the view from the window slipped away. She wasn't sure if she believed Fotheringay when he said they were going home, the fact he hadn't finished his sentence increased her distrust of him.

Partners. Sure.

One thing he was right about, however — she was exhausted. Berd closed her eyes and inhaled deeply. The languid air inside the cabin tingled enticingly with the scent of peppermint. Opening her eyes, her gaze fell on the luxuriously soft white bed, the sole non-metallic thing in the room.

It looked so safe, it made her wonder if it really wasn't.

She remembered the many transformations of the blocks of metal and groaned. Charles had said to rest. Again she was unsure if she could trust him on anything in this place. The bed… It *looked* soft. But its softness beckoned like Circe's island of dreams, and she was not game to be Odysseus, the lost traveller, to test the bed in case it snapped shut like the leaves of a Venus Fly Trap. She had read about them in those awful Penny Dreadful stories ladies really shouldn't be seen reading. Any longing dissipated as she imagined those lotus-like sheets wrapping drowsily around her like a tongue, and she never waking from that enchanted sleep.

The train continued to chug along, building up speed as it left the station behind. Her exhausted body alternately relaxed and tensed in the rhythm of its movement as she stood there, considering whether it was a prison cell or a princess's chamber.

She dragged her gaze to the window, determined to strike out on her own. Charles said they were leaving, so logically they would head for the Output Section. If only she knew what it looked like.

They passed a red-arrowed sign.

It read 'STORE'.

Her eyes widened.

Not the Output but the Store: not a commercial store like a grocery, but the storage like a silo. In a computer it was where the current program's instructions were held in memory. He had said they were going home. It took a few seconds for the implication to register.

Charles had lied.

Sound and time passed like clouds over her. Then she hiccoughed and began breathing again. She rubbed and blew on her hands to warm them, but there was a deep hollowness inside her, as if she had lost something of value.

Charles had been deceiving her.

For too long she had been blind. The signs had probably been there from the beginning. It had all begun when she thought the Engine was dead.

How wrong she was.

With the battery bugs as receptacles, the Engine was alive. Barely alive, but alive like a man in a deep sleep, who to an observer, would at a distance appear dead until one came closer and saw the unmistakable signs of breathing. She was sure she knew what kept the Engine alive.

Energy.

It streamed in the rivers. It powered the Engine. It modified everything it touched.

The buildings. The moths. Charles.

And she had lain in the river, which meant that whatever happened to him would end up happening to her, for there was no sustenance inside the Engine. She did not know how long she would be able to hold out before she also partook. She licked her cracked lips sure thirst was already beginning to affect her ability to reason.

She had to get out.

Berd removed the pins from her hair, then finger-combed her tangled tresses off her face. The rhythmic movement brought her breathing back to normal. Except for the slight jostling of the carriages and the ever-present hum, she heard nothing. Charles could be in the next compartment or carriage or even off the train by now. She should have asked for a map when she had the chance.

She opened the door and slipped out. Red and yellow flames burned without flicker in the two brass lamps lighting the passageway. At the end was a silver door. Beyond it was another passageway similar to the first. Stepping in, she took a breath of minty air and examined her surroundings. Besides the door she had come through there were two other doors: a matching silver door directly opposite that probably led to the third carriage, and a single door half-way down the passage on the right. All no doubt composed from energy.

Brass lamps also burned on either side of this second door, making it appear as if its mercurial surface was on fire. This had to be the cargo door. Perhaps if she found out what cargo they were carrying, she would have a clue as to what was going on.

The first lamp seemed to stare at her like an eye as she passed. But if it was an eye, then the door was a mouth and it would devour her if she opened it. Yet in a way she had been already eaten whole, rattling around in the belly of the steel snake that was the train. She had willingly travelled down its gullet.

Snakes were predators, but they were also prey, to everything from cats and boars to birds. If the Engine wanted to throw something else at her, it certainly could. In the belly of a snake. She grinned, wryly. James, she was positive, would never appreciate the analogy, but would Charles?

She took a deep breath then placed the tips of her fingers on the door handle. Cold prickled up the length of her arm. Her breath came in noisy heaves as she squeezed back the lump of fear in her stomach, lifted the latch then teased the door open a fraction.

Radiant white light blazed along the crack. Bits! She slammed the door shut. This was a data train! Argh, of course! The payload of the data train was bits! That arrogant ass and his puns! The last thing she wanted was to be attacked by any more, so she whirled around. And squealed.

A silvery ball was racing furiously towards one end of the corridor. Its desperate efforts to flee left zigzagging tracks of gold burning upon the air, long after it had passed.

It must have escaped from the compartment!

But the corridor was sealed. There was no escape for the ball. Both she and it were in an enclosed space, and sooner or later—more likely sooner—at the speed the ball was travelling, it would end up crashing into her.

Petrified, she shrunk against the wall.

The ball veered recklessly away before impacting the closed door. It made a tremendous zap noise and then bounced off and zipped past her.

She flattened even further against the wall.

It crashed into one of the lamps, extinguishing the flame before it pinged off again. This time, it angled straight for her.

Before she could react, it grazed the hand she held over her face. Berd flinched as its tiny feet snagged against her fingertips. The taste of charred metal stung the tip of her tongue. Her mouth opened in a scream, her eyes widened in terror, her muscles clenched in anticipation of pain, but to her amazement, there wasn't any…

Instead light, glorious shimmering light blossomed like a rose before her.

Knowledge.

Illumination.

Exploding like a firework within her brain.

Tiny truths twirled, star-like, through her loose hair, whispering in dulcet harp notes before winging off like comets as fast as Hermes.

Her hand fell limply to her side.

Intelligence. Understanding. For a split second, she knew everything. Nothing was beyond her.

The brightness drained away and she was herself once more, only duller, humbler. After the brilliant performance, the shining metal passageway seemed dim. She squinted as her eyes adjusted.

But she was not the only one trying to escape. Something buzzed by her feet, spinning in smaller and smaller circles, trying to burrow its way into the floor. She picked it up, cradling it in the palm of her hand. The ball hummed vigorously, tickling her — an electrical firefly in the last throes of life, barely larger than a tennis ball, gasping.

Whatever it was, it was more than a bit.

Berd pulled open the passage door she had come through and slowly slid it out into the next passage. It trembled and then as if it had found new strength, flew off. Hopefully one of them would be successful in their escape attempt.

Charles had said this was a data train. Data. This must have been how the Engine passed data from one section to another. Or, even within a section. What the ball had shown her was surely a sample of the knowledge the Engine held. No wonder she had felt intelligent. This was possibly what a computerised future would bring: knowledge on hand.

But the ball had been larger than the bits and contact with it held no pain. This must have been what Charles had been trying to show her only he had confused the attacking bits with these spheres. But what of the doppelganger…

She brushed her tongue across her teeth. This was no dream. She would not be waking up from this. When she saw Charles again, *if* she saw him again, she would have a lot of questions. But would he tell her the truth and would she be able to recognise it if he did…

Berd shut the door and padded down the passageway before stumbling into the next carriage. Her steps grew heavier. Shadows grasped at her. Though she had been in trains before, she had never experienced this nightmare. In the trains back home, opening doors did not lead to disaster, to being electrocuted, or to being killed.

She eyed each lamp she passed, unable to blink in case she missed some significant change. When she gathered the courage to proceed, she would turn back to stare, to make sure the lamp had not transformed into something gruesome once her back was turned.

At the door of the eleventh carriage, Berd paused. If she had expected to find something, she was not disappointed. Here was proof finally. Evidence.

Two voices drifted from the eleventh carriage.

Strangely, both voices sounded like Charles.

Bitter disappointment mixed with anger filled her at this discovery. He had said there was no twin, but here he was, deep in conversation, with whoever the second figure was. This was simply more confirmation he had lied.

Yet, though he had shown himself not for the first time to be untrustworthy, she was disappointed.

It made no sense that it should matter so much to her.

Chapter 9

OMEONE WAS CONVERSING with Charles.
Whoever the speaker was, he was on the other side of the door. Leaning in, she found the second voice to be identical, like one person having two sides of a conversation. It had to be the doppelganger.

Berd's heart raced as she wrenched the door open, but instead of hard yellow lamplight, soft golden rays poured over her. What she saw almost caused her heart to stop.

She was seeing the whole of the bright green enamelled computerscape through which the train travelled. At the same time, she was also seeing the whole of the interior of the carriage. In some spine-chilling fashion, the outside had flowed into the inside. Her breathing quickened and her stomach twisted, and she clung desperately to the lintel as if clinging onto reality, as she gaped at the ghostly outlines.

Berd took a moment to let all the information filter in, like with the ball of light, and the secret came to her.

And she decided that it was not meant as a trick after all, but simply a whim of the Engine's creator.

She was looking at the last carriage or, more correctly, through it. Except for the floor and door, the last carriage was composed entirely from glass: the four walls, the door opposite, and the roof, a thick glass dome. Just like the elevator.

Only, here everything vibrated gently, thanks to the rattling motion of the train. This was what had given her the initial uneasy feeling. She felt more exposed than if she was riding in an open-top carriage, and was not sure if she liked it. A single glance revealed everything, and yet nothing.

The sole piece of furniture in the carriage was a lime-green Chesterfield perched in the middle of the room. It blended effortlessly against the verdant backdrop as it faced the back of the train. A lone figure was seated in it. As she stumbled forward, the figure turned and stared at her.

Charles.

His gaze lingered on her face, before he stood and gestured elegantly to the opposite end of the sofa. "Ah, princess, didn't you find your cabin suitable? I'm afraid we can't offer first class accommodation."

If this was a joke, she was not impressed. Berd glared at him, and he shrugged good-naturedly. The tension in the air was palpable as she scanned the carriage.

She had heard voices nearby, so it had to be a trick: an illusion, or a portal. It was impossible for anyone to duck out through the opposite door without being spotted. No one clung to the dome outside. No carriage followed. Yet the second person had disappeared. Again.

The uncanny feeling in her stomach doubled. She forced her voice to remain steady, and for her face to show no fear. "I heard voices."

"All the way from your cabin?" Charles's eyes twinkled in amusement. "You *must* be tired, princess. Or did you find a pea under your mattress?" He patted the sofa accommodatingly. "I suggest you take a seat."

Furious, she remained standing. "I want answers, Mr Fotheringay. The truth."

He met her gaze, his eyes smooth blue seas. "When have I not? You make it sound as though I have been lying to you all along." He actually appeared wounded.

"You said we were leaving."

His mouth tightened as if she had accused him of lying. "We *are*."

"But we can't be. The sign said the train was heading towards the Store."

"We are leaving and it is," he said, full of confidence.

She almost stamped her foot. "Leaving to where."

Charles shrugged. "Very well. As you keep on insisting, I will tell you. We are stopping by the Store to get the settings we need. That way, when we leave, we don't end up blowing ourselves up."

The sod was actually serious. She stared at him, unsure if she should believe him.

"If we don't escape soon, we will find ourselves trapped in the Engine forever." He held out one hand, calculating as he ticked off long, elegant fingers. "We have 202 battery beasts. According to my calculations, we need 100 each at least in order to leave. Remember, it's not one person, but two to attempt this journey.

That's 200 beasts all up. The Engine uses the energy from one battery beast a week.

"I give us a week to ten days with the energy from the two spare battery beasts. Then we start eating into the energy we need."

She had wanted answers. Now she had them. Her voice was thin when she spoke, "Can't the battery beasts be topped up?"

He smiled patiently. "I triggered the first lightning strike. A year later, you triggered the second. Do you envisage that happening in the near future?"

Again the sod was right! Even though the Engine was now hooked up to the lightning rod, there was no guarantee that there would be another lightning strike. "But if we have two hundred, couldn't one of us at the very least go first?"

"Then try to get the other out?" He gazed at her searchingly. "Would you trust me to go first? Or say you went first. Would you know what to do to get me out? Or what if, as we speak, the Engine is being sold for scrap? Or worse, dismantled."

That was true. If she knew James, he would get rid of the Engine immediately, or perhaps even dismantle it. She still had problems forgiving James for having their home renovated when their mother passed away. His reason was that it hurt him to live in a house where almost everything reminded him of Mother.

Berd pressed one hand against her chest, in hopes of quelling the pain within. It was in vain. The trouble was everything Charles said made sense.

"Do not worry, my lady."

She looked up to find his gaze locked upon her, intense.

"If it does come to that, I have made the decision that *you* will be the one to leave."

There was no reason that he should do that. Especially when she had told him she didn't trust him. Such an accusation did not normally make for cordial relations.

As if exhausted, he sank onto the Chesterfield. "What happens when the Engine runs out of energy?" he muttered, gazing out the glass dome.

She stared blankly at him, thinking he was asking her, but then he answered his own question.

He sounded almost comfortable as he said, "When the Engine runs out of energy, it will die. And if we are in it when it dies, we die with it."

For a long time, Berd stared out the glass dome, seeing the endless emerald computerscape as the train chugged on.

When the Engine runs out of energy, it will die. And if we are in it when it dies, we die with it.

If anybody knew what it was like to live within the Engine as it slowly ran out of energy, it was Charles.

He was seated on the opposite end of the lime Chesterfield and gazing into the distance.

"Is there nothing else we can do?" she asked.

He looked at her, and she thought his eyes appeared unfocused. Then he blinked, and the brilliant blue clarity returned to them. She must have been mistaken about the earlier green, but it made no sense why she could never tell what colour his eyes were.

"We're doing everything we can. At the Store, we'll get the settings needed to ensure our safe departure."

"Why did you not tell me of this earlier?"

He cocked one brow. "How could I? We know the Engine allowed us both to enter successfully. Leaving the Engine, however, has never been done. I was willing to sacrifice all to get out of this place at a moment's notice, but suddenly, with another person here, it feels like I must question everything again. I could not give you my uncertainty, as that was not what you were asking for." He shook his head. "I don't wish to find I've left something out of the equation and thus jeopardise the endeavour."

"Were you ever going to mention it?" she persisted.

"Of course! But following the encounter with the bits, had I told you immediately, I doubt you'd have believed me." He paused and scratched a brow. "I felt perhaps after a little rest you'd be in the right frame of mind."

Charles probably thought because she was a woman, she would not be able to handle the strain.

But it *was* all too much, though she doubted it was because she was female, judging by Charles's appearance. She had been sucked into an engine and was now dealing with what was the supposed ghost of said engine. Most people would have gone mad already. No, she simply needed time alone to process what was happening. Time.

"How long will it take us to do everything we need before we can leave?" she asked.

"About a day. Another day to get to the Output."

Two days. If nothing went wrong. If the ground didn't shake again. If blocks didn't explode, and if they weren't attacked by another swarm of bits. She wanted to be out now.

What else he was he not telling her, she wondered. She rose and approached the glass wall at the back of the carriage, some vague idea in her head that if she pressed herself against it, she might see a glimpse of the world outside the Engine.

Instead, she saw only her own troubled reflection.

Was she in the eye of the train looking out, or in an upside-down glass bowl? If so, who might be looking in? And why could she never catch sight of him?

Her breath formed a wall of condensation, hiding her like a fish behind its own bubbles.

She could see nothing outside but flat, green, enamelled emptiness unrolling to the computer's horizon under a gold sky. Even the blocks were gone. It only she could see her world again with all its trees and mountains. Crush real grass beneath her feet, and smell its sticky residue in her hands…

She turned to Charles, who was draped over the couch, brooding. "To whom were you conversing to earlier?"

Charles set his shoulders, appearing determined to answer, but as he opened his mouth, the train whistle screamed. He sprang to his feet, holding one hand palm-up towards her, every muscle in his body tense.

Danger.

By the time he reached the door, she was right behind him. Just before he stepped over the threshold, though, he braced himself in the doorway. She ran into him full-body and he whirled on her in the moment of confusion.

The siren was so loud, she wasn't sure whether he had actually shouted or mouthed the word 'No'.

But he was a fool if he believed she would just wait here; she had seen the terror in his face. Though she had made up her mind to escape without him, she would be an idiot if she didn't find out the cause of the whistling. She had to know what was going on, or more precisely, what was going wrong.

He tried three times to turn her back.

She smiled daintily at each attempt, and in the end, she followed him.

As he hurried through the first freight car, he scrubbed his hand through his hair then threw his hand down in contempt. She thought a flash of sound went by her head, some curse of his, but comprehension was stolen by the siren's shrill, which seemed to palpate the air.

Let him seethe.

As they reached the next car, she expected the whistle to stop.

It didn't.

It shrilled on and on and on, shrieking through her head like a banshee, regardless of which car they were in. Regardless of time.

The train slowed.

Charles quickened his pace, flinging open doors in his path, and she, following through, neither bothered to shut them. And still the train slowed.

Each time they entered a carriage, she felt that the front of the carriage deliberately shot away from her, growing distance between her and Charles. By the time she entered the fifth carriage, she saw only the heel of his boot as he raced out the door to the next one. By now, her breath was coming in long gasps. She had to stop. Blasted corset!

She slowed to a brisk walk, digging her fingers hard into her side to ease the pain of the stitch. When she reached the sixth carriage, Charles was nowhere in sight.

It didn't matter, she told herself. She knew where he was headed. The Engine was obviously malfunctioning. That was probably the explanation for everything going wrong. No wonder Charles always looked haughty when she tried to ask him questions; he must think she was trying to find fault.

Insulting his Engine was insulting him.

No doubt he was proud of the Engine, and he had every right to be. He and his late father had come further than any other inventor, but it was clear the Engine still had a few flaws. A few bugs in it. She smiled at a vision of the battery bugs. The swarm of bits had to be a symptom of the Engine's malfunction, an energy leakage.

By the time she reached the passenger compartment, the train had come to a complete stop. At the opposite end of the passage was a cream door edged with gold that she had never noticed before. Charles, with his abilities, must have caused it to appear. Hopefully, the door bypassed the tender and led straight to the footplate, just like The Flying Scotsman.

She was reaching for the knob when a brown scorch mark on the thick green carpet stopped her. The mark reminded her of the ball of light, but there was no sign of it anywhere. She assumed it had fizzled out like a firecracker though there was no smell of extinguished gunpowder. Perhaps it had escaped when Charles opened the door to get out.

When she reached the locomotive cab, she found Charles fiddling with switches at the driver's console. The minute he spotted her, he dropped what he was doing and grasped her arm, at once easing her off the train. His mouth opened to form words she couldn't hear, but his actions expressed his intentions quite clearly.

Go away.

Go far away.

His dismissal stunned her. She was unwanted. She nodded curtly, about to stride off when he grasped her by the wrist, yanking her back. The shock of his touch went right up her arm and into her heart, sending it aflutter.

For one tremulous moment, he stared into her face as if he were about to speak. It made her breath catch in her throat, to have those eyes look so wantingly upon her. Heat from the boiler rose in hazy waves around them, blurring the gold of the train. Her face grew hotter.

His eyes were like diamonds. Melting blue diamonds.

Sparks from the locomotive's engine landed, hissing on the ground around them. She itched to shift her feet, and stared down at the ground, suddenly shy. Her pulse was roaring in her head when, with the same swift motion, Charles released her and climbed back inside the locomotive.

All without speaking a word…

The whistle continued to scream.

She turned away at once, her chest heaving as she

ran from the train. Her eyes smarted with unshed tears. He was playing games with her. That look…

But it made no difference even if it was romantic interest.

We're partners. Just partners, she reminded herself.

The truth was she had never intended to marry.

That was why she had been so hard on Charles from the beginning. She had no wish to be Cinderella. Even with his glass elevator and glass carriage, he was not a Prince Charming. She did not wish for one.

I do not want your glass slippers to contain me.

Charles had not been in the least bit sympathetic. Though he had allowed her to help with the bugs, he had ended up commandeering the whole action. He was like every other boy. The incident with the balls of energy proved he was a stubborn fool who only wanted his own way. If he were genuinely sincere, he would have allowed her to help him now. Unless he was worried the locomotive would explode.

She slowed.

But if the locomotive were that dangerous, then the solution was to leave. Escape. With her. At this very moment. Not risk being blown up.

By now she had walked some distance across the exposed area of green plains, but the sound of the whistle was still painful. In fact, it appeared louder than when she was on the train. She cupped her hands over her ears and turned shakily to watch Charles scrabble around inside the open cab.

He touched, tapped, twisted, and examined every movable part. The speedometer, pressure and temperature gauges, water level indicators, the fire door, the regulator valve, the whistle cord, the brake lever, as well as every other lever she could not name, he went at least twice over, all in the span of minutes. But it was to no avail. He jumped out of the cab and strode around the locomotive, all the while muttering to himself. He kicked the great metal wheels and ran his hands gingerly over the valves, flinching whenever he touched something hot.

Good. She smiled to herself as he shook a sting off his hand.

He glanced at her from time to time, nodding as if pleased she had stayed where she was. After more ardent examination of the wheels, he scrambled under the train. She hoped the pistons would leak oil on him.

Crossing her arms, she waited.

And waited.

The whistle continued to shrill.

Berd tapped her foot. She was becoming more cross with it than him. It didn't make sense why the whistle was sounding. The train had stopped, so the boiler couldn't be overheating. Yet the whistle was still going. He should have found the cause by now. The trouble with this world was that everything was not as it seemed.

Unless it was an alarm for something not on the train!

She halted her tapping and turned slowly away from the train. If it wasn't coming from inside the train, the answer had to be outside. She scanned the green plains that stretched to the computer horizon all around her. No blocks. No buildings. No trees. She could see everything, but there was nothing to see. As she lifted one hand to shade her eyes, the whistling wrenched to a halt.

Charles was shaking his head as he clambered out from under the train, bewildered.

Berd could think of only two reasons why the noise had stopped: because the cause of alarm was over or because the person running it knew she was onto the idea of the source being external and was about to go looking for it.

She had to find out who it was and where they were. But what worried her most was that the only way the perpetrator would have known was if they had been watching her the whole time.

It had be the mysterious third person in the Fotheringay Engine.

The one who tried to kill her.

Twice.

Chapter 10

PREDATORS SENSE FEAR in prey. I am prey.

The bright green enamelled computerscape with its dull gold sky was now menacing. The image of the monstrous eye she had seen in her stables had returned.

Berd was in its domain. Its hunting ground.

Though she saw nothing watching her, she was convinced it was out there, that it had been there all along, biding its time. She was a fool to think it had been Charles she had to fear. He was merely the decoy.

Her lungs burned as she raced forward, desperate to get back to the train.

The train.

If the train would but wait!

Already a puff of smoke issued from the funnel. In her mind's eye, the train was pulling away…

Berd transferred her fear into her feet and charged across the green enamel ground, her boots smacking the surface. Smoke now billowed from the train's funnel. A terrible sweat was coming on, but she would not be left behind. By the time Berd reached her carriage, she was trembling. She pounded up the steps and pushed past Charles, who had been waiting at the bottom for her.

"My lady?"

Though she heard the concern in his voice, she was in such a state she could not stop to explain. Then the train lurched forward, and she heard him scramble aboard.

That's twice now, she thought, twice she had heard him fumbling to board the train. It confirmed a suspicion.

Charles was not in command.

Had he been, she was sure the train would have waited.

Something or someone else was Lord Almighty in this place.

"Might I suggest you would be more comfortable in your compartment?" he called out.

She didn't slow. Instead, she flew past her compartment, one hand working the open neckline of her blouse as she fought to keep her composure. She was right to reject him, she told herself. She was right. The hard knot of pain curled in her chest squeezed even tighter.

Charles, however, had other ideas. He ducked his head as he moved past and as she approached the door at the end of the passageway, he lunged to open it. "Have I upset you, my lady?"

She did not answer. Though he opened each successive door for her, she continued to ignore him. When she reached the last compartment, she sank onto the Chesterfield. In the glass opposite, she saw his reflection pause in the middle of the doorway, unsure if he should enter.

"I believe I have wronged you, my lady." His voice was deep, breathless, but she couldn't quite make out the emotion behind it. His long dark hair partially hid his face.

Plus his secrets.

She had to push him away especially since she wished for no commitment from him. "I do not wish to discuss it, Mr Fotheringay."

"I had hoped you would address me—"

"Your actions made it clear the fire plate of a locomotive is no place for a lady. I see that you believe society dictates we all know our place," she said. "So please know yours."

Charles inhaled sharply then searched her face. "I know you are a lady."

"Mr Fotheringay, if you want me to trust you, you must first trust me. Before the whistle blew, tell me with whom you were conversing."

The whistle shrilled again.

In the glass reflection, surprise shot across Charles's face. His mouth opened, his eyes narrowed, and she did not think she was imagining it. Twice she had tried to ask him who he had been speaking with, and twice the whistle had shrilled. This was too much of a coincidence.

Beyond them, the green computerscape flashed past as the train continued rocking on its journey. No blocks. No buildings. No eye. Yet it was obvious he had been looking at something. She swung round to glance at him, just in time to catch him give her a wink.

Surely that was not meant for her! Her hand flew

to cover her mouth. But it was too late.

Charles had seen the effect his wink had on her and the grin on his face simply broadened. He squared his shoulders and stood taller.

Berd's solitary defence was to turn swiftly away.

"I'll return shortly, princess." It was hard not to miss the note of jubilation in his voice.

"You have not won," she said, under her breath to the already closing door.

I do not need this. She kept her gaze stonily on the floor, her pulse beating strongly in her throat, not looking up in case she caught his reflection in the glass. Only when she heard the door click shut did she raise her head.

The computerscape outside was going by at a clip, nearly twenty miles per hour.

Again I find myself alone, locked away by my 'protectors.'

He was gone. And she was not going to waste a further minute thinking about that ingrate. Her heart continued to thump loudly in her ears, and she waved her hand to cool her hot face. He had seemed so worried earlier when the first whistle had blown that she had thought it a matter of life and death. But now he seemed to take it in stride, not even bothering to run! She had to find out the reason. She pushed her lower lip out, furious at herself for letting her guard down and allowing him to see…see what? She cared not for him surely!

But while the whistle screamed, he was gone which meant in his absence she was safe to search for the doppelganger. She waited a good five minutes in case Charles returned.

The whistle was still blowing when she rose and poked round the Chesterfield, but as she expected, there was nothing suspicious in the carriage. Even in all the nooks and crannies nothing revealed itself.

They had been travelling a good half hour by the time she concluded her inspection, the whistle screaming all the while. Her head felt fit to explode. She had originally suspected someone was outside spying on them, but she would have spotted the perpetrator as he ran to keep up with the train. The train hadn't slowed, so the logical move was to check the rest of the carriages.

Slowly, she turned to look at the door.

But as she tried to leave the compartment her body grew heavier, it seemed harder to move her feet. She stood before the door, her breath coming in dry heaves as she struggled to find the courage to leave.

I can do this. I can do this.

If she found the doppelganger, she needed a plan of action for he would easily overpower her and she would be at his mercy. Yet if she didn't find him, she dreaded to think what he would do when she wasn't looking.

If someone was trying to kill her, she needed to know exactly where he was.

I am running out of time before Charles returns.

By now her breath was pumping in and out of her lungs and she saw spots before her eyes as she stepped out into the passageway.

The silver door opposite that led into the next carriage was half open, but the cargo door she wished to open wasn't. It was a high possibility that the doppelganger was inside the cargo hold. He had to be somewhere and this was the closest place she could think of, especially if he had overheard her when she asked Charles who he had been talking to the second time.

She reached for the door.

Even as her hand closed on the knob, the hairs on the back of her neck stood on end. She sprang back. Something powerful was inside. Perhaps it was simply more energy. Static electricity. Bytes. Death.

Berd was cold, so cold she knew she was close to passing out. There was no reason for the fear, she told herself. She had experienced the ball of energy earlier and escaped uninjured. There was no need to fear.

Breathing through her mouth, she reached forward once more, feeling the sleeve of her blouse push back up to rub against her arm.

She lifted the latch.

The cargo door swung open effortlessly and silently on its hinges. But there was no blazing white light. Instead, solid darkness glared malevolently back at her.

Pins and needles danced upon her shoulders. Her arms lost their strength. A sudden inexplicable weight pressed the air out of her lungs.

The impenetrable darkness…

The darkness was waiting for her to enter.

Waiting to devour her.

The corridor swayed. And somehow, somehow though she couldn't explain it, the darkness and the cargo door seemed to grow larger before her eyes while the gleaming steel corridor seemed to shrink away behind. There was now only the door. Only the door and the darkness… And it was waiting.

How long Berd stood there, she did not know. She grew colder, nauseous. If someone had told her she had been standing outside for all eternity, she would have believed them.

Her hand lifted. She wasn't sure if she was controlling it, or if it was moving of its own accord. Her legs, however, were a different matter. They did not want to enter the room and they didn't, because she was falling.

"Princess!" the darkness called.

A dazzling object flashed before her.

Something grabbed Berd and together they rolled. She wanted to scream, but her mouth was too dry. She wanted to shove him away, but she had no strength. Oh, but if she only hadn't opened that door…

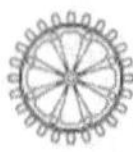

Berd was lying on something soft. She was also swaying gently, like aboard a boat or a train…

She snapped her eyes open. Fuzzy grey cleared into mild darkness as her greeting, and she found it to be the haziness of dusk. But this was the Engine. They mustn't have night and day in this world.

Berd inhaled fragrant peppermint as she raised her head. Unsurprisingly, she was back in her compartment. What was surprising was that Charles lay on another bed opposite. Asleep.

Her face flushed hot as she realised she had been sleeping in the same room with a stranger, albeit in different beds.

In more ways than one, Charles had turned her life

upside-down. If he had not created the Engine, she would not have been sucked inside; she would not have been nearly disowned by her brother; she would not be possibly dead. But most of all, she would not have met Charles…

She rose from the bed; the bed she had earlier declined because she did not trust him. He certainly did not warrant it. He lay with one hand across his eyes, his breathing deep and steady. As she stared, his arm slid away to reveal a face in repose; dried blood from their encounter with the swarm of bits still stained the tip of his nose.

It made him look almost comical, yet his defencelessness was alluring. Asleep, the tension around his eyes was gone. She guessed he was not much older than her, but living alone for a year inside this madhouse had probably aged him. And he had risked his life to save her.

Did he love her?

At that thought, her face crumpled. Though bitter joy welled inside her, she refused to cave in to the possibility he did. If she succeeded in her objective of programming the Engine, lives could be saved. It also wouldn't hurt to be the world's first programmer. What a difference that would mean for women! Men would have to start taking them seriously. It was the golden opportunity women had been searching for, and she could not afford any errors in judgement. Nor any weakness.

She could not afford to be in love with Charles. It would simply wreck everything.

"It's just coincidence. You have been trapped inside the Engine for too long, and I am the first person you have seen," she whispered. "Yet you are the first person to have ever wanted me."

Little rapid motions started under his eyelids; had he heard her? Was he waking?

His hair was damp at the hairline and if she stayed, she would be tempted to smooth it back. It was high time she left.

"Good-bye." She turned on her heel and in two swift steps, she reached the door, twisted the knob, and before she could change her mind, she stepped into the passageway. Even as the door closed, she realised she was not alone. The voice greeted her first.

"My lady."

The doppelganger.

Chapter 11

THE AIR WITHIN the passageway seemed too thin. The light too bright. The walls far too close.

Berd leaned back against the cabin door, needing its support as strength ebbed from her.

The doppelganger rested against the wall in front of her, his feet crossed and looking — if it were possible — more devastatingly handsome than Charles. But then the doppelganger's face was clean, his hair neat and clipped perfectly, and he was attired as any young buck prepared for a night out on the town. He was the embodiment of what any civilised Victorian gentleman should resemble. The ideal.

Compared to him, Charles appeared distinctly savage.

The doppelganger bowed, low and elegant, and when he straightened, eyes filled with mirth met hers. They were such a deep emerald, she felt she was drowning in a sea of jewels. "A distinct pleasure to meet you, my lady." He grinned.

Charles's looks. Charles's voice. Yet the doppelganger was…more.

More powerful. More elegant. More… Charles.

A corner of the doppelganger's mouth tilted mischievously, and when he spoke, it was with the ease of requesting a dance. "I have a proposition."

She pushed herself off the door and glowered at him. "You have been trying to kill me. Why?"

To her annoyance, his boyish face lit with amusement. "Why not?"

Berd almost choked. "I beg your pardon?"

At that, the doppelganger's face creased with laughter, and he did it so much better than Charles. There were no lines of worry at the corners of his eyes, no parched lips. The doppelganger cleared his throat and then perfectly serious, spoke as if in answer to his own question, "You are killing him."

That gave her pause. "What? Why would I want to kill him?" It seemed easier to refer to Charles in the third person, especially if she was supposed to be killing him.

To add to Berd's confusion, the doppelganger's eyes widened in mock disbelief. "And *you…you* wished to program *me*?"

Program him? The only thing that could possibly be programmed was the Engine, which could only mean…she was talking to the Engine itself. The Engine, in the guise of the doppelganger, who'd run circles around her.

Berd placed her hand on her throat, discomfited, but she had to confirm this. "Who are you?"

"Gine, my lady. At your service. Think of me as your portable genie." He held out pristine gloved hands, and winked.

"You *are* the Engine," she croaked. It shouldn't be possible. And yet here it was…

And she was staring at him. Staring in the rudest possible fashion she had ever stared at anyone, or anything; poring hungrily over every inch of him like a starving beggar eyeing her first meal in days. Yet she could not stop.

This was the face of the computer.

The very Engine she'd hoped to program, and here it was. Smiling at her. Talking to her. Insulting her. And yet not a single operation card to be seen. It had even tried to kill her, and now it was doing a stand-up job of befuddling her.

The whole idea seemed absurd. The Engine, standing right there, a living, breathing…

No, not breathing, she realized. It might smile and speak, but its chest never rose or fell. No blush coloured his cheeks. It was no more human than the metal shell surrounding them.

Gine rubbed his cultured hands briskly as she studied him, and she had to admit, to her chagrin, that Charles had done an excellent job in programming Gine. The way he tilted his chin, at just the right angle to portray a raffish demeanour, was perfect. He could conduct lessons. No need for her to teach the Engine anything, not that she had been about to teach Gine deportment. Now she could sympathise with the Luddites—the men and women working in the mills who had been replaced by machines. She knew how they must have felt.

Redundant.

Charles had built her dream. But he had also destroyed it.

"Let's come to an agreement," said Gine, his tone cool, confident and civilised.

She frowned. "Agreement?"

"Charles will not survive if he does not partake of the energy. When he was pulled in, he programmed me to do anything I had to in order to save his life. He will not survive the two days before you depart. That is why I must take action."

'Take action?' That sounded more like a euphemism for 'trying to kill her.' "Why didn't he say anything?" she demanded.

Gine raised one brow slowly. "Incredible. You haven't worked it out yet."

Just like Charles, Gine had not bothered to answer her question. Apparently, there were no men, breathing or otherwise, who understood the proper decorum of conversation in this place. She would have pressed her case, except she suspected the answer to his question was vitally important to her health.

Then the realisation of what she had done hit her: she had asked Charles to refrain from partaking of the energy, thinking they would soon be out of the Engine and he could easily survive without it. While he, with all his stupid male pride, well, he would do everything to abide by the agreement even if it…killed him. That had to be it.

"I will speak to him," she said, wishing she didn't sound so uncertain.

Gine gave a short laugh. He wiped his eye with one finger. "That will make him more determined not to agree. There is only one way to prevent this."

Numb, she nodded. *Remove the threat. Me. I am an undesired event in the operations and here is the Engine's Exception Handler.* "You want me to leave the Engine."

The doppelganger beamed expansively like a king.

"You are as clever as he said you were. Impressive, my lady. Or should I say, *princess*?"

"Do not mock a woman you are trying to persuade." She did not trust him. "I'm not leaving."

Gine's eyes widened dangerously. "No?"

It was good to put the Engine on the back foot for a change. "No. How do I know I can believe you? You did try to kill me. Twice."

"How you're harping on it. 'Twice'!" he mimicked. "If I wanted to kill you, you'd be dead."

Before she could protest, Gine tapped her on the tip of her nose with a bare finger.

She hadn't even seen him remove his glove or take a step forward. One minute she was staring at him as he leaned against the wall opposite, the next his lemon-silk cravat was in her face, as he stood before her, watching placidly as a frisson of electricity razed through her.

She jerked back and screamed as pain shot through her body.

Frantic scrambling was heard from the cabin behind her. Charles!

"Elizabeth!" came Charles's' muffled cry, through the door.

Gine bowed. "I will not try anything for twenty-four hours. You decide. After all, you were saying goodbye to him in your own way."

He pressed himself backwards against the wall. His features greyed and dissolved, and Berd was left staring at blank steel, so eerily like the time he had tried to reach out and grab her.

"I was not trying to kill him," she muttered to herself, aggrieved, as the door behind her banged open, and Charles burst into the passageway.

He collided neatly into her. Relief washed over his face as he clutched her in his arms, trying to maintain their balance. They spun in a circle before he released her, only to stand on shaky legs in the hall.

"Kill who?" he asked, his eyes widening. He peered around the passageway, which was empty except for the two of them. "You didn't mean me, did you?" He grinned, brilliantly.

He would have disarmed her with that smile of his, but more important matters owned her. If Gine wanted her gone, he could have killed her. He had demonstrated he could. There had been nothing to stop him. Charles may have appeared all-powerful, but he was weakening, possibly even dying, and Gine was clearly the most powerful player here.

She had to find out what game Gine was playing.

The train slowed then came to a halt. A station; a simple slab of steel, in the midst of a metal forest. When Berd took to the platform, she found those trees were growing, just like the blocks.

As she watched, a tower of coiled copper about ten yards to her right, sprouted into a tree. Tendrils unfurled into leaves, while steel bushes bristled up out of the glass-green ground to line their way. Then she caught the calming fragrance of lavender. If the grove was trying to say it wasn't dangerous, it would have to do far more than this to prove it.

However, dangerous or not, it didn't appear as if

she had a choice, as Charles gave a wave to show their path threaded through the metal grove. If he was brave enough to venture in, so would she. At least for now, there was no evidence of anything untoward.

She pressed her lips together and nodded, thankful Charles had not offered his arm. After his wink, she had expected him to pursue the matter further. There was of course, the other matter of whether she was killing him.

If, by removing Charles from his sole source of sustenance, she was 'killing him', then she could see Gine's motivation in separating her from Charles. The solution seemed straight forward—she should leave the Engine immediately. But, while she had no qualms in departing the Engine, she had to know what would happen to Charles if she did.

Gine had not said anything about it. If Charles was doomed to remain within the Engine, he would have no choice but to partake of the energy yet again. She would have to live with the knowledge she had left Charles behind to his demise.

She was pulling at her lower lip, trying to decide when Charles reached across as if to take her hand.

She flung her hand out, pretending she had meant to point to a tree shooting up in front of them. "Isn't that beautiful!" she said, a little too loudly.

"Why, yes." He coughed, also a little too loudly, into his fist, then turned dutifully to watch the tree.

Balls of gold blossomed at the end of each branch. As they approached, pomegranate-sized metallic apples dropped softly, clinking onto the ground. Orange blossom lovingly scented the air.

"I have never seen trees such as these. And to grow out of what appears solid enamel."

To her surprise, he answered immediately.

"Well spotted. It is indeed enamel—an excellent insulator."

"And the green?"

He scratched his nose with his little finger, looking a trifle embarrassed. "Learning from earlier prototypes, it made sense to place the Engine upon a wide board. Far easier to transport when the need arose. And so thanks to the idea of Mother Earth, I painted it green and called it…" He cleared his throat. "The Motherboard."

"Where life begins." She tilted her head at him, unable to believe they were actually having a decent conversation. "But how would Gine know about trees?"

Charles shook his head, looking wistful. "From me. Our conversations. Stuck in a laboratory, all he's ever known really is metal."

"It sounds almost sad."

"But now you've met him. Gine that is," he said suddenly.

So Charles had only answered her questions because he wanted something from her. She should have trusted her suspicions. "Yes."

"May I ask what he said?"

The vulnerability in his tone made her glance at him. Guilt flushed through her. Living in the Engine for a year, it was probably normal for him to think that death could come at any time. And now she shared his fate.

"He promised to behave for twenty-four hours."

"Might I ask why?"

If only his voice wasn't velvet. "I presume it was a sort of…a good-will gesture? Surely you would understand his reasoning. You created him."

Charles's response was to peer at the sky. When he spoke, his tone was sombre. "Gine said he would not try anything for twenty-four hours," he repeated.

She nodded. That was the truth. Not the whole truth, but how could she tell Charles that Gine had thought he would not last two days?

The roof of a building gleamed from amongst the branches of a filigree silver tree. She turned to inquire, to find Charles gazing at her.

"Extremely beautiful," he whispered. His eyes were the midnight blue of the sky.

Heat rushed up her throat. She glanced away and hurried on. Her boors tapped noisily on the surface of the glass-green path. Then she blinked and rubbed her eyes. It was either her imagination, or the path was imperceptibly widening the distance between her and Charles. Just like the carriages on the train…

When she turned back to look, she saw that Charles had halted to pick up a golden apple. Or at least he tried to. He struggled for a while before abandoning his attempt. How heavy must the apple be, especially if it was solid gold…or perhaps this was a sign he was weakening.

A corner of his mouth tugged upwards when he saw her observing him, and there was nothing frail in the way he strode after her. They went on, he walking quietly beside her, she viewing the active scenery, but the strange beauty continued to affect her. "I would never have imagined any of this happening inside the Engine." And she meant it. The metal forest was stunning. And curious.

"Well, Gine is rather remarkable. In his own fashion. Especially when it comes to making apples one cannot eat or pick."

The sarcasm in Charles's voice stunned her, and she stole a glance at him but regretted it immediately. Something in the way his eyes gleamed worried her. She was sure he was going to try and kiss her. Before he could close the distance, a copper branch snaked its way between them. Nutmeg spiced the air.

Charles hadn't forgotten about the wink. He *had* wanted to kiss her. Thankfully, Gine was keeping them apart.

Charles groaned as he eyed the sky then ducked under the branch. "Are you going to tell me?" His tone was grave, as he propped one hand on his hip.

Golden light fell upon his face, highlighting his features, especially the piercing curve of his brows as he stood lithe and tall in his suit of stunning black leather. He had never looked more serious. Or beautiful. Or sad. The fragrance of lilies filled the air. She sucked in a breath and looked away.

"Gine. What else did he say?"

She stiffened, but their eyes met. And she found herself staring for an eternity.

He could almost be a prince on a quest…

The humming increased, as if an angry dog were growling.

Berd frowned and shook her head, breaking the contact. That humming…she had to determine what was causing it. She tried to recall if she had noticed any humming when she had been speaking with Gine. That humming… Gine…

Horror filled the pit of her stomach. The humming was the humming from the Engine. And the Engine, why the Engine was Gine!

The humming was Gine!

And to think she had been so blind! "I would have thought Gine would have informed you of every single one of his ideas, as he conceived them. You are, after all, his maker," she accused.

Charles rolled his eyes. "I think Gine would give God a run for His money."

At that remark, Berd couldn't help but burst out laughing. She sobered a second later when she felt Charles clasp her hand. How swiftly he had moved! She knew she should pull away, but she didn't. Unlike everything else in the Engine, he was warm. Breathless, she looked up to find him gazing at her.

His words were half-plea, half-desire. "Don't, please."

She swallowed hard, her belly roiling. She dropped her gaze to his chest, following its rapid rise and fall. The black leather of his outfit gleamed strangely in the soft light, as if it were alive. Charles started to bend his head. She poised to run.

"My la—" Before he could proceed, the road beneath Berd reared up, yanking her hand out of Charles's grasp.

Berd screamed as she was swept up in the air. Arms flailing, she was about to topple when a railing conveniently stretched out in front of her. She grabbed at it, balanced shakily, then turned and stared agog at Charles, who was left behind.

He was swearing furiously, "Gine! You promised!" He flicked a wrist and the path beneath him rose. Like her, he was ensconced on a solid, flat disc, the roadway beneath surging and carrying them forward like a green wave.

Like a damson stone or a pebble, they were bobbing across the surface of a pond. Only instead of skipping up and down, there was merely a forward motion. That motion grew faster. Outlines of trees whirled past and she smelt newly-polished metal as she veered perilously close to the trees on either side.

Berd gasped as the transport she was crouched on swerved and darted dangerously amongst the tops of the trees. Leaves, sharp as knives, flickered past her face.

"What do I do?" she yelled, as her transport narrowly missed colliding with a silver branch.

"Control it!"

She ducked, barely avoiding getting sideswiped by another branch full of razor-sharp silver leaves. "How?" she cried back.

"Like that! Use your body. *Bend!*"

She did, and just in time, as her transport wheeled round the trunk of an enormously tall steel tree. Her heart was in her mouth as she swung from side to side, but her confidence built. Just as she felt in control, two arms grabbed her.

She screamed and lashed out!

Too late did she realise Charles's transport had come alongside hers, and he had leapt across. She flung her arms out, overbalanced and promptly toppled off the transport.

Charles swore in her ear as he cradled her against him.

The world blurred. The ground loomed up. She covered her eyes, too stunned to do anything but hide her head in her hands. Their bodies smacked into the green-enamelled surface.

She squealed as they barrelled ingloriously along the ground which somehow…softened. When they tumbled to a stop, she was stupefied to find herself still in one piece, though flat on her back, breathing hard from the fright.

"Princess, are you all right?" His blue eyes were wild with concern, as wild as his hair falling around his face. Weight lifted as he rolled off her.

She had never had such fun and such a fright in her life! Unable to stop the spinning inside her head, she clutched at his waving hand and to her great embarrassment, snorted.

"It's not true! It's not true, you know. You can go faster than thirty miles per hour and not have brain madness!" She giggled, feeling truly like she had gone mad, unable to stop laughing. Maybe she had spoken too soon, judging by the way she was unable to stop.

"Forty," he said in a tight voice, staring at her as if horrified he had lost her. "We were going at forty miles per hour."

The stars in her head fled. She released his arm, snapped her mouth shut, and sat up, brushing her hair out of her face with her fingers. "I should have put it up before we left the train. Look at me. What a mess! Look at me. I a—"

"I *am* looking at you." The tone had changed, the words spoken with a breathless burr.

Her hand stilled in mid-air. She babbled again, raking her hair so furiously that Charles, who was next to her, was forced to back away to avoid getting elbowed in the eye.

"I have to find my comb and pins. Must put my hair up and I can't do a thing without my ha—"

Before she finished her sentence, Charles reached over to gently brush a tendril of brown hair out of her eyes.

The tips of his fingers just barely touched her brow causing a shiver to run through her.

He smiled, slow and sure. "It appears I have saved your life. This is twice now, princess, and…" He paused, searching her face. "I would like to claim my reward." He began to bend down.

Strange feelings again streamed through her, emotions she could not name or understand. Every part of her body electrified. And Charles was the cause.

Terrified, she twisted her hair and draped it over one shoulder, but not before she had flicked him in the face with the end of her braid.

"Don't be ridiculous! Now where did I put those dratted pins?" Her voice was louder, higher.

His breath warmed the side of her face.

She twisted away. "Charles, please! Don't be absurd. This isn't a game. You're *not* Prince Charming!"

The words had been spoken with a laugh, but he stiffened and a shadow passed over his face. His lips had been inches from hers, but now he backed away. "*Prince?* And that is important to you?" he whispered.

If only she hadn't said that! She spoke lightly, "You know what I mean."

Charles frowned and sat up. "No, I assure you, my lady, I do not. Absurd. Ridiculous. And not Prince

Charming. Not quite the description I was hoping to hear. I'm beginning to think you truly believe that."

He rose to his feet.

A ragged tear in the back of his leather outfit flapped open, and she caught a glimpse of bloody gashes on his back. A whiff of coppery blood caused her nostrils to crinkle.

How poorly she had rewarded him!

Berd watched as he retied the strings of his leather garb. She told herself she had done the right thing, but there was a dreadful emptiness in her she could not name. When he reached down to offer his hand, she took it, stiffly getting to her feet. His skin was icy cold, his touch indifferent, utilitarian. Whatever magic there had been earlier was gone.

Chapter 12

A S SOON AS Berd was on her feet, Charles relinquished her hand. She watched as he clenched his jaw, pushed his shoulders back, and aimed for the path a few steps away. Except to check she was by his side, he took no more notice of her.

I have done the right thing.

To add to her confusion, the forest of steel, copper, gold and silver grew abruptly quiet as the metallic eruptions slowed to a stop. Berd had never seen anything like it. Had her altercation with Charles been the cause? Or had the growth reached its natural conclusion?

Or was the forest silent, because it was *listening* to them?

She shuddered.

While they had travelled by train, the green-enamelled computerscape had been a desert; yet they were now walking through a metal forest. Something had caused the drastic change, this sudden growth of trees. There had to be meaning to everything she had seen and experienced, and she knew she needed to find the answer. She suspected it was a matter of life and death.

Specifically, hers.

As they came around the bend, the whiff of metal pressed upon her tongue. The air misted and soon the clatter of their feet on the green was drowned out by a roar. A peculiar muffled thudding shook the ground as if giant Clydesdales, their hooves wrapped in pillows, trampled the soil nearby. Surely it had to be a sign another earthquake was imminent.

"Charles?"

"We're here," he announced softly.

Ahead the road straightened, and the wall of trees parted to reveal hazy golden sky looming from the ground up. If the forest of metal trees they were leaving behind seemed strange, then the sight in front of them was even queerer. They were on the edge of a plateau, below them stretching a flat plain studded with…monstrous formations.

Gigantic boulders balanced on columns—ringed columns—if they could even be called that, rose in strange, precipitous structures.

"Book stacks!" she cried out in sheer amazement. "They look like stacks of books."

Charles flourished his arm, silver-blue eyes blazing with pride. "Therefore its nickname: the Stack. Welcome to the Store!"

So this was the Store. Another cry of wonder escaped her lips at the incredible sight.

Each pile was propped on two columns. Steam emerged from funnels at the top of every book stack. The books themselves were of polished iron, about the height of a cottage and from each, copper wires trailed down to the ground, glinting in the golden light. With about a dozen books on each pair of columns, and every column the height of Big Ben, Berd couldn't help but feel intimidated by the collection — there were hundreds of them. Mostly walking.

But it made sense. Books were the repository of knowledge, so books seemed the logical choice. Only these were books like no other.

She turned to Charles, a sinking feeling in her stomach. "How on earth are we going to find the answer in *there?*"

He raised his brows. "We?"

The stack closest to them moved, or more precisely, staggered; its columns bent at the centre just like knees would flex when walking. Now she understood the origin of the muffled thuds.

"They're alive!" she gasped.

"No!" Charles scowled. "They're autonomous machines dredging the ground for data."

Autonomous machines were machines that governed themselves. But of course, these things were possible, she reminded herself. She had seen one such automaton sketch a picture, and she had also read about them in books; after all this was the Industrial Age. Even Babbage had his Silver Lady, one of two automatic dolls. If Berd wanted evidence of the impossible, here she was, herself, within an engine. She turned to watch as the book stack pulled its wiry roots out of what she had thought solid green enamel, then clomp clumsily about a hundred yards, where it shifted its load and settled into its new spot, sending down new copper roots. Clouds of steam puffed happily out of its funnel, dissipating quickly in the open air.

Grandmother Bird had often quoted Babbage, stating that in order to study anything, one ought firstly to place oneself at a distance from it and then to approach gradually to investigate the details. Well, soon Berd would be amongst these clanking giants.

"Our path lies that way." He pointed to their left where a small waterfall glistened half a mile away. Spray shot into the air in a luminescent blue halo as if angels danced in the skies above. Skeins of silken liquid dashed onto the rocks below while a thundering banter reached her ears. The waterfall was laughing.

So this was the cause of the roar. But no water ever gleamed with such iridescence. It was energy and not water gushing along.

Energy.

Like the river of energy she had lain in. The battery bugs… The computerscape and everything in it was energy.

"Come." But while Charles strode forward fearlessly, her feet would not move.

This is a trap.

The joke was on her.

Gine was tempting Charles, hoping Charles would give in. Or perhaps Charles had deliberately planned this route so he would appear to have no choice but to yield to such great temptation. Already the waterfall's closeness affected her. Her throat was noticeably drier, her stomach emptier.

"It's not what you think," Charles called out when he had gone a few steps and noticed she had not followed.

She flicked a glance heavenwards and scrambled after him. "You *knew* we had to come this way," she said, when she caught up.

"Of course I did, but it's not what you think," he answered, his voice strained.

In the open light, the blue half-circles under his eyes were deeper. The energy *was* affecting him. Only he seemed to be resisting, every muscle in his body taut. Now she wondered if it really was true that he would not survive two days without the energy.

"Are we to enter the energy?"

"There's a funicular rail along the side."

She couldn't help but notice how his hand shook slightly as he pointed to a tiny bubble-shaped car hunched beside the edge of the waterfall, almost invisible in the blue ethereal glow. The stink of grease and paraffin blew in her face.

"Why not summon a hot air balloon or some other form of transport that would not require us draw near the waterfall?"

"Why? The car is perfectly safe. You're not planning on jumping into the waterfall, are you?" His face brightened, the thought clearly entertaining him greatly.

She turned and tossed her head. "No, of course not, but—"

"Trust me, princess." His tone was husky.

They walked the half mile together. The odour of grease and paraffin grew stronger as they neared, and the wavering blue glow enclosed them. Hunger blazed within her.

Yet, it was Charles she found herself looking at. Outlined in the shimmering blue translucence emitted from the energy, his lean face appeared fey. His eyes glinted ravenously. His lips curled back slightly, as if he already tasted the energy.

This is what will become of me if I do not partake. I will go feral and die. But partaking is not a choice.

She dug her nails into the palms of her hands until pain came. She should not do this. It was foolish to continue. She had to turn back. Now. She was about to bolt when she felt his hand grasp hers.

Warmth filled her, replacing the chill from the spray; the chill that permeated the entire Engine.

"Princess." Charles's face was all planes and angles in the blue glow. He bared his teeth at the waterfall and snarled, a predator readying to attack.

"Charles, I d—"

"Don't look at the waterfall or it will be harder to resist jumping in." He winked. His chest was rising and falling with effort, yet he still teased her.

Peeved, she narrowed her eyes at him.

A corner of his mouth tugged upwards in a half-smile, and for a moment she thought he was about to lean forward and try to kiss her again, but all he said was, "Concentrate on the car. Remember. I have never lied to you."

He has never lied to me.

The thought flickered, brightening through her mind, like red and gold leaves flying through the autumn sky.

He has never lied to me, but I cannot say the same for Gine.

Berd pressed her lips together, hard, fixed her gaze on the car and despite the emptiness whipping in her stomach, kept walking.

"Look only at the car," Charles said, again master of the situation.

The car was constructed of steel. Completely spherical. She imagined entering and Charles sealing the door. They would be completely enclosed. Exactly like in a t—

"Tomb!" She inhaled sharply, whipping her head from side to side as if awakened from a nightmare. "It's a coffin!"

Her hands thrashed as she tried to pull free. She should have seen that Charles was leading them to their deaths!

"Princess," his strong voice commanded as he gathered her to his chest.

The world stilled. As if in a dream, she lowered her hands.

Soft silver eyes met her gaze.

Please enter.

Somehow they were already at the car, and Charles had opened the door for her.

In a daze, Berd found herself sinking onto a seat. If only she could sleep. Sleep and not wake. She was weak. So weak. And Charles was mean not to let her partake. Just because he was bigger than her. Just because he was stronger than her. Just because he was in lov—

The door slammed.

A pop went off within her head. And sound, harsh and painful, swam back into her ears, almost deafening her. But her mind cleared and she could see again. Think again.

She moaned, instinctively cupping her hands over her ears, and blinked away tears. It had been that painful. She must have been in a trance.

"Wake up! Wake up, now." Charles was shaking her. Heat from his hands seeped into her being. "I meant it. We're safe. Not just safe from the waterfall, but the energy, too. And Gine. The car's a Faraday shield which means we're enclosed so Gine can't hear us. Now quick, I have so much to tell you and we haven't enough time. First of all, are you all right?" He scanned her face.

"I'm fine. Fine," she said then realised that she was supporting her head in her hands.

Berd stared in front of her as the world blurred and then cleared in turns. She heard Charles rifling in a cupboard. Something brushed her lips and a familiar odour reached her. Instinctively, she gulped, swallowing the cool liquid.

"Water," she muttered, when she was able to stop drinking. She hiccoughed then focused on the object that Charles was now drinking from. It was a bladder.

Dim yellow light from the glass overhead shone on rounded metal walls. She was seated on a narrow curving bench that circled a third of the wall's circumference. Directly in front of the door to her right was a small, built-in cupboard. Its hinged metal door was open, blocking its contents from her view, but the ever-present humming was gone.

Except for Charles's soft swallowing, all was quiet.

No sound came to her of the car's motor as it travelled down the side of the plateau. She had to believe it was moving.

"How on earth did you get water?" she asked, for as far as she remembered neither the Difference, Analytical nor the Ghost Engines required steam to function.

He lowered the bladder from his mouth then flung it back into the cupboard. Only one bladder and she had nearly finished it. She bit her lip.

But if she was upset with her selfishness, Charles did not appear to be. Rummaging in the cupboard, his voice was muffled, excited.

"The book stacks. I collected steam from their engines the last time I was here and stored a bladder in the car for emergencies. There was water in the locomotive tender, too, but that was undrinkable. When I placed the car here, I didn't think its nearness to the energy would be a problem. The waterfall powers it, so it made sense at the time to have the Faraday car close. Since the second lightning strike, the volume of the waterfall has increased massively. I just never thought one day I would see the energy in a different light."

That was probably the closest he was going to come to admitting the energy was dangerous, but what she really wanted was for him to confess that *Gine* was dangerous. She had to know whose side Charles was on. She sighed. Still, it was poor manners to be ungrateful when he had shared his water with her.

Gingerly, she rubbed her hands over her face. When they came away, there were brownish-red stains on them. It must have come from when he had grasped her hand to encourage her on.

Blood.

Blood from when he was injured trying to shield her from the impact of the fall when the road lifted. She attempted to wipe it off on her woollen pants. It seemed having her in the Engine was a liability to Charles. But the Engine had allowed her in.

"Did we come this way for the water?" Her voice was tight.

Charles closed the cupboard door and then plunked himself down beside her. "No, we do need the settings. It was handy the car was here. I created the car assuming that, should ever the waterfall overflow, a Faraday shield would provide protection from the excess energy. I only wish I had placed the car further away from the falls. Didn't occur to me at the time. I could move it now, but it would require energy, and the last thing I want is to drain the Engine of any energy."

This was probably why he hadn't created a hot-air balloon. He was trying to conserve energy. He was the expert on it. "You survived one whole year in here," she said.

He shrugged. "Had I known what to do when I was first pulled in, I would have been able to escape. But I didn't, and by the time I did, it was too late. There was insufficient energy to get me out. But now you're here, and we have sufficient."

Charles clapped his hands together. "Now quick, what did Gine speak to you about? The whole story this time," he demanded. "How many days did he give me?"

She had to tell him he was dying, she would be wrong not to. He had the right to know. "Two."

Unperturbed, Charles nodded, as if he expected that answer. "That is Gine. Exactitude is his forte, but we have the advantage. He has promised not to try anything for twenty-four hours."

"Nothing? What did you call that episode earlier amongst the tree tops?"

"When the road erupted?" His voice lowered. "You've made yourself very clear on *that* matter. It won't occur again."

The road had erupted because Gine was trying to separate Charles from me. To prevent a kiss.

She turned her head to the side so he could not see her blush, and busied herself with a ruffle on her blouse.

"We have twenty-two hours left. It will be tight, but if Gine does nothing, we should be able to make it." He rubbed his hands on his thighs, as if getting rid of nervous energy. The whole car vibrated around her with his movement, the scent of leather strengthening dizzyingly. His shoulders kept bumping against hers; his legs seemed to stretch from one end of the car to the other.

She moved to the furthest end of the seat, as far away from him as possible.

"What you need right now is a map. I'm surprised you never asked for one." He pulled out a pen, pulled the cupboard door open, then leaned across her and started sketching on the blank inner door in front of her. "That way, if anything were to happen to me, you will be able to find your way out. Now we are here. In the middle." He stabbed his finger against the centre of the cupboard door.

A map? A map meant he *trusted* her, because it meant she could use the map to go anywhere she wanted, without him. He trusted her in his Engine.

Not only had Charles never lied to her, he trusted her.

If only she could hide. She had been a fool for ever doubting him and she groaned inwardly. There was only one way she could think to make it up to him, to show him she trusted him. "No," she said firmly.

"No?" He frowned then paused in his scribbling and lowered the pen.

"No. No time," she lied brazenly.

His frown deepened.

"I—I have a few questions. I can understand not summoning a hot-air balloon because you don't want to use up too much energy, but the blocks when I first came were exploding into buildings."

"Ah!" He straightened, looking pleased with her question. "Energy. After the second lightning strike, the one that brought you in, the Engine was flooded with energy. That was the runoff Gine used." He slipped his pen away, took out some strips of leather, then shut the cupboard door and began attaching, one by one, the strips of leather to his outfit, as though repairing the damage to his suit.

She stared at the floor. "So that explains why the train had travelled through such desolation. That was the normal state of affairs; but the trees back there?"

"A distraction," he answered quietly, as he continued to tear strips of leather into lengths.

She frowned. Gine, trying to distract her from Charles must have been desperate enough to have gone to the extent of sacrificing energy. And when it didn't work, Gine felt he had to take things in hand with the road lifting.

"At all times you were safe." Charles tugged viciously at the leather, engrossed in his wrapping.

Safe but only because Charles had been nearby to stop, at the last second each time an out-of-control automaton with god-like powers. But his remark proved that Charles was still on Gine's side, believing the best of Gine. If she had been injured she had no doubt that Gine would use that as an opportunity to treat her with energy. Though Gine had said otherwise, she wondered if he would even try to injure her.

"I know you believe Gine is trying to hurt you. At this stage, I do not know what to do to convince you otherwise. Gine is clever, but Gine is only an engine. A computer. And we are smarter than he."

She eyed Charles curiously. It was almost as if he had read her mind.

"Sometimes you can be fairly transparent, my lady," he murmured.

She glowered at him, but his words made sense and there was no malice in them. Or taunt. She hoped she was smarter than Gine, though her first and only conversation with Gine did not prove that. Charles was obviously smarter than Gine, but then Charles had beaten her to her goal of being the world's first computer programmer, but that was not his fault. He had sped up his research, pushed it beyond safety and sanity because he had to survive. But she didn't want just to survive. She wanted to escape.

"If anyone knows Gine, it is you. After all, Gine is in your own image," she challenged.

Charles shrugged self-deprecatingly, but his eyes glinted with pride. "I hope the Almighty Himself forgives me for that, but it was none of my doing. I am, of course, terribly conceited and filled with delight that Gine chose my visage. Gine obviously knows a good-looking fellow when he sees one."

She crossed her arms. "You're the *only* fellow he's seen."

Charles rubbed his chest, feigning hurt. "You really know how to wound a *fellow*, don't you, princess?"

She ignored his comment. "One thing I don't understand. If Gine is the Engine, and you are his creator, then why can't Gine give you the answer you want? Why can't he let you out?"

When Charles's face flushed, she knew she had hit a sore point.

He sighed heavily. "Ah, that's simple. Gine doesn't want me to leave."

Chapter 13

CHARLES WAS TRAPPED.

For some time, Berd had suspected that Charles was not in control of the Engine.

Yet, he had seemed so Godlike in the beginning.

"This is why we had to come all this way to the Store. To get the settings Gine won't give you," she whispered.

Charles swept a lock of black hair off his forehead, leaned back against the rounded wall, and clasped his pale hands over his stomach. In the dim yellow light, she saw the laborious movements of his chest, rising and falling. By now the air inside the car was staler, but then the car had been built to carry one occupant, not two. Even Charles's black leather outfit seemed to have lost its normal sheen.

They had been in the car too long.

"When I programmed Gine, I made it part of his operating system that he'd always do whatever it took to keep me alive. Made sense. Still does," Charles said, staunchly meeting her gaze.

She had to find out if 'whatever' included killing her. "You programmed Gine. You programmed Gine without the use of operational cards…" For, had she not spoken with the Engine itself?

Charles looked away for a moment as he stretched his long legs, apparently finished with his strips of leather. "I programmed Gine, but so is Gine."

This did not make sense. "Pardon?"

He met her gaze again, but this time held it. There was some emotion in his deep blue eyes she could not read. "Gine, you see, is learning to teach himself. You understand programming, right?"

"I know a program is basically a set of instructions. And there are only three types."

"So you will know that all programs are made of a combination of these structures: sequence, selection and iteration."

There was no condescension in his tone, if anything he was speaking to her as an equal. This was the first time a man had ever done that to her regarding her pursuit. She couldn't help but preen slightly. "'Sequence' meaning to complete the instructions a user gives, 'selection' involving a decision and lastly 'iteration', which means to repeat an action a finite number of times."

"Or infinite," he added softly.

"Infinite?" Her heart skipped a beat. She pulled the meaning deeper into her. Infinite repetition, if done unwisely, could mean the possibility of the program never ending. When her eyes met his again, she read the answer. "How is that possible?"

"Recursion." Charles rolled the word on his tongue. "I made the control structure for Gine recursive, to protect both him and myself."

Berd pressed one hand against the wall, steadying herself. A shiver ran through her, but it was not because of the metallic coldness. "That's an endless loop. Gine has to keep repeating that instruction again and again. Ad nauseum."

Her stomach tightened. Charles had programmed Gine to teach himself, just like a human being. On one hand it made sense, because if Charles were ever to be incapacitated, having someone, or more precisely something, who could do the thinking for him was the only way to preserve Charles's life, but on the other hand, to know Gine would keep doing that action infinitum — would make it harder to stop Gine.

Gine: a being not created by God but one who could think and generate ideas, and act in an independent capacity. And who would not give up his objectives. Ever.

In doing so, Charles had moved away from the world of engines and machines. He had become like a god. A creator. For only God could create life. Maybe in the future, such things would become normal, ordinary, but for now it was revolutionary. Blasphemy, even.

Gine was more than a computer. He was more or less a sentient being, but without reason. A monster, like the ancient Titans.

She had thought Charles was explaining all this to her in the hope they could work together, yet this sounded more like a warning.

She looked up to find Charles studying the door. His face was sombre. "We are almost at the bottom. When the car stops, the door will open automatically.

A word before we go. Pray do not judge Gine too harshly. Instead, think of him as a human child. Still learning. Still prone to making mistakes. At least he has a sense of humour."

She almost hit her head against the back of the wall. "Sense of humour? That is what you call the darkness that almost swallowed me! A jest!"

Charles shrugged, but he was dead serious. "Of course, there are sections of the Engine that are dangerous. Would you walk in front of a moving train? You came to no harm. Gine sent a messenger to warn me."

"Gine is an engine. An engine! Why are we even referring to Gine as a 'he'? It's an engine! An 'it'. Not a 'he.'"

Charles's face hardened. "He saved your life more than once. He could have allowed you to be electrocuted."

So he truly believed Gine was alive and sane. She had seen Gine, too. But 'alive'? And 'sane'? This felt like a bad dream. One thing however, she had to get clear. "Gine had a reason. You tell me. Tell me what Gine is trying to do. If all you say is true then why did Gine save my life?"

The door clicked open.

Hazy golden light swung into the car, along with life-giving fresh air and the scent of fresh-cut pine so strong she was dying to sneeze. Her nose watered. The humming droned loudly in her ears. Before she could move, Charles was out the door, gone with not even a backward glance or a 'by your leave' or 'let's work together'.

If anything, Charles's action convinced her that he

was not keen on answering the questions that mattered. He must truly think women indeed the weaker sex, despite his earlier spiel. No doubt he expected her to wait until he, the great hunter-gatherer, returned. Or perhaps he was going to warn Gine.

She stumbled out the door, expecting to find herself surrounded by gigantic monsters.

Outside, the humming, pressed in on all sides, causing her to feel as if she had been stuffed into an invisible pillow. It reminded her once more of how alone she was.

But she wasn't alone.

Charles stood a few feet away, facing the car, his face white. He was staring at something behind her, his mouth slowly opening as he raised his head. What he was staring at must have been extremely tall. Monstrously tall.

She whipped round.

The waterfall of energy that had earlier on clouded them in ethereal blue light was gone. Only the bright green enamel of the plateau met her eyes. Flat like polished glass. Unscaleable.

"Finished," Charles muttered.

Berd nodded, understanding. If the waterfall was gone, then it meant one thing.

The Engine had run out of energy.

They were doomed.

The air around them pulsed. But slowly between the beats, Berd heard a sound.

The chaotic chimes of a thousand church bells tolled by the damned. She caught a glimpse of a celestial stream of stars, glittering as they hurled themselves over the top edge of the empty waterfall.

The bits were back.

"Run!" Charles yelled, slipping his calloused hand into hers. Warmth filled her. He ran, tugging her along.

"But the car? Surely we would be safe inside."

"No energy. Door won't close."

That was good enough reason for her. Berd stumbled after Charles, but all she could think of was how beautiful the bits looked as they skimmed down the side of the plateau. A pack of glowing silver wolves following a trail…

But wolves were predators.

And if the wolf-bits were predators, she and Charles were prey.

She turned to find him smiling, but she was not surprised. He liked these dratted bits. Once again this reaction, like his reaction back in the hot air balloon stumped her. At least this time round, he was running in the opposite direction of the bits.

"The bits, see them, my lady?"

"Of course I see them!" It annoyed her that they constantly had to make conversation as they ran. "How can you smile at a time like this?" she choked out.

"Because we're still alive," he shouted, his face flushed with exhilaration. "We have a chance. When I first saw the waterfall had receded, I thought we were done for. I knew Gine had used up energy creating the forest above. I flatly refused to believe he had used it all."

Charles's confession made sense. He was smiling because they still had a chance. She seemed to be making progress in understanding him.

The distance between them widened as their arms stretched out. Berd battled to keep up with Charles. If only their fingers were locked. It was all she could do to make sure her hand did not slip out of his grasp.

"You—you saw the waterfall vanishing as a sign?"

"I thought it was the end. The Engine had run out of energy. We were done for." He jerked his head at the silver stream hunting them. "Obviously, we're not. Gine simply moved the energy so we can't return up the plateau. We've a chance if we can reach the book stacks. Come on!" Charles whooped with joy and ran faster.

If only she could be as confident as he. Her mouth was dry, a stitch was coming on, and they were a hundred yards away from the nearest book stack. Somehow she had to make it.

The bits reached the bottom of the plateau.

"Do you wish a problem to solve, my lady?" he cried out almost joyfully at her.

He was mad! "Surely, running for our lives is enough!" Her heart was pounding so hard she was sure her ribs were about to crack. Perspiration loosened her grip on his hand. She clenched her teeth at him in annoyance.

"Ha! I have rather an interesting one on hand: which book stack holds the settings we need."

He had to be jesting! "What do you mean, you don't know?" she wailed.

Charles gave a hearty laugh when he saw her face. "I'm not God, my lady! Even though you may think I am." Then he winked and veered away from the nearest book stack. His grip on her hand continued to loosen. Now it was only their fingers clutching.

The nerve of that man! Berd was sure her heart would not hold up much longer. The second book stack was much farther away. She was barely able to keep up with his long, untiring legs.

Run. Run. Run.

The bits were halfway to them.

Charles seemed engrossed in his own dilemma, unaware of her plight.

"Look around at the volumes of book stacks. In one is the answer, only I am not sure which."

"Don't jest!" She wanted to weep, close to collapse as pain radiated up and down her legs.

"Wish I was!"

There were hundreds of book stacks. The whole horizon was littered with these towering monsters and the air seemed to spiral above her head each time she peered up. The stacks cast deep pools of shadow on the ground; the icy wind buffeted her face.

They passed the second book stack.

The bits were almost upon them now; a blaze of white lightning snaking across the surface of the plains. Blue sparks smacked into the ground, releasing the scent of charred pine.

"Faster!" Charles yelled as he headed for the third book stack. "Blast! There's so much I wanted to say to you, so much. Look, if I'm not back, whatever you do, do not ingest any energy. My suit is made from the leather of the battery beasts. They were once black. Black. Not silver. You were right. The energy will change you. Whatever you do, do not allow Gine t—"

He yanked her forward, but their hands were so delicately connected that it was that little bit too much. Berd lost her hold on him. She lunged, desperate to regain it, but tripped.

The terrifying music of the bits drowned out her shriek. At the loss of contact, Charles twisted. He saw her go down and dove to catch her, but it was too late. She landed with a jolt on the ground, skinning her elbows and palms. She rolled, hard metal smacking her ankles and joints.

The world was spinning as she tried to rise. She was vaguely aware of bits whirling dizzyingly over her head, lethal, silver, one-pound cannonballs. The scent of gunpowder and iron was strong in the air when in a flurry of leather, arms and legs, Charles crashed into her. As she lay stunned from the second impact, she felt him tuck her knees under her, then wrap her arms around her legs.

"We have an hour to search. Meet back at the car. Regardless of whether you've found the answer. Or not."

The last thing she remembered was Charles pushing her head between her knees. She smelt the familiar aroma of the leather hide he wrapped around her, and felt its thick, soapy texture against her bare skin. Then it tightened around her, cocooning her in a ball of leather.

With her ears shielded by her arms, his voice sounded muffled. "I'll draw them off! Just run!"

Then everything went topsy-turvy.

He had rolled her away from him.

She gagged, but a moment later, she was unrolling. She shook her head, horribly dizzy. The smouldering, charred piece of leather lay beside her on the ground.

But the air around her was clear. Clear of noise, clear of bits.

Charles had wrapped her in the leather hide to protect her when he pushed her out of the circle of bits.

He had sacrificed himself for her.

And now she was free.

Even as she rose, bits whizzed blindingly over her, leaving smoke trails of black and gold. Again the scent of gunpowder spiked the air, now laced with sulphur.

Desperate, she needed to know what had happened to Charles, but the bits were circling her once more. If she did not run, she would be trapped.

"Run! Elizabeth!" Charles's voice called out.

She turned and ran towards the nearest book stack.

He continued to instruct, but his voice was melding into the sea of noise from the bits whistling round him, becoming more chime-like, as if he were being absorbed. "Promise me this. Promise me you will meet me here in an hour's time and if I am not here, you will proceed to the Output!"

"Promise!" She dared a glance behind her, but Charles was nothing more than a mass of brilliant blue-and-white particles.

Tears blurred her vision as she turned and raced for the nearest book stack — a towering structure to her right.

Charles's voice grew softer and softer behind her. "Run! Elizabeth, I lo—"

A guttural roar filled her ears.

Charles's.

Berd screamed as she twisted back to look. An explosion of white and yellow flashes! Fragments of dots and dashes. Then smoke. Then nothing, as the smoke cleared.

Nothing.

There was nothing to see.

Nothing, except brilliant blue-and-silver bits circling the spot where Charles last stood. Wolves hungering for scraps.

He was gone.

"Charles!" she screamed as tears blinded her. The lump in her chest twisted. She couldn't go on. She couldn't. But she had to, because Charles would want her to.

She ran, picking up speed, the silver metal of the towers filling her vision as she searched for the right book stack. That way, Charles would not have died in vain.

The world grew hazy. The stink of gunpowder and metal in the air dazed her so that she crashed into a glass wall. She jerked back and stared, her sweaty palms squeaking over the smooth, cool surface of transparent glass that had stunned her.

A panel slid aside, and for a while she was not quite seeing it for what it was.

An elevator.

Berd threw herself inside and sank to the ground. Quietly, the glass door closed behind her, and the stink and noise of the bits was no more.

Charles was dead.

He had sacrificed himself for her.

He had loved her.

Chapter 14

WITH A HUM, the elevator door slid shut as Berd lay on the mica-grey floor. The sense of emptiness in her heart only grew as the elevator shot up.

Seen through the glass walls, the plains stretched away, and the book stacks stood silent. In the darkening light, the Faraday car glinted like a fallen tear, mirroring the ones on her cheeks. Somewhere…somewhere between the car and her, were Charles's…*remains*.

It had only been yesterday, when he lifted a finger to calm the world.

Right now, all she wanted to do was to curl into a ball and give in to her grief, but the world of the Engine wouldn't even let her have that.

Bits swirled suddenly, spearing out of the air, exploding and crashing against the outer glass of the elevator. She jerked upright.

The car rocked.

Cables screeched.

Blue smoke billowed.

Bits smashed against the glass walls, shattering into blazing clouds of blue, yellow, and grey smoke. Pray the elevator did not jam halfway! Were Charles here now, no doubt he would be cradling her in his arms, shielding her. He had spoken to her like an equal. And yet she had treated him cruelly. She had never thought such a man as he existed.

In a life-and-death struggle, Charles had given up his life to protect her whereas Gine would sacrifice her to protect Charles. This attack of the bits was most likely Gine avenging Charles.

But it didn't make sense that Charles was dead. Gine would not have allowed Charles to be killed.

Charles had said that Gine would do everything it could to keep Charles safe. That meant it should have done everything possible to protect him. Charles may still be alive… Hope flared, only to die in the next second. Most likely the bits had been meant for her and slain Charles by mistake.

Charles had explained that it took a while to redirect the bits, so maybe that was what had happened. The bits were really meant for her, and now they were finally on target.

Berd sat in numbed silence as the elevator rocked and shuddered, ascending at twice the rate the Faraday car had taken to descend. Soon, the shimmering assault of bits halted. She pressed her face against the scorched glass, trying to peer past the yellow-and-black discolourations. Warmth from the heated glass permeated her cheeks and forehead.

She doubted that Gine had run out of bits. He'd be too clever to use them all. Still the elevator was travelling, which meant the Engine possessed energy.

Gine was probably waiting for his next opportunity.

Pray the bits only attacked out in the open. And that the elevator kept ascending.

The sky was now a dull gold. As the elevator levelled with the top of the plateau, lightning stabbed a corner of the metal forest and illuminated a building sitting in the darkness.

A tower of cast iron and glass rose from amongst the metal trees, courtesy of her new perspective. Twice the height of the Crystal Palace in Penge judging by the trees, it was the strangest glass-house she had ever seen. Mist mysteriously shrouded its contents. Silver balls of lightning burst within the structure itself, tailing off in dazzling streams that veined across the surface of the glass walls.

The rough map Charles had attempted to sketch… He had thumped his finger on the centre of the cupboard door, indicating the centre of the Engine where they were now. There was only one answer that seemed appropriate: the structure had to be the Mill.

The brain and heart of the Engine. Its soul.

She sucked in a breath. The building hadn't appeared. It had been there all along. She had seen its roof when she was up on the plateau, only she had been distracted at the time. And now she understood what Gine had been up to.

Gine hadn't been reckless; he hadn't used the energy to create trees to distract her from Charles, but from the Mill.

And that was far more important, for if she were within reach of the Mill, she could enter and rip out every part of Gine's heartless machinery.

She was clenching her hands, imaging the havoc she

would wreak when a door opposite sprung open into an ice-blue room about ten yards in diameter. Cool air, scented lavender, blew into her face as water rippled down the walls, sounding like a multitude of raindrops plopping into a multitude of ponds to gurgle away into a finger-thin channel that lined the room. This was not the devilishly complicated and deafening clockwork mechanism she had imagined. She was unsure if she were really seeing the true innards of the book stack, or if Gine was playing tricks again.

Her throat was so parched that when she swallowed, she tasted only stale, salty dryness. Charles had said he had gathered water when he was here last, but she wouldn't be surprised if Gine was disguising the energy as water by making them appear alike. She cast one last look at the plains. That was when she saw it.

The figure.

She gave a little cry. Dressed in black, a figure stood right where she had last seen Charles.

Almost as she recognised him, she realised it could be a master stroke of a last-ditch ploy, for Gine looked identical to Charles.

"You clever devil, Gine," Berd muttered, torn between entering the room to find the setting she needed and going back down. If that was really Charles below, then her decision was clear.

She paused in the middle of the elevator doorway.

If she could see the colour of the figure's eyes, she would know.

Charles: Blue. Gine: Green.

And Gine knew she was trying to find the settings. This dilemma was the one thing that would prevent her from searching the book stack.

She was chewing at her lower lip, trying to decide, when a section of the room's wall bulged. A figure peeled off and strode towards her. It took no great science to recognise him.

She jumped back into the elevator, fear and relief flooding through her. Fear, because it was Gine who had appeared. Relief, because she knew, now, it was Charles who waited down below.

He wasn't dead!

Gine, attired in a morning coat and grey pants, stood in the doorway and calmly pressed one hand against the door, effectively preventing the elevator from closing. "Thank-you. At least, I think. It was a compliment, the bit about me being a clever devil?"

Berd could almost smell the burning in the air from his scorching gaze. She clenched her hands and lifted her chin defiantly. "You made me think he was dead."

Gine said nothing, but calmly strode past into the elevator. At the glass edge he peered down then shrugged. "He looks perfectly fine to me."

She ignored him, instead searching the glass walls for a lever or panel of buttons, anything to get the elevator moving, even if it meant travelling down with Gine, who was currently observing her as if entertained by her discomfiture.

"What's the hurry, my lady? You just got here." He waved to the left of the door, and a series of buttons protruded from the surface of the inner glass wall of the elevator.

Only one button had a letter on it: the letter 'G'. Berd stabbed at it, scowling when she heard Gine laugh. When the door closed and the elevator began to travel down, she braced herself, unsure what kind of attack to expect from Gine.

"Can you explain your obsession with killing, my lady? The first time I met you, apparently I was trying to kill you. Now I am 'trying to kill him'. Are you afraid of something?" he smirked, leaning near. "Death perhaps?"

Gine's words stung and for a moment Berd was stuck fast to the floor, all her limbs trembling.

"But whose?" he continued, his hands behind his back. "And by whom?" He turned back to her, suddenly serious. "I think perhaps you are so afraid of your own death, you're striving to cause ours!"

He's only trying to confuse me. I'm not a killer. But he could be.

There seemed nothing lethal in the way the young man folded his arms across his chest, and leaned against the glass wall that had a view of sweeping metal plains behind it. Nothing, until he tut-tutted and his gaze swept down to meet hers. His bright eyes turned liquid, and a strange, mesmerising tingling hollowed out her stomach, frightening but a little warm.

The attack had started.

Berd opened her mouth, about to reply when she caught a whiff of something devastatingly familiar. So familiar that whatever answer she had planned completely slipped her mind, and though she tried to recall her words, her mind remained filled with the scent and its memories. It occupied her entire focus. Her nostrils twitched frantically as she tried to place it.

She inhaled deeper, aware Gine was studying her, ever smiling. "Stop playing games, Gine. This isn't funny. What is…?"

She recognised the black leather from Charles's suit, and of course the ubiquitous paraffin, but mixed within the blend was something else…a note of something unique, important. And then with a gasp of horror, she knew.

She knew what it was. Whose it was…

Charles.

She blinked rapidly at her discovery. This was not possible! The scent had to be Gine's doing. If he could manufacture other scents, he would be able to imitate Charles's. It might be just in her mind, or it just might be that he was able to simulate organic compounds in very small amounts. The revelation that such a thing was possible stunned her. But why wouldn't it be possible here, if nowhere else.

She was in a world where Gine was God. And right now, that God was watching her as if she were the most interesting thing he had ever seen. But then he hadn't seen many living beings. She just hoped he was more interested in living things than dead.

Gine cleared his throat and the scent faded away. "I agree. Not funny. Not funny at all. There are things here I can do that you do not understand, wonderful things, and I would like to keep doing them. What do you think will happen if you destroy the Mill? Effectively, you will be killing me. And him. And yourself. Now, I haven't killed you, or Charles for that matter. You, on the other hand, have thought about killing me on several occasions. Who's the real murderer here?"

Berd frowned, trying to stay calm even though she did not feel it. It horrified her that he knew she had been thinking of destroying the Engine. But he was the paranoid one.

"It is true," she said cautiously. "I did think of destroying the Mill, but you're only an engine. You make it sound like a crime to turn an engine off." She glanced at his chest, long enough to confirm it wasn't moving.

Gine is an engine. An engine. He's not alive. Or a god.

She took one last gaze out the glass wall, and then forced herself to face him.

To her shock, Gine's face had paled. The muscles in his throat had tightened, as if her words had stabbed him.

It was almost as if the Engine had feelings.

"Turn an engine off. Turn the power off. What would happen if we were to do either now?" His voice faltered, and he drew in a long, shuddering breath. "I would have thought that you of all people would know how it feels to be a possession."

Even a possession can have feelings. My exact words.

In disbelief, she stared at him. "How did you know I wanted to destroy the Mill?"

"The movements of your hands gave the game away." He mimed her throttling him.

"The glass walls of the elevators…and the railway carriage…" she breathed, finally understanding.

Gine lifted one finger and prodded the air. "Each time Charles lifted his head to the sky he did so because he was referring to me. He talked to me through the glass walls. Sound is just vibration and I am the Engine itself, so I can hear anything pointed at a wall capable of catching vibrations and ringing with them.

"And this." He waved a hand at his form. "Is a new development, made possible thanks to the energy you brought with you!" He smirked and bowed, appearing extremely pleased.

The energy she had brought with the second lightning strike.

All this while she had been in a goldfish bowl, and it had been Gine who was looking in.

The Engine was a doll's house, a child's plaything with Gine, the child, moving his toys about. Perhaps that was why Charles had referred to Gine as child-like. Gine, a young boy, filled with dreams of glory, moving his little tin soldiers across a battlefield, and not caring if the pieces got destroyed.

"You've been spying on us."

"I prefer the term protector."

"What from? The only danger is you."

Gine gave an over dramatic-flinch, but his emerald eyes danced. "Ouch! She bites and has claws! Has Charles ever seen this side to you?"

She dug her fists into her hips. "I'm not playing games, Gine."

"Did your world end when you thought he was dead?" he taunted.

"You know nothing of human emotion. You're like a child who only knows relationships from his nanny and what he reads in trashy nickel novels!" she huffed. "So let me ask you this: why did you rescue me when I was electrocuted?"

"Did you ever ask yourself why I would rescue you, only to want to kill you?" His smile broadened.

Once again Gine had a point. It made no sense for him to rescue her, because if he wanted her dead, he could have let her die when the lightning struck.

Gine gave a lazy wave of his hand, the movement

so exactly like Charles's that Berd's chest grew tight. A heavy thump shook the ground as a book stack stumbled into view.

A tiny dark figure was riding down its elevator.

The figure was dressed in a mauve blouse and fawn pants, the silk shimmering like a war standard as it caught the light. Long coal-brown hair lay loose across the figure's shoulders.

It was a doppelganger of her!

Berd drew back, shaking her head in disbelief. "Stop, do not do this!"

"Do you think he will be able to tell you apart?" Gine tapped his lower lip with one finger as if musing.

When the faraway elevator reached the ground, the door opened and the figure started running straight towards Charles, who pivoted towards her.

"You know, just a thought…" Gine's breath tickled her ears, causing her to jump. "If he picks the other you, why…there's no need for *you* any more, is there?"

He pushed himself backwards into the glass. Like the Cheshire cat, he took on the colours of the glass and melted away, until only his features remained. And then, even they vanished one by one, leaving only his glowing green eyes. They seemed to swallow her up…

The door to her elevator opened, with an enormous moan of a bell.

Berd shook herself. She'd been drowning in his eyes so long she hadn't even heard the elevator reach the ground. There was no time to wonder on it.

She was back on the ground.

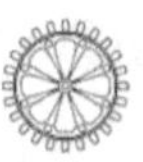

The overpowering scent of fresh pine blew into her face as Berd stepped out of the elevator, but as her foot touched the ground, the plains tilted, physically. Her body swayed. The sky stretched dizzying over her head. She almost went down. The ground around her rippled as if someone had shaken a cloth.

No doubt Gine was using another trick to delay her. She had to shift her body, wondering if this was what being drunk must feel like, as she struggled to stay on her feet. Across the way, the doppelganger was already running, her path unobstructed towards Charles.

Berd ran on, at an angle, constantly about to topple. Her ankles wobbled, on the verge of twisting, yet she managed to pound her feet as she raced against her mirror image, each trying to reach Charles first. As she neared, she noticed his right arm was bare and her heart swelled as she remembered how he had wrapped her up with the leather.

The doppelganger reached Charles first. "Charles!"

At its tinny cry, Berd almost laughed. There! The doppelganger did not sound like her at all. Surely Charles would know which was her. All she knew was that she longed to rejoice in his survival, not try to persuade him it was her. And that would make the difference!

He will know.

As Berd reached them, the doppelganger twisted to look at her. Close-up and face-to-face, it was impossible not to stare, especially since the doppelganger had flesh just like her.

So it was true then. If Gine can create such a life-like being out of energy, I should not be surprised that I seem real to myself.

The doppelganger's nut-brown hair, loose like Berd's, had frizzed during the run and now resembled an unkempt lion's mane. Its dark eyes glinted, wolf-like in its wildness. Through the rips and tears in its own mauve silk blouse, its undergarments gleamed bone white. Its hands were curved as if ready to claw…

Then the world tilted even more: a massive uplifting of earth roared to life. As the glass green floor slanted, all three slumped to the ground.

Berd screamed.

The doppelganger screamed.

At the synchronised scream, both women cupped their mouths. Both elbowed the ground together. Both turned to Charles. Both pushed back up with one hand, desperate to remain upright.

A hand grasped Berd's arm.

She looked up to see Charles had hold of her, but he also had hold of the doppelganger. Her heart sank slightly, but she refused to give in.

She squeezed his hand reassuringly, only to find cuts and burns there. "Charles, it's me." But before she could go on, the doppelganger interrupted.

"No, it's me, and I'll prove it. I know why the metal forest was created. To distract you from me."

"There's a second reason!" Berd inched closer.

The doppelganger inched closer, too. "Of course. The first was really a red herring."

Charles sat back on his knees, alarmed.

Berd and the doppelganger chorused in unison, "Gine stopping me from finding the Mill."

Their words merely caused Charles's already haggard face to crease further in confusion. His breathing was ragged and as they moved forward, he moved back and pushed his messy hair out of his eyes.

Nothing like this had every happened before, and Berd stilled, unsure how to proceed. The doppelganger stilled also. Both had their hands pressed against their chests, and Berd was sure the horrified expression on the doppelganger's face was the exact same as on her own.

She frowned at the creature and the creature frowned back.

"Tramp," Berd said, and the doppelganger gasped.

"I am not!"

Berd smirked.

All the while Charles's desperate gaze darted from her to the doppelganger. He couldn't tell them apart! That scoundrel! To go after her so hard and then not be able to tell her apart from a twin!

The doppelganger's voice shrilled louder and louder, growing more and more insistent. "But of course, there's the third reason. I know the third reason."

It was Berd's turn to be incredulous. The third reason, she knew of no third reason.

"Charles, please! It's me." Berd's voice was a whisper against the din of the doppelganger's. The yap, yap, yapping of the doppelganger, like a clockwork toy newly wound, jarred every thought, but it was from her whisper, close to his ear, from which he flinched.

"It's me. I know all three reasons why Gine created the forest of metal trees," said the doppelganger, its voice nice and strong and loud. Then it dispensed with all its earlier insistence and instead gazed calmly at Charles, exactly the way Berd had done.

Berd was starting to wonder if Gine could read her mind. Regardless, he must have been fine tuning the doppelganger even as it proceeded onward with its mission. Berd could think of nothing to say, and she shook her head, frustrated. Unless she did something, the doppelganger had won. And then Gine no doubt would do away with her like an erroneous line of code.

She had to persuade Charles.

The answer came, and she gasped, blinded by its simplicity. It was the only method she knew to persuade Charles it was her. Only it wasn't an easy undertaking and her body seemed to swirl into smoke at the thought of carrying it out.

She would have to give him the kiss he had wanted for so long.

Berd had never kissed a boy before. Not in that fashion. Not ever. If it was anything else but this!

But she had to. As Charles continued to look bewildered, between her and her double, she knew with certainty what she had to do, and her resolve solidified.

I have to do this.

Charles eyed her suspiciously as she leaned forward. Her heart beat wildly. Her arms were marble. Her waist was stone. She shut her eyes, squeezed her lips together tight as she struggled against her inhibitions. Perspiration plastered her hair to her throat. She was sure Charles was laughing at her. He probably thought her forward.

Before she knew it, their lips connected, only it was not the reaction she had hoped for.

His lips bit with electricity!

Berd jerked back with the dry sting of electricity ringing through her from finger to toe! She screamed. Her lips were burning, alternately scorched and then frozen. Her mouth stung as if filled with burning coal. This must be some new trick of Gine's to stop her from convincing Charles.

Her gaze flew to Charles, frantic. Her evident negative reaction to him could not have made him happy.

Through her chaos, Charles was smiling. Only his eyes were now green.

It was Gine.

And it had been Gine all along.

Out of the corner of her eye, the doppelganger stared dumfounded at what was happening.

"He's dead. You've actually killed him," Berd stammered, reeling as if her heart had been ripped in half.

"Nonsense, he's alive. Look!" Gine pointed over to his left.

The world levelled physically as a figure stepped out from behind one of the legs of a book stack about a hundred yards away.

"Charles!" Berd shouted.

At her scream, the figure looked at her, then at the doppelganger beside her. It certainly looked like Charles, at the very least.

Gine stood and bowed, dusting himself off. "Princess, I won't offer a hand as I know you won't take it, but I would hurry if I were you. She knows what the real Berd would do to persuade Charles to her."

Berd scrambled to her feet. Even before Gine vanished away the doppelganger had lifted up her skirts and was racing away to the figure in black.

The real Charles.

Chapter 15

IT WAS A nightmare.

Again the doppelganger reached Charles first.

This time it said nothing as it stood before him, but looked at Charles as though joyful to have him returned to the land of the living. Berd did not doubt that it would even go so far as to tell him it loved him. Or kiss…

Strength ebbed from Berd and she was cold, so cold, as she came panting up behind them, her hands on her sides and her head bowed as she sucked in deep breaths.

Blast that Gine! He knew exactly how to trick Charles. Even kissing wasn't going to work this time.

Charles's blue eyes were bright with wretchedness as he stared from her to the doppelganger, the doppelganger that seemed to be made of flesh.

Berd brushed her fingers through her hair. They caught, stuck in the tangled mess that seemed to have ballooned around her head like a lion's mane… A bone-white chemise flashed through the rips and burns

174

of her mauve silk blouse. She lifted her hands to her face, only to discover she was curving them.

The doppelganger spoke, its voice nice and strong as Berd's. "It's me. I know all three reasons as to why Gine created the forest of metal trees."

Then the doppelganger leaned forward stiffly. Its lips puckered, its eyes shut.

Had I looked that awkward when I'd done it? Oh, Lord alive...

Charles cleared his throat, eyes wide and frantic then took a wary step back.

"So, you know all three reasons why Gine created the forest of metal trees," Berd said, her voice raw with emotion, as the doppelganger leaned towards the man.

It nodded primly, its lips inches from Charles's. Its eyes closed.

"Good!" Berd gave a vicious shove, and the doppelganger fell to one side.

It was surprisingly light. It collapsed, crashing to the ground like a toppling tree. There hadn't even been any flailing of arms, but Berd didn't wait to see what happened to it. She'd had enough of Gine's little games.

"And you," Berd accused the figure that looked like Charles with a pointed finger, "*you're* not Charles!"

She swivelled away from it and would have crashed into another figure, this one standing right behind her, had not two hands reached out to grasp her firmly, steadying her.

Berd barely noticed the pressure on her upper arms, because she was staring into eyes so blue she was lost in them. She didn't need the hint of any aroma to tell her who this was.

Now she knew that deep down she would never have thought Gine was him.

"Are you all right, princess?" Charles's voice burred.

Her heart began to hammer. And for one intense moment as he reached down, she thought he was going to kiss her —

He grasped her hand.

"Run!" He pulled her along, and they were running again.

She glanced back at the spot where the doppelgangers had been, but both body doubles were gone. No doubt they had disappeared back into the Engine. She snuck a peek at Charles, but he was looking straight ahead. Her heart beat faster but she knew it wasn't solely because of the exertion. And she was warm, but again she didn't think it was all because of the running…

Their run this time was nothing compared to the wild madness earlier, their pace distinctly slower. They could have conversed, and there was nothing chasing them — no bits, no disrupted earth. Yet, she sensed Charles was putting every ounce of strength he had into moving. He slowed even further as they reached the nearest book stack and then, to her horror, he tripped over his feet and pulled her down, tumbling into a heap together. As soon as her head cleared, she pushed herself up from the reflective floor, expecting Charles to follow, or to give her a hand, only he remained on the ground, his dark hair damp, and his eyes closed.

"No… No! Charles!" Her voice wavered, thinning away in the twilight of the Engine.

There was no response. He stayed exactly as he had landed, his eyes shut and his head turned aside. Hesitantly, Berd placed her hand on his cheek. The skin was cold and clammy.

"Charles!" she screamed again, her hands desperately shaking his inert body. He jiggled back and forth like a massaged piece of meat, but did not stir; as soon as her hands ceased their movement so did he. Berd sat back on her heels, unsure of what to do. His breathing was ragged. His eyes fluttered, opening long enough for her to see they had turned silver, and then closed again.

He was dying.

At first she thought the shudder she felt was her grief and shock, but then a shadow passed over her. Another deep metallic groan and shockwaves went through the ground. The book stacks were moving.

Berd jumped to her feet, hooking her arms around Charles. They had to get out of the way before a book stack trod on them. She tried to lift, then to drag him, anything, to shift him out of the way of those monstrous giants. But she failed.

The ground trembled. Charles's head lolled from side to side. Berd, on her knees, had to brace herself with her hands, palms flattened against the green enamel floor or risk falling forward. Shadows swayed back and forth. The ground crunched and shook as a large column landed with an explosion of force, barely ten yards away.

Charles was simply too heavy. She had just about given up trying to roll him, when a voice nearby cursed.

Gine.

She almost wept in relief when she heard it.

"You pretty little fools!" Gine swore as he bore down.

Had Gine appeared at any other time she would have flown at him, but as he scooped Charles up into his arms, Berd saw him solely as a rescuer. Gine ducked under the leg of one of the monstrous nook stacks. Berd hesitated then followed, her heart in her throat.

No matter what Gine had attempted before, all was forgiven so long as he saved Charles. Gine, the god in the image of the man, strode away carrying his creator. Berd followed, praying that whatever Gine had in mind, it wouldn't be too late.

In minutes, they were in the elevator of one of the book stacks, travelling up. Gine had taken control of it, moving it without the help of buttons. It was difficult to look at Gine and not see Charles as he gazed silently in her direction, but she had to thank him.

In the dying light, Gine's black lashes glittered with tears.

Berd took a step back. "You — you really love him, don't you?"

"I'm an engine. What is an engine supposed to know about love?" He replied, soft and bitter.

That was true enough. She glanced away, unsure.

"He loves you," Gine said simply. His eyes, steady and begrudging, burned into her when she looked up.

Berd folded her arms, but her voice was a whisper. "You weren't trying to kill him. Or me."

He snorted. "Back on the subject of killing again? You certainly do have a one-track mind."

She thought she detected a trace of laughter in his

tone. "That horde of bits on the plain… I thought we were running for our lives, but you were simply trying to save Charles from dying. Surround him with energy so he would be tempted to partake."

Gine's gaze shifted down to Charles where his gaze softened. "Stubborn fool."

"Like someone else I know," Berd said. "You *were* trying to provide him with energy. I wondered why we were never actually hit."

"You'll make me a pair of wings next and then I'll have to hide my horns." He rolled his eyes, but a corner of his mouth twitched up.

It was all beginning to make sense. "My incident with my doppelganger…"

Gine said nothing, only pushed his lower lip out. She found herself noting the shape of his mouth — Charles's mouth — yet somehow…different. Gine continued to study her, and Charles, in his arms, did not stir.

She spoke slowly, as the pieces fell into place. "You wouldn't have created that doppelganger of me simply so that Charles could tell the difference between it and me. It's too obvious. Though the doppelganger was flesh, it wasn't me. I don't look like that…"

Gine's eyes only widened provocatively as if daring her to continue. The space outside slid by, and the mechanical whir of levers and pulleys continued.

"Oh stop it. I know you enjoy watching me squirm." She rubbed her chin, no longer afraid of him. "So was it to see if *I* could tell the difference between the real you and him?"

The mechanical man gave a little laugh. "You obviously failed there. I mean…you did kiss…*me*." His eyes caught hers, and the curious sensation of drowning in green returned.

Kiss me. Kiss... Berd shook the stupor off then clapped her hands together. "I know! You did it to get me to kiss Charles. That was it. That was the real reason all along. But ha! He fooled you."

"Well..." Gine's nostrils flared slightly, a flicker of reluctant admiration in his voice. "Ever think that maybe I would want to kiss you?"

A pause.

"That can't be true."

Gine raised an eyebrow. "Maybe Charles was right. There is something in you after all." He shrugged, shifting Charles a bit.

The door to the elevator opened, and cold, lavender-scented air pressed upon her sweat-drenched body, causing a shiver to go through her.

Gine strode into the ice-blue room as if he were the master of the place, carrying Charles in his arms. Somehow his shoulders seemed broader than the man's had ever been. Easily, he deposited Charles on the metallic floor, but as Berd stepped off the elevator, he stood, and began running his fingers through his jet hair. Had she not known Gine any better, she would have sworn he was nervous, but this was his domain.

"Charles will recover if you give him water. At this stage, he's merely suffering from the effects of dehydration." Gine's tone was emotionless as he stared down at Charles.

Berd nodded. She had, after all, drained the bladder.

Gine placed one of his palms flat on the wall, watching as the water rippled over his fingers and hand. "And yes, what is stored here *is* water, not energy. Not that to become like me would be so terrible a fate, would it?"

"I am in your debt, Gine," she said.

He swivelled to face her. Watery reflections played upon his features, revealing a sudden vulnerability until he twirled one finger arrogantly in the air and pointed at her. "Before I go, how *did* you tell us apart that second time?"

It was only her disgust with Charles's inability to pick them apart that had alerted her to the fact it might not have been him, but merely another ploy. It had been a guess, but something inside her screamed not to reveal this fact to Gine. Berd gave the most confident laugh she could. "Are you trying to tell me, I wouldn't know the real you?"

A roguish smile spread across Gine's face, brightening him as if the dawn had come. "Touche!" Gine crossed his arms over his chest and regarded her lazily, as he leaned against the wall. "You'd better beware your tongue, my lady. We could end up mutually admiring each other. And that would be *dangerous*." He spoke the last word as if it were a promise, his eyes shimmering twin emeralds as seen beneath the surface of a lake.

She frowned, unsure what he was alluding to. He was pushing himself back into the wall when she shook herself and called out. "Wait! Gine! I have a question."

He stopped and reversed out. No matter how many times she had seen him do this, her stomach still turned each time it happened — his skin taking on the colour of whatever he was touching.

"What is it, my lady?" He frowned, as if he were in a great hurry and she was holding him up.

"Why did you rescue me?"

Gine cocked his head at Charles. "Ah, why don't you ask him?" he challenged.

Charles? Berd swung her gaze onto his prone figure on his side. When she turned back, Gine was gone. Only clear water rippled down the blue walls while the scent of lavender pressed upon her face like a cold towel.

So all along Charles was responsible for rescuing her. Yet he had never mentioned it. Even as she asked herself the question, she remembered his dire need of water. She should not have spent minutes talking! Pray she was not too late to save him.

She ran over to the walls, washed her dusty hands in the cascade, scooped some up and then hurried back to Charles. His face was pallid, and she had to lift his head onto her knee in order to get the water into him without drowning him. It took several trips and many long minutes before she was able to get any water into him.

"Charles?" She watched anxiously.

In the end, she had to cradle his head in the crook of one arm to do so. She had just managed to rest his upper body partially on her lap when his lashes fluttered and he spluttered and choked.

He opened his eyes. They were silver-rimmed, as if he had woken from a beautiful dream. As she stared, the glazed expression disappeared and a sharpened one settled on her.

Heat flared up her throat. They were too close. She let go his head and it hit the ground.

"Ow!"

"I'm sorry!" she slapped her hand over her mouth then reached out to help only he waved her away, rubbing the sore spot on his head vigorously.

Thankfully, the difference was mere inches. But he was finally sitting up, his weight off her. "Where are we?"

"In one of the book stacks," she answered, wishing her voice did not sound so shrill. She dared a glance at him then; his face was terribly pale, but his eyes glowed, alert as he looked around. "Are you all right?"

He nodded, his chest heaving from the exertion of sitting up, and if he had noticed her staring at him earlier, there was no sign of it. "You saved me. Again," he said quietly.

She tilted her head at him, puzzled. "You did save *me*, earlier." And so he had, at risk of his life.

"Colleagues."

She frowned, not sure what he was alluding to.

"Colleagues," he said again, insistent. "We are colleagues who work well together. You are my Enchantress of Numbers."

Warmth flushed over Berd's shoulders at the compliment for that was what Charles Babbage had christened her grandmother. And now Berd understood what Charles Fotheringay was trying to say.

Perhaps in the olden days, a knight would have rescued a damsel in distress, but if she was fighting for equality, it would be just as right for a damsel to save a knight if he needed it. Of course, she couldn't take all the credit. In fact, most of the credit belonged to Gine. Well. She had been brave, and done her part. Small steps. Equality was a road, not a cliff to jump.

Equals.

Charles began to rise to his feet.

"Let me."

He held out a hand to stop her.

"I believe 'I' can do this." And so saying, he stood, and looked around at the room. "I admit I'm impressed. I thought I collapsed outside. You could have left me, but you didn't. And you obviously managed to…?" He eyed her questioningly.

She opened her mouth to explain when Charles held one finger up.

"No, don't tell me. Let me guess. You dragged me here?" Despite the paleness of his face, the laughter was back in his blue eyes.

She prepared to humour him, glad he was alive.

He persisted his questioning, his eyes gleaming curiously. "Well, carrying me would be out of the question. Hmmm, roll?"

She shook her head again, her stomach clenched as she tried not to laugh. He did look so puzzled. And beautiful.

Charles knotted his brows together. He concentrated as he gestured with his hands, miming solution after solution only to discard each one. "I give up. How did you get me here?" he finally said with a wave of one arm.

"Gine." She smiled as she revealed the truth.

At the sound of Gine's name, Charles's face darkened. "Gine! Damn him, the treacherous bastard!" He glared at her as if she had betrayed him.

Chapter 16

ERD FROWNED, UNSURE if she had heard right, but in the moment that passed between them, he seemed only more upset. Charles grasped her hand. "Come!" he ordered, and hurried her towards the elevator. His palm was unnaturally warm and damp.

Confusion washed through her. "But didn't you want to come here to find the settings?"

Charles did not answer. As if he were still recovering from his ordeal, his feet dragged. He swung his arms as if to give impetus to his movement, his face so ashen she shuddered with worry.

"Charles, please, what's wrong—"

He swivelled to stare at her, and the eyes that gazed at her were fully silver. Tiny sparks of electricity glinted on his lashes.

Suddenly, his body tensed as if he had received a huge shock. His skin shimmered as if he was being devoured alive from the inside by molten metal. His eyes were silver.

"Charles!" She was sure she smelt smoke.

She reached out to support him just as his grip on her other hand tightened. Belying his previous weakness, he began to crush her hand. Tears sprang to her eyes. She attempted to yank herself free from his grasp, but her hand was caught in a grip as tight as a vice.

A thin wail erupted from her mouth. She had made a mistake. Charles was like every other man. "You're hurting me."

But he continued to squeeze.

"Charles, please!" The bones in her hand were grinding together, skin giving way in hopes of saving what lay beneath. Tears ran down her cheeks at the pain.

Berd reached her free hand back and slapped him, hard, so hard the sound of her palm on his cheek reverberated around the room, making the water jump. But it worked. He staggered back and released her.

"How dare you! How dare you hurt me!" Holding her injured hand to her chest, she backed away.

Charles blinked then shook his head as if waking from a dream, horrified contrition on his face. "What's going on?" he asked as she bent forward and cried, cradling her fingers to her chest.

"My lady, please accept my humble apology. I do not know what came over me. I cannot express the deep regret I feel at my actions."

Berd stared up at him, barely able to see through the tears. His eyes had returned to their normal iridescent blue, now wide with anguish. His right hand was open in a gesture of conciliation. He took a step forward and she took a step back. At that, he dropped his hand.

Something was responsible for this aberrant

behaviour. Whatever it was, it terrified her. "I'm not staying a moment long—"

The ground swayed beneath their feet.

As she stumbled, Charles reached out to grasp hold of her. She slapped and shoved at him but he was stronger than her and determined to hold her still.

"Let go! Let me go damn it! Stop this!"

At first she thought she was causing the shift, but it was strange, because he was as powerless as she against the earthquake motions of the book stack. They rolled together, slipping and sliding along the water-strewn floor, water from the walls splashed onto them.

"Calm down, my lady, please calm down!"

He was trying to protect her after attacking her. This did not make sense.

In moments, the jerky movement of the book stack walking settled into a gentle rhythm. He released her then, and she scrambled to the opposite wall to get as far away from him as possible. There, she glared at him, still clutching her injured fingers.

Charles remained on the ground; he made no attempt to reach her. "Gine's causing the book stack to move. It's his way of stopping us from leaving the stack."

"Why?" she asked, suspicious.

"To remove me as far as possible from the Mill." His voice was a whisper.

"I thought you wanted to go to the Output."

"I needed to go to the Mill so I can reprogram him. The reason I gave regarding the settings was true. I do need them, but it was also an excuse to get close to the Mill."

She stared at him, the meaning hitting home.

"You can reprogram him?" From what she understood of computers, that was impossible. "How can you reprogram a computer unless you first turn it off?"

Reprogramming a computer required taking out physical components and either rearranging or switching them out for something else entirely, or else swapping the operational cards, which was why they had to be turned off. "If you turn an engine off, especially this one, don't we perish?"

He smiled bitterly. "Do you understand the term bootstrap?"

"When a computer is turned on, it has only one instruction: to load its operating system. So in analogy, if a computer were a human being, it would be the equivalent of inserting its brain."

"Exactly. Hence the term bootstrap. Because it is such a difficult operation, it is likened to a man lying prone, attempting to raise himself up by his bootstraps."

"But once a computer has loaded its operating system and in turn loaded the application program it wishes to execute, the program runs until concluded, correct?"

"In the earlier prototypes they did. Gine, however…"

She exhaled heavily, seeing where he was headed with this conversation. "Is at the cutting edge of technology," she breathed out.

He snorted. "I am too clever for myself. I saw the benefits of reprogramming the Engine as it was running. Even better, the Engine stores all its old instructions. The book stacks are not what you think they are, my lady. They are the Store, but they don't just hold the current stack of instructions, they also hold old programs. Every single program that Gine has ever executed is in storage here."

So that explained why there were so many book stacks. Despite her anger, she understood the impact of such an invention. "That's brilliant. So when you turn the computer off, it won't lose its memory."

"I certainly thought so at the time. Auxiliary memory I call it. Permanent memory."

Permanent memory as compared to temporary memory! That was indeed a breakthrough. She had never heard it done before. For a moment, the pain in her hand was gone, lost to the swell of epiphany.

He lifted his chin. "So to explain my erratic behaviour…in the book stacks are parts of me."

"I don't quite understand."

"Do you remember when we were running towards the book stacks and we were being 'attacked' by bits?"

She had never seen Charles so disgusted with Gine before. "But Gine wasn't really attacking us. He was just being childish and trying to surround you with energy in the vague hope that you would imbibe some of it." She was stunned to find herself actually defending Gine!

But if Charles hadn't really sacrificed himself for her, then why had he pushed her away?

"It was foolish and dangerous of Gine. Do you not remember what happened the last time it occurred?"

She nodded, recalling Charles's bloody nose after the attack of the bits and how she had been injured. She was surprised how quickly she had forgotten. But the world was all madness now, so one piece of confusion was easy to overlook.

He rested his elbows on his knees and gazed up at her through his dark hair. "I called out something to you then."

"Something about me not taking any energy…about how the energy changed you." She found herself staring down at his chest, watching him breathe.

He followed her gaze. "The leather from my outfit is from the battery beasts. They were black once, but because they imbibed the energy, it changed them. Do you understand? It *changed* them."

Her skin prickled. "I understand."

"They began to take on some of Gine's being. I can't quite call it characteristics or traits or even emotions. Their beings *merged*. They became part Engine while he became part them."

"So are you saying that…"

He couldn't look her in the eye as he spoke. "I am part Gine and Gine is part me." His voice cracked, and he dropped his head to his hands.

Charles had never accused Gine of being anything other than good because it was as good as accusing himself. He'd attacked her because the energy was affecting him.

"But Gine's a child. You said so yourself. Surely we could reason with him."

Charles exhaled heavily. "Pray Gine stays a child."

That stunned her. "What do you mean?"

"Have you ever asked yourself why Gine keeps playing games?"

It was true. Gine had been playing game after game since she'd entered the Engine. "Why?"

He lifted his head as he gave an ironic smile. "How else does a child learn? It's when he stops playing games we must worry. He's grown, and at his most dangerous."

And Gine was learning how to imitate people…

"Why did Gine rescue me?"

Charles's back stiffened, his shoulders tensed and his hands closed into fists. Back on the train he'd done the same; she had received answers then, only it had made the situation worse. But she had to know.

"We *saw* you. Remember before the explosion?"

She had thought then that she had seen an angel and a devil with the same face. Berd looked away, and when she glanced back their eyes locked. His were wide and defenceless. And then she understood.

"So did you fall for me then?" she asked, the words out of her mouth before she could stop them. "Or did you simply feel desperate for someone to save you?" Was that when he had fallen in love with her? Only…was Charles in love with her…? Her heartbeat quickened. "What are the three reasons Gine created the forest of trees? I know the first was to distract you from me. And the second was to distract me from the Mill. But what was the third reason?"

"The first two reasons were to distract, but the third…" He stared at the floor. "The third was to *attract*."

"Attract what?"

He exhaled slowly. "Not what. Who."

She knew the answer, but she needed to hear him say it.

"You," Charles answered. "He doesn't want you to leave. When you first entered the Engine, he produced a swathe of buildings to make you feel at home; to impress you. He wants to keep you just like he wants to keep me. Here, in the Engine. Forever."

Chapter 17

L OVE.

Love was the cause of Berd's imprisonment.

Charles, who had fallen for her from that first moment in the stable; Charles whose 'being' was partially merged and operational within Gine…it was inevitable Gine would also fall for her, or at least think he was.

An engine in love with a human…

"No! That's not possible. I want to get out. I want to get out, *now*."

Berd scrambled to her feet, but as she flung herself towards the elevator, Charles seized her arm. He yanked her to him.

She clenched her hands into fists, anticipating another attack. But though his grip was iron strong, it was his gaze that imprisoned her. Anguish shone in those sapphire eyes. His mouth parted, and they were sharing breath; his sweet boy scent mixed with paraffin and sweat.

It was clear what she had to do; Gine believed he

was in love with her, at least to some degree, thanks to Charles. She had to destroy that love. If that meant also destroying the love Charles had for her…so be it. It was her only chance to escape and she could not afford to be weak. She would do anything. *Anything*. Even hurt Charles.

"Let go," she pleaded.

He released the pressure on her arm, and she jerked out of his hold and moved toward the elevator.

"We can't leave while the book stack is moving or we'll be crushed," Charles said from behind her, his voice hoarse with tenderness.

"But Gine promised," she said, as stubbornly as only the daughter of an earl could. "He *promised* to let me out."

"What do you mean?"

At the door of the elevator, Berd turned to face him. "Gine thought I was a danger to you. He said that because of me, you refused to partake of any more energy."

"I see." Charles's voice was curt. "But if Gine wanted to let you go, why didn't you take him up on his offer?"

"Back on the train he gave me twenty-four hours."

Charles's brows shot up in surprise. He straightened then flicked his black hair off his face. "If Gine's still keeping his promise then you have twenty hours by my estimate before you know if he will."

Berd glared at him. "*Gine* wouldn't injure me if I wanted to leave."

"I suspect that as soon as Gine changed his mind, all bets were off about releasing you."

She stiffened, stung by Charles's accusation. This

was as close as he was probably going to come to admitting that Gine was now in love with her.

Then Charles groaned. "I thought Gine would behave honourably towards you until I saw what he did with the doppels. I curse my own stupidity for that." He ran his hand through his hair; a frustrated movement. "Gine was trying to pacify me after I gave him a piece of my mind regarding his idiotic attack with the bits. When I saw how he was prepared to play with you, I realised what he was planning. He wasn't trying to steal a kiss for me, but…for himself. Thankfully, you saw through it in the end. But if you'll let me, I'll prove my words."

She met Charles's gaze and did not flinch. "Show me."

Berd watched as Charles approached the elevator. It had been waiting with its door open. Inside, he nodded at the panel of buttons.

Eager, Berd stretched her hand toward them, just as the panel melted, like a bar of glass chocolate, back into the wall. She gave a cry of disappointment and shock. So this is what he meant. She was truly trapped. Charles was right.

"Elizabeth." And so saying, Charles reached to comfort her, only she whipped one hand up. "No."

He halted, confusion clear in his face; the outstretched hand stilled.

Never, she mouthed as she rejected him.

Charles lowered his hand, his face paling. "Blast you, Gine," he muttered under his breath, and stared at the wall.

It was done.

Her lower lip trembled and then she was still. The

price for freedom was love. It cost Berd everything in her to lift her chin proudly and feign disinterest.

"My lady." Charles pursed his lips, his face calm and cold as a marble statue. He nodded stiffly, squared his shoulders, and then marched out of the elevator back into the room, head held high—a lone warrior about to face his final defeat.

Again he was attempting to be noble. A commoner thinking he could rise to her level simply with words and bows. How laughable! Good riddance! But it was false bravado. When he was gone, she sank to the floor, a deep hollowness gouging at her. She had never seen Charles so angry. So hurt. It was all thanks to Gine, who had lied and deceived her; trapped her.

The thought she would never escape were like agonising bites that gnawed away at her. She tapped her fingers against her lips, trying to get her brain to work, trying to make sense of what she had learnt, but her mind was dominated by how dangerous Gine was. Each time he had tried to fool her, he had succeeded brilliantly. Each time she thought she knew his motives, it had been a half-truth or an outright lie.

A loud pounding jolted her from her trance. She peered into the room. Charles had pried apart one of the wall panels to reveal a confusion of copper pipes in the cavity.

"What are you doing?" she called.

He arched one brow, but kept working. "I was thinking that if we can't go down, we might as well try to go up."

"Up?"

He was still trying to get to the settings.

Charles raised a finger, sketching patterns in the air

to demonstrate the circulation of water through pipes. "When the stack moves, the water is piped to the Engine to provide steam, which in turns powers the stack. This stack has been going a while, so the pipes will be hot. But we should be able to use them as a ladder."

She pushed herself off the ground and headed toward him. As she neared, heat emitted from the pipes fanned her face. Steam — sweet and clean — filled her senses.

Charles was already unwinding some of the leather strips that he had bound around him when in the Faraday car. "I had hoped it would not come to this, however, we are not totally unprepared." He handed a couple of strips over to her.

Taking the leather would mean she would be beholden to him again, and that was the last thing she needed. "I'll be fine."

"I must insist that—"

"I shall manage."

Charles studied her for a moment before exhaling heavily. Without another word, he wrapped some of the leather around his own hands, then leapt and grasped a pipe. It hissed and spat at him. The odour of charred leather clouded the air, and she screwed up her nose at the stench.

He swung himself high, scuffling and kicking against the pipes. The terrifying ring of metal echoed about the room, causing the fine hairs on her arms to stand on end, but in a few wild seconds, he was out of sight.

"Your turn," he called, his voice muffled.

Easy as climbing a burning tree. Pity she had never done so.

She reached a hand out tentatively, but even before she could touch the nearest length, the heat made her withdraw. She stared, tempted by the lengths of leather Charles had left behind for her.

No, he had referred to her as his colleague, but she would do this her way.

Gine, if you're watching, I hope you are gentleman enough to look away.

Berd sucked in a deep breath before unbuttoning her blouse and pulling it off. Then she stared down in annoyance. She had forgotten that she was still wearing James's pants. Had she not, she would have had her petticoat for the purpose she had in mind. For the first time since donning the trousers, she wished she were wearing skirts. But only for a second.

Another deep breath and this time she undid the pants, stepping out of them. Her under drawers would have to do. She stretched the silken undergarment, hoping it would be thick enough. Then she ripped off two of the pants' pockets. *There!*

They would suffice. Berd redressed then stuffed each pants' pocket with part of her under drawers. Finally, she slipped her hands into each pocket as if it were a glove. When done, she exhaled heavily.

Her pulse quickened as she reached out to grasp the first pipe. The odour of smouldering silk scorched the air, but the pipe was comfortably warm so she did not panic only tightened her grip and started to pull herself up. Within seconds though, the warmth changed, intensifying into a burning sensation. Heat seared her flesh and she screamed, released the pipe, and fell. When she hit the floor, she lay sprawled and dazed.

"Elizabeth!" Charles leaped down beside her. "Show me your hands!"

"No! Don't touch me," she ordered, stunned and embarrassed to see him next to her.

But Charles was not put off. "Give me your hand!"

"It's merely a burn." She hugged her scalded hand to her breast.

Despite her deliberate refusal, he seized her hand. "I'm sorry to disregard your wishes, my lady, but I must insist, and I have to be quick or risk the injury worsening. One hand or both?" His tone was brusque; his face dark. Nor did he wait for an answer, but tore the silk inner pockets free from her hands.

She gritted her teeth, ready to explode from pain and frustration that everything was constantly going wrong, but even she could see the skin was inflamed.

After a swift assessment, he banged on one of the panels. "Water. Cold water and plenty of it."

She watched as a trickle began to reflow down one wall panel. Then cradling her injured hand in his as if it was a fragile rose — she resented the idea immediately — he placed it in the stream.

The same hand she had slapped him with.

Cold soothed the pain away.

Berd had opened her mouth to object; now she snapped it shut. He had been right again. About everything. She had been deliberately stupid.

She glanced away, determined not to say a word while the healing took place. Yet, even in this minor attempt at independence she was defeated, because the cold which had been so kind before now turned cruel, as if wreaking its vengeance on her for her ill-treatment of Charles.

Her pain was disappearing because the water was freezing, and she began to shiver, her body shaking uncontrollably and forcing her to speak.

"Charles," she said, almost apologetically, as she tried to stop her teeth from chattering, "It's not that bad, truly. We have no time to waste."

His face tightened with annoyance. "The process of healing a scald takes a while, and to remove your hand as soon as the pain vanishes will merely cause the pain to return swiftly. Trust me. I know. We may as well sit and wait."

Again, without waiting for a response, he settled himself on the floor, half-pulling her down as he did, so she ended up hunched at an awkward angle with her arm across his chest. If she looked over her right shoulder, their faces would be inches apart. The only way to regain her dignity was if she sat.

She remained bent over, uncomfortable. With one arm across his chest, she was receiving some of his body heat. She wasn't sure if this actually made it worse, the knowledge that what she needed was so close to hand.

After allowing some time to pass, he winked. "Why don't you sit?"

"I—I don't li—like sit—sitting on the floor."

Perhaps he sensed she was close to defeat for his tone changed to one curious but pleasant, as if asking the time of day. "I see. Might I inquire as to the reason?"

"I don't know." How she wished she didn't sound so petulant. Or frozen.

"*I* dropped down to your level."

She knew she was being silly, childish even.

"That's — that's dif — different. You're a fool. Men are fools."

He gave a little laugh, leaned back and shut his eyes, relaxed and comfortable while she shook violently.

Her gaze took in her right arm, snug and warm against his chest, then followed it all the way to where her numb hand rested in the icy water.

Her hand. Charles had taken her hand once again. Allowing him to take her hand meant she would have to follow him down to his level. The gesture was almost symbolic of marriage.

"We — we really don't have m-much time left," she grumbled, trying to annoy him into moving. "Less than a day. Haven't y-you been thinking about it?"

His eyes flicked opened, perfect lashes framing iridescent blue eyes as his lips twitched. "Oh trust me I have. I asked myself, if I had one day left to live, how would I live it?" He raised his eyebrows, and smiled pointedly at her.

Berd sucked in her breath. The realisation struck like the sun in all its golden glory, blinding and dazzling as its rays reached out to warm her.

If she had less than a day of life left, how would she live it? Fighting Charles or loving him? He appeared to have made his decision.

But of course he'd made *that* decision. He was a boy. But she was a woman. It was her priority not to give in to silly things like feelings! She would be single until the day she died. It was the best thing. *It was.*

It was her body that betrayed her; weak from hunger, exhaustion and cold, she slid down beside him.

For a moment, Charles did nothing then he wrapped one arm around her. Just a minute or two, she told herself, until she was warm and her hand was healed. She closed her eyes, sighing at the bliss already filling her.

When she stopped shivering, she lifted her head. "I don't understand. Why didn't your hands blister?"

"They did. Like hell in the beginning. But now, having done it for so long, I guess they toughened up."

The admission made her feel a tiny bit better. "We need to get going. Now. Please." They had to; for with each step the stack was moving further away from the Mill. They were running out of time.

"Another minute," he said softly, seemingly unwilling to move, unwilling to release her. She let him have his minute.

"Charles?"

"Yes?"

"I've been thinking. That flow of water down the walls. Why did it stop when the book stack started moving?"

"Because the water was needed to make steam, obviously when the book…" his words died away. He glanced at the walls and then at her. Then he tilted his head and gave her a long, slow smile. His tone was full of praise. "Brilliant plan, my lady. If we divert the water, the stack will run out of steam and be forced to stop."

She gave him a tentative smile, the first since she had slapped him. "Can we? Can we actually do that?" She stilled, hoping beyond hope that finally she had an effective idea.

He beamed back at her, his eyes shining as if the full

moon shone from behind. "Come. I'll show you what to do."

They circled the room, banging on the walls, and before long water again trickled down the walls. The scent of lavender thickened the air and she felt dizzy with excitement. Gine wasn't going to get it all his own way! They were going to get out. She was about to bang on the last panel when Charles stopped her.

"No, we don't need that one. That conducts signals to be stored. Now watch!" He wrenched the finger-thin channel that lined the room away from the walls. With no exit, water began to flow, pouring into the room in great quantities.

Waves of frigid water rolled across the floor, pouring towards the centre of the room. She had no idea this would be the result, but logically, the water had to go somewhere and this place seemed designed as the overflow area. Pray the stack stopped before the room filled completely.

Water lapped at her feet, swelling up to her ankles in minutes. As thick as her leather boots were, they were no defence against the biting cold. She was about to rub her shoulders for warmth when Charles scooped her up.

"What are you doing?" She kicked and struggled, trying to get him to put her down. He was being idiotic. He was so close to exhaustion it would be fatal for him to do all this unrestrained.

"What does it look like I'm doing?" He gave a little laugh and then unexpectedly kissed the tip of her nose.

Heat filled her. She stopped struggling. "You knew this would happen, didn't you? Was this why you never suggested it?"

"Nonsense. It was a good idea and I should have known. I helped create the Engine."

The water had now reached his knees. Waves of cold shimmered upwards, chilling her derriere. She trembled.

"You knew, didn't you, that by doing this it would be dangerous. Why did you agree?"

"We had to stop the book stack somehow."

He was going to help her escape no matter the cost to himself. His words on the train came back to haunt her now.

'You will be the one to leave…'

The water reached his hips, and though he tried to keep her above the water level, cold streaked painfully through her body like iron veining into her. Yet he still carried her.

"Why?" she whispered, tightening her hold around his neck, the strands of his hair soft against her fingers.

"Why not? Nothing is going to happen to me. Gine will intervene long before anything happens."

Hot tears filled her eyes; that was the problem — Gine would intervene.

"Don't cry, my lady," Charles said, his voice husky. "If you really want me to put you down, I will." He smiled wryly. "Do you want me to?"

It seemed a ludicrous question as the water was now up to the middle of his torso and they were both wet, but she understood what he was asking.

He had just proposed.

He bent down to kiss her forehead. "I'll always carry you."

The strength of his words seeped into her, warming her from head to toe. But even as his words warmed her, his muscles began to harden. His eyes silvered.

The water reached his shoulders.

"No!" Berd gasped, pressing herself against his chest, but it was like trying to embrace a rock. She ran her fingers through his hair, clutching at the ends and lifting them to her lips. Then she kissed his poor frozen face, working her way down to his mouth as she muttered. "Charles, please, please, come back to me." And all the while the water roared maddeningly in her ears.

His skin was turning blue. His lips blistered and peeled. She had to stop or risk tearing her own to bits on the jagged surface. She drew back and stared anxiously into his eyes. Though open, they saw nothing. Charles was now as sightless as a statue. Snow-white crystals formed like miniature diamonds on the tips of his lashes and brows. She gave a strangled cry and heard her frightened voice echo about the room.

"Berd. My name is Berd."

There was no response.

"Charles!"

She held her breath as she waited for a response, blood pounding in her temples as though someone was trying to hammer her head open from the inside.

Cold water enveloped her.

In sheer panic, she kicked, freeing herself from his rigid grasp and began to float upwards. Berd took a gasp of air from the surface and despite the water pressure, hauled herself once more against his chest.

I am not leaving. I love you, Charles.

Warmth flowed through her body and she flinched, feeling as if she were being steamed alive as waves of sleepiness overcame her.

Chapter 18

A VOICE WAS roaring deep inside Berd's head, causing her ears to ring as she hovered on the edge of consciousness.

"Berd? Berd!"

Light flared; a red glow that flickered and danced upon her inner eyelids. Opening her eyes, she squinted but saw nothing except an almost impenetrable grey, through which a faceless figure loomed. All around her, odours hung in the air, a vague memory, only she could not grasp it or its meaning. A whiff of paraffin, followed by the stench of charring…

"Damn you! What have you done to my sister?"

The voice rippled through the grey, but it only closed into black.

"Charles!" she shouted into the darkness, not because that was who she had heard but because that was who she wanted. And it was as she was watching her brother's furious face with its dreadful shadows that Charles's voice rumbled down to her.

"Berd, my darling, wake up." His voice sent a

delicious tremor through her, and she leant into the hollow of his shoulder. The rules of etiquette now long passed.

His dark shape surrounded her, holding her up. It was soft and warm and stationed on the ground with her. She craned her head in his direction, feeling like a newborn kitten in her blindness. Large, warm hands slid protectively around her, and calm enveloped her.

The first voice battered on, "I have sent for the servants. You had better be prepared to provide answers as to why my sister has been missing these three days, you savage."

Oh blast! That was definitely James. What a fool he sounded. Charles would never send servants to take care of a situation like this. He would do so himself. Yet, James was her brother, and he was trying to protect her. Only the last time she and James had conversed, they had had a difference of opinion regarding her spinsterhood. This made the current situation almost ludicrous: he, who wanted her to marry, was attempting to protect her from the man she intended to marry.

Berd rubbed her eyes and stared again. She was able to distinguish not one, but two figures: James, standing at the door to the stables. The second was Harold, the butler, hovering behind her brother and carrying a lamp that cast deep shadows that contoured the landscape of James's face so that in his anger her brother appeared almost alien, barely recognisable.

And as her brother shouted, lips brushed the top of her head. "Shh, my darling."

"James, this is Charles Babbage Fotheringay. And Charles, that loud noise is my brother, lord…lord…

James, be a dear and help out. What are you lord of? I forget; my mind's such a blank." Her words ended in a yawn. "Can I retire, now?"

At her statement, Harold's eyes nearly popped out of his head. A feminine gasp of astonished horror rose from behind the two men. That had to be Rose.

James, however, pointed a white-gloved finger at Charles as he demanded, "What have you to say, blackguard? A ruination of womanhood lies before you in your care and thievery."

Berd jerked upright, and one foot kicked the air as she turned in a panic to Charles. "No! Charles has done nothing wrong!"

His face was a concentration in tranquillity. "Go with them. I will explain."

She felt his parting words like gentle smoke against her brow, but it was the iridescent blue fire in his eyes that cradled her with hope. She stared at him, and her breathing slowed even when Rose and James materialised beside her.

"Let me escort her," Charles insisted.

James's face only tightened. He held out his arms.

Charles kissed Berd on the forehead before releasing her. "My darling, I will brave a word with your brother when he returns. Go with them for now. I will come for you, I promise."

James, once encumbered with her in his arms, swiftly headed towards the door, leaving Harold to guard the stables. Outside, stars glittered in the black sky like diamonds spilled on a velvet chaise. If Berd wanted further proof she was in the world, as they turned the corner, her aunt's townhouse appeared, all aglow with burnished light, as welcoming as

Cleopatra's barge must have been to the ruler herself on the dark Nile.

I am home.

Surely things would sort themselves out. Berd pressed her hands against her face, inhaling the lanolin from his leather outfit. Charles…

But the storm in James was not over. He manoeuvred her through the front door. "I have our family's reputation to think of," he seethed.

"James, everything is fine. You don't understand," Berd mumbled as he carried her up the stairs, the dark mahogany banisters streaming like debris on either side of her after a flood.

Though the house appeared empty, she was aware of a listening and waiting silence. No doubt the servants had prudently sought shelter and disappeared at their approach, but she knew they were all watching. One thing puzzled her though and that was the absence of her aunt.

"It is you who does not understand. You are ruined, Berd. Ruined. You will never inherit now." James's voice was softer, his anger more concentrated.

"Do you think I ever cared? I have done nothing wrong. I am engaged. To Charles."

James pounded down the passageway, Rose hurrying ahead to open her bedroom door. "You have no idea the uproar. Three whole days. Policemen—"

"James," she pleaded. "Charles will explain when you return."

"Charles?" reprimanded James. "Who is this man you would be on a first name basis with? How long have you known him, you harlot! You never worried about inheriting because you had him in your pocket the whole time! You want to ruin me with scandal. That's it, isn't it?"

She groaned as he deposited her on her bed. "James, please, *please*; stop, all of this."

James paused at her doorway. "Berd, listen to me. Even if you are engaged, do you think I will let you marry a savage? I'm getting my pistol."

Before she could leap out of bed, the door slammed shut behind James.

"Don't try to think of getting out, my men shan't let you." At that he bawled orders at the footmen to do just that.

All night long Berd listened, waiting to hear a shot, or for Charles to come for her. Neither happened. When pink tinged the sky, she sent Rose down to investigate. That had been two hours ago.

Now Berd was on the point of bursting. She hadn't slept and hunger gnawed in her belly, a ravenous rat caged to a tortured man's stomach. If anything, the dreadful feeling that something was wrong permanently anchored itself in her chest as she looked around the familiar dark walls, tinged with unfamiliar shadows.

I will come for you.

Rose's recognizable fingernail scratching on Berd's bedroom door made her look up, just as it opened and Rose peered round the doorway.

"Is my lady awake?" she asked, her hazel eyes dull with tiredness as she gazed at her mistress.

"Any news?" Berd craned forward in bed.

Rose did not answer, but entered the bedroom lugging a small portable table. Berd understood why, when Rose was followed in by the parlourmaid, Hilary, carrying a tray.

Berd waited with mild irritation as the table was placed at her bedside and the tray set down on it. A glass of barley water along with a basin of milk and bread sat on the tray: an invalid's breakfast. No doubt James had informed the staff she was unwell and was using illness to explain her disappearance. The louse!

"Glad you're feeling better, my lady." Hilary bobbed a curtsey, her gaze deliberately downcast.

Berd nodded, but she was not fooled. She had seen the girl's eyes widen at her dishevelled appearance. As soon as Hilary departed, and the door closed, Berd turned to Rose who had seated herself opposite on a divan. "What's happening? Tell me."

Rose's face creased in apology. "I'm afraid I have little news, my lady. His lordship has informed the entire staff that you are ill, and so you are to be confined to your bed."

"But what of my brother? And Mr Fotheringay?" She bit her lip.

"His lordship returned empty-handed from the barn last night. Harold checked his pistol, but it hadn't been fired." Rose cringed as if she did not like what she was about to say next. "And as for Mr Fotheringay, Harold confirmed his lordship ordered the carriage return him to his home. From what Harold could gather from the coachman, the servants were in the process of shutting up his house and were astounded to see Mr Fotheringay return."

"But what did he say? What did my brother and Mr Fotheringay converse about when my brother returned to the stables?"

Rose gazed at Berd warily. "I know that's what you wanted me to find out, my lady, but according to Harold, Mr Fotheringay simply requested passage home."

Charles had not mentioned our engagement.

"But, but didn't my brother ask..." Berd pressed her lips together tightly. No. She would not let Rose see her humiliation like some normal woman who couldn't keep her man interested. There had to be some mistake. Charles must have been exhausted. Harold was only a butler; though he had twenty years of service he must have misinterpreted what passed between James and Charles. James obviously had second thoughts about the pistol. He must have relented when he saw how Charles had taken care of her. Or perhaps he had seen how exhausted Charles was and they would speak today.

I will come for you. If only he had specified when.

"My lady?"

Berd looked up.

Rose was visibly shaking, colour rising to her cheeks.

"Yes, Rose."

"There's one more thing." Rose sniffled.

"What is it, Rose."

"His lordship paid a visit to Mr Fotheringay early this morning."

Berd's heart lifted. "And?"

"He came back an hour ago and said, apparently that Mr Fotheringay asked him for one thing alone to make up for his transgressions with you. To bring them to an end."

Berd swallowed. One thing. "What was it?" she whispered, not wanting to know, yet unable to stop herself. One thing. One hand in—

"The Engine," answered Rose. "He will be coming by to pick up the Engine this morning, and you are not to be let out until afterwards." Rose nodded, as if this were a well and good conclusion.

Despite her pride, Berd could not help the sob of bitterness that escaped her.

The Engine?

She must have mistaken Charles's proposal. She felt Rose's hand on hers.

"I'm sorry, my lady. But you've been away…"

"Three days."

"Three days without explanation. No unmarried female can afford such a liberty."

"Do you think I care if I'm ruined?"

Rose squeezed her hand. "Perhaps Mr Fotheringay is coming to express his intentions to his lordship?" She looked up hopefully.

"What was the expression on my brother's face when he returned?"

Rose sighed heavily and her shoulders drooped.

Berd glanced away, focussing her attention on the old violet ottoman by the bay window, her late mother's favourite seat, and the only piece she had been able to salvage when James had ordered everything removed. Everything that reminded him of Mother…

"I'll come with you, my lady, if his lordship lets me," Rose said softly.

They were not idle words, but there was no need for Rose to explain what she meant. Exile. Banishment. Disgrace.

James was no doubt planning to keep her locked up in her room until he had someplace in the country in order to bury her. Berd tried to convince herself that it really wasn't so bad. After all, she had never wanted to marry. The irony was that she had never cared about society and only wanted to be left alone to do her work.

But I love him. I thought he wanted me. I thought we were to be partners…

Her heart twisted; a dead weight that grew and grew until it forced all the air out of her so that she struggled to breathe.

"It would be good if my lady could eat something," said Rose. "It's a pity, Her Grace is away."

Berd nodded. Yes, perhaps if her aunt had been home, she could have sought assistance from her. But according to Rose, her aunt was enjoying a weekend of fox hunting. She had apparently wanted to cancel the engagement when Berd went missing, but decided in the end that her absence might have aroused suspicion and decided to proceed. She would be back sometime late on the morrow.

Berd picked up the glass of barley water, but as she brought it towards her, she noticed the clear unblemished skin of her hand. The same hand Charles had cradled like a precious rose. The same hand she had slapped him with…

The room blurred. The glass slipped. Thankfully, it was a few inches from the base of the tray and landed without spilling a drop. It was loud, though, rattling her and when the room came into focus again, she found herself staring at her white and flawless hand. Any injury had vanished. Any external injury. She rubbed her palms together briskly, and heard the rasp of skin on skin. Surely, surely it must have all been a dream, the sort of thing a mathematics professor might have written to amuse a little girl.

She had been Alice in Wonderland.

Gine had really tried to kill her. Yet, she was back in the world. She was out of Gine's reach.

She and Charles had come back. Alive. Whole. Clearly, Gine had no further use for her.

The Engine had been in the stables. It must have been there upon her return as well, as that was where she came to. And it was Harold at the door, but he would have been little defence against...

Berd fingered her throat nervously, aware Rose watched her every action. Determined to appear normal, she picked up the drink, brought it to her lips and drank.

He was coming for the Engine. The Engine. Not her.

All she knew was that she had to be there when he returned.

Gine must be controlling Charles from the Engine.

Chapter 19

GINE HAD TO be at the bottom of all of this chaos. He just... No, not he. *It.* It had to be responsible. Gine. *The Engine.*

Berd gritted her teeth and before Rose's astonished eyes, sprang out of bed. "Draw my bath at once," she ordered.

Rose's mouth dropped. "I—I...yes, my lady."

"And press my green riding habit." Pity she had to dress like a lady again, but leaving the house dressed in pants would attract too much interest.

"Hurry!" Berd pushed the baffled maid out of the room and into the arms of the startled footman stationed outside.

Rose blushed furiously and disappeared as Henry gawked and swallowed. No doubt he would have a tale to tell down in the servant's quarters later, but it didn't matter. None of this mattered. Berd knew now what was important and was prepared to fight for it.

While Rose was gone, Berd undid her blouse and then tried to undo her corset. Thank goodness she was no longer in a child's corset! Still the task was nigh impossible without a maid to assist, especially since her chemise appeared stuck to her skin. Though after what she had been through in the Engine, she was not surprised. But it was evident she needed hot water. At least the pants slipped off easily enough. She just hoped Rose did not notice that her under drawers were missing.

Berd shook her head warily. Even in the area of attire, women were trapped. Women should have the freedoms of a man in dress. Or, however, they chose! This subtle and insidious control by men in every aspect of a woman's life was all the more reason for her to succeed in her endeavour and to prove to the world that women were just as good as men and that they weren't to be seen only as housekeepers. Domestic angels.

I am no angel, she thought. In fact, it was time to be that demigod's devil.

Rose returned with two maids carrying a bath tub and copper buckets of hot water.

"Laundry day. Had water already boiling," explained Rose, then she made a face as she saw the red welts on Berd's skin in her attempt to peel her corset off.

Berd nodded. Once on laundry day, she had mistakenly entered the kitchen, looking for Rose. She had gasped at the alien world with its massive coppers of boiling water. Steam clouded the air. Scents of Sunlight soap and starch had made her light-headed.

The bath was soon ready and the maids gone. Rose's brow crinkled in worry as she undressed Berd. "My lady, forgive me for asking, but you aren't thinking of..."

Rose was certainly getting braver to be actually querying her. Or more worried. "Eloping?" Berd eyed the window. Escape had entered her thoughts. If she did, she would be unaccompanied for she doubted she would be able to persuade Rose to come with her. This year one or two brave ladies had attempted to walk about unaccompanied, but they were in the minority. And they had attracted such a crowd.

Those women had been hard-pressed to persuade men that they were not whores. Pray the suffragist movement gave women the freedom to roam independent from such slurs on their character. Even though Mayfair was one of the best areas, it was too close to the sea, and an unaccompanied woman was fair game for kidnap, which was the last thing she needed, even though James had already assumed that was what had happened.

A footman below and a footman at the door. She would tackle the one at the door first.

She stepped into the bath. "Not as far as I am aware. I believe one also needs a man, if one is to elope and there I fall short." She winked, as she tried to lighten the tension in the room. To some extent, she succeeded as Rose nodded, her face softening as she scrubbed the dirt from Berd.

The act of winking, however, reminded her too much of Charles; but then everything reminded her of him. It had to be love, what else? Only she had never realised love could be so painful.

She blinked rapidly to dry her tears and her gaze slid about her room. The air danced with buttery light, pouring in through the white lace curtains across the French windows. Every wooden surface gleamed as if polished with honeyed beeswax. She was back. She had her wish. She should be happy, only she had been happy in the Engine and had not realised. Charles had protected her and loved her, but she had not appreciated him until he was gone.

If Gine was responsible for this, then it was to Gine she would repair. She would fight him for Charles if need be.

She had to persuade Aunt Agatha to help, not see that she was ruined. Perhaps Aunt Agatha would blame herself and not be as lenient as she had been in the past. No, Berd decided, it was up to her to escape. Charles was returning to the stables for the Engine. She had to be there before him if she wanted to confront Gine.

"Where is my brother this morning?"

"I believe at his club, my lady."

Perfect. James was probably trying to gather information on Charles. But with James gone, maybe, just maybe, her plan would work. If she didn't lose confidence. Or James returned too early. Or Charles called for the Engine before she was ready.

An hour later, her heart pounding like a piston, Berd was prepared. "Open the door, please, Rose."

To his credit, Henry, the footman on guard, straightened when he saw her, like a junior officer upon seeing a higher-ranked officer. His hands even opened as if he was preparing to bodily seize her but then they closed the next.

Good. Berd smiled inwardly. It was as she had predicted. Henry remembered his place. She was a lady and he, a mere footman. He should not lay a finger on her, which would make it difficult for him to restrain her.

She stepped out.

"My lady," he gasped, his face flushing.

"Good morning, Henry." Taking advantage of his confusion, Berd coolly headed for the stairs, barely glancing at him. Rose followed close behind.

"I'm sorry, my lady, but you need, umm, to return to your room."

Berd halted with all the grace at her disposal. She cocked her head at the cringing footman and simply stared at him, as if she could not believe he was actually stopping her. Behind her she heard Rose draw a deep breath.

Henry, barely twenty years of age at a pinch, wilted even further under Berd's gaze. He tried once more. "I'm sorry, my lady, but his lordship insisted you remain in your room."

She arched one brow. "I see." Then she turned to give Rose a reassuring smile before once again proceeding towards the stairs.

At her flagrant disregard of her brother's order, Henry whisked in front of her, his face mottled crimson in embarrassment, but determined to stop her.

Despite her annoyance, Berd had to give him credit for attempting, despite the awkward situation, to carry out James's orders. Again, she drew to a halt. She lifted her chin. "I'm afraid I don't find this at all amusing. I shall have a word with my aunt when she returns."

A look of confusion crossed Henry's face. As if he had just realised it was the duchess who employed him and not the earl, and that the duchess had given no such command to confine Berd to her room. "Yes, my lady." He glanced at Berd then at the room she had vacated then back at her again. A corner of his eye twitched.

But Berd had little sympathy for the footman. Time was running out and she had to enforce her will swiftly or James would be back. She glared at Henry impatiently as she played her final card. "Where is his lordship? I need a word with him."

To her surprise, she received an answer immediately. Only it wasn't from Henry.

"Here." James's voice was suave.

Berd's stomach knotted. Somehow she managed a curtsey.

James, leaning against the banister at the bottom of the stairs, bowed back in greeting, his manner unruffled. "Would you care to join me in the library?"

Her smile broadened as if she really was glad to see her brother. Head held high, she glided away from the petrified footman, down the stairs and straight into the library. At the appearance of the earl, Rose had conveniently disappeared.

When Berd heard the door shut behind her, she turned to face her brother. "James," she breathed.

"Please be seated, Berd."

She sat, clasped her hands in her lap and fixed her gaze on the large brass globe of the world in front of her.

James pursed his lips then headed to the array of decanters to pour a brandy. He raised his glass to ask Berd if she wanted a drink, but she shook her head. It was tempting, but she had learnt a hard lesson that when dealing with Gine, she needed all her wits about her. And more.

"Well," said James. He took a good swig of the brandy. "It appears we have a delicate situation." He swirled the amber liquid round in the glass, before he looked up at her. "You weren't about to head to the stables by any chance?"

"The Engine is mine, James. I purchased it."

"With my money." He narrowed his gaze at her.

"My allowance." She glared at him.

"Oh blast it! Let Fotheringay have the damned Engine. He's taken far more from you. Why do you want a reminder of him?"

Berd gave a cry of shock. How dare James believe she had let Charles have his way with her!

To her relief, James's face contorted guiltily. He jumped up, and reached out one hand to console. "I apologise."

"Nothing happened. I can swear on the Bible that nothing happened."

James's voice was soft, bitter. "Whether or not anything happened is not the point though, is it?"

Heat flared in her cheeks. She pressed her lips together stubbornly, refusing to look at him.

He sighed heavily, and she smelled brandy on his breath. "I took my pistol last night."

"You didn't fire it."

He gave a little laugh. "Should I have? It almost sounds as if you wanted me to. I went down thinking to use it on Fotheringay so he wouldn't marry you. Only by the time I got there, I was thinking, I should use it to threaten him to marry you."

Berd frowned, confused.

"In the interval, one thing became clear. You love him."

I love him. Berd swallowed hard as the blood rushed up her throat, but she refused to cry and instead dug the heel of her palms into her eyes.

James sighed heavily as he slid onto the sofa beside her.

She allowed him to gather her up in his arms.

"Now I have my answer. Though it was a foregone conclusion," he muttered.

She said nothing, simply allowed him to hold her as her body shuddered. He had comforted her in this manner when she was little. It had always made her feel better, but not today. Only she could make herself feel better. "What made you change your mind?" she croaked as she pushed away from him.

"At first, I thought it was Fotheringay who abducted you, however I was wrong. Apparently, he was just as much victim as you."

Berd nodded. That was true.

James stood, picked up his glass and stared at the amber contents. "So if I had shot him, I would have shot a victim rather than the perpetrator."

"If you know he is innocent…"

"Ah…but once again it's not me, you see. It's what the rest of society thinks."

James was right. Society would condemn her whether or not she had done the wrong thing. She had gone missing for three days. It didn't matter that Charles had gone missing for a year. He would survive. She would not.

He was a man. She was not.

Berd wet her lips and waited.

"I called on Fotheringay this morning. Hoped he would see sense. After all, he had demonstrated affection for you last night."

James put the drink down without another sip. His expression was wary. Almost as she asked herself that question, a wagon rumbled up outside.

She jumped up. "Charles! I must—"

Before she could cross the room, James seized her arm. "Do not go to him. I warn you." He spoke rapidly, "Fotheringay is a very busy man. He was in a hurry to return last night. I gathered his father has recently passed away and his estate was to be passed on to the next in line. I believe he has trustees at his bank to convince as well as the chancery that he has returned. Then the police."

There was only one reason she could think of, as to why James was telling her all of this now. To delay her. "Please, I must…"

The squeak of the stable doors opening drowned everything else out. She struggled, but it was as if she had been grasped by a metal statue, her arm in its grip as the molten metal had been poured and now the statue had cooled and she was trapped.

James's jaw locked. "Are there to be any surprises, Berd?"

She gasped, stunned. "What?"

"Promise me there will be no unexpected… Will you need to retire?" He waited, the unsaid implication hanging in the air.

Retire? Her heart almost stopped. He meant a baby. "No," she whispered, unable to believe that James was betraying her like this. First, he offered comfort then insult, acting like Jekyll and Hyde, but then she had treated Charles the same way…yet he had forgiven her.

James forced a bright smile at her. "I could arrange a place in Wales. Perhaps Harold…"

She frowned.

James gave a helpless shrug. "Harold knows the situation. I could set both of you up in a little cottage..."

James expected Harold to marry her should she be in a family way. The butler was thrice her age!

Shakily, she lifted her gaze to her brother. The trouble was that in James's own mind, he was doing the right thing by her. He was showing her he cared. However, she cared not for his method. "No," she whispered, her voice taut with anger. "There will be no surprises."

James nodded, but the muscles on his face were still rigid. "Good. Good." He appeared to be listening intently.

Men's voices muffled in the morning air... The squeak of something metallic and heavy being shifted, grinding in the dirt...and then the crunch of boots on cobblestones.

The Engine was being loaded.

"James, I must speak with him," she rasped, desperate to get away.

The stable door slammed shut with a bang. She hurled herself once more at the library door, but James twisted her arm, holding her back. The scent of his white carnation swept over her, bringing tears.

"No." He glared. "I forbid you to go near Fotheringay."

A whip cracked the morning air.

Berd startled as if the full force of the lash had been unleashed upon her. She jerked, trying to wrench herself free. "Let me go. Please." If she ran she could catch them. Him.

The tears in her eyes spilled over, rolling down her hot cheeks.

"Berd, please!" James swung her round, grasping her by the shoulders.

His grip was gentler. She could have escaped…except something in his tone made her pause. She stared into his hazel eyes, stunned. James wasn't angry. Instead, he was pleading. She had never seen him in such agony.

"He didn't want you. Fotheringay made it very clear he did not want to ever see you again. That's why I kept you inside."

Chapter 20

ERD GAVE A hoarse scream as her heart shattered. Sharp pain shut everything else out. She blathered. Words flew out of her mouth. She heard herself, and it was as if someone else spoke. Someone else acted.

A madwoman.

"No! It's not him, James. It's Gine. And Gine's a machine. An Engine. And he, I mean it, it is controlling Charles. Only Gine's Charles and Charles is Gine!" she wailed.

"Please, stop this," James urged, pinning her against him as she raged.

"We're engaged. I need a word with Char—"

"Berd!"

White light flashed over her, cutting out sight and sound. She froze as a different sort of pain blinded her. Black spots hung before her eyes, dropping as they faded. Her cheek throbbed.

James had slapped her.

"Berd?" Her brother's voice was extremely mild.

The sole sign of violence present in the stark lines of his face and the hollow slits of his eyes as he stared open-mouthed at his hand.

He must have released her in order to do so. It was an illusion to think she had broken free. Once more it demonstrated how powerless she was. But the pain of being slapped and the acknowledgement of her powerlessness was nothing compared to the grief that now surged through her: she had lost Charles.

The enormity of her loss crushed all the fight out of her. She could not even respond to James's overtures of calm. He hauled her to the sofa where she slumped like a ragdoll upon the cushions.

In frustration, he ran one hand through his blond hair. "Rose! Damn it. Rose!"

Her maid appeared.

Rose had been listening. Likely, all the servants were. Berd felt her body go through the motion of stiffening back into control as she pushed herself upright.

James half-turned away as if unable to bear the sight of her. He linked his hands behind his back and stared into the distance, the impassive lord of the manor. "Escort your mistress to her room," he said brusquely.

But before Rose could move, Berd had risen gracefully to her feet. She pressed her arms to her sides, refusing to let her maid touch her. Before she left the room, she turned to her brother, who was gazing out the window.

She lifted her chin. "You do not know what you have done," she said quietly.

James continued to stare out the window. The solitary sign he had heard her was a hardening around his mouth.

Back in her room, Berd allowed Rose to undress her and help her into a nightgown. Worn out, hurt beyond belief, she crept into bed, thinking she would be unable to sleep. Giant hands were squeezing her insides, wringing and wringing until all that was left of her were scattered threads.

She awoke to find the room lit by a pair of candlesticks on the mantelpiece and another pair on her dressing table.

An elegant voice was calling her. "Berd? Berd, my dear girl, you have no idea the amount of worrying I have undergone." The dulcet tones purred, mixed with the scent of lavender, horses and earth.

Aunt Agatha.

Berd threw herself into her aunt's arms, startling the duchess, so it was a good thing the older woman was seated.

"You're back! When did you get home?" Berd clung to her saviour, like a drowning man a plank of wood.

"Hush, child," Aunt Agatha soothed as she stroked Berd's hair.

Berd pushed herself out of her aunt's arms and stared into those sparkling grey eyes. Aunt Agatha had always been her staunch supporter, the one person Berd had never disappointed. No doubt James had brought their aunt up-to-date with what he thought had happened. But he was wrong.

It was time she told her aunt the truth: what really happened. It was also the only way Berd could see to extricate herself from this mess. "I was simply trying to get the Engine going."

Aunt Agatha's forehead creased with the effort of trying to understand. "Your autocar."

Autocar? The trouble with telling the truth, Berd suddenly realised, was that she would also be revealing how much she had lied. But perhaps all was not lost. Her aunt's own mother, Ada Lovelace, had worked with the inventor of the Difference and the Analytical Engines, Charles Babbage. Surely Berd should not be chastened, but applauded for having done the same thing, with another inventor.

She put on her most serious expression as she willed her aunt to believe her. "No, a computer."

Aunt Agatha brightened with pride. "You built it?"

If only Berd knew how. Too late did she remember that seventeen-year old heiresses should not be attending auction houses even if it was to purchase computer engines.

"I was merely emulating grandmother," Berd said in a firm voice. She prayed her aunt did not inquire further. "I er, purchased it."

Purchased? Aunt Agatha mouthed. Her eyes glassed over as if trying to understand how and where Berd could have obtained the device. She stiffened and when she gazed at her niece, Berd knew that whatever trust remained was being swiftly eroded.

Telling the truth was not going well.

Berd's voice wobbled even more as she hurried on. "I wanted to use the computer as a tool. For research. So no more women need die prematurely like Grandmother. I tried to program it."

"You disappeared for three days. What really happened?" Anguish laced the duchess's words.

"I—I ended up being abducted by the Engine." As Berd spoke, she felt she teetered on the edge of a precipice. With each wrong word, she was slowly overbalancing. It wouldn't be a good idea to mention Gine wanting to kill her, but at the least she should explain about Charles.

"Charles Babbage *Fotheringay*. He's the one I'm engaged to. The inventor named him after his good friend, Charles Babbage. You remember him, don't you? His house in Marylebone? The inventor of the Difference and the Analytical Engines? He worked with Grandmother. Well, I met Charles in the Engine and—"

"Charles? Isn't that the man you were found with? The one attired like a savage."

Savage? Oh, how Aunt Agatha was harping on the wrong things! "Yes, but—"

Aunt Agatha gave a horrified gasp. "Charles Babbage is dead!"

"No, Aunt. *Fotheringay*."

"There's no need to snap. Why was he attired in that fashion?"

Berd almost growled, 'Wasn't it obvious?' But then it probably wasn't. Aunt Agatha never had to fend for herself. She had never to fight to survive or search for food or water. Or wonder if anyone was out to kill her.

Aunt Agatha had participated in a fox-hunt, but there she was the hunter; whereas in Berd's case, she had been the fox.

Berd tried not to ground the words out, but she knew her explanation would not sound good. "The reason he was attired in that fashion was because his clothing wore out. He couldn't go around unclothed. He used the skins from, from…these moths, you see…"

"Moths?" Aunt Agatha stared at her, stark horror in her gentle eyes. "Oh my darling, my poor, poor darling."

"Auntie, please believe me. I know it sounds incredible, but…"

Aunt Agatha swallowed. She rose rapidly from her chair. "My brother's child. My poor brother's child," she muttered, looking lost as she swept out of the bedroom.

Berd opened her mouth, but no words came out, which, she decided was probably just as well after what she had said. Aunt Agatha had been her last hope, but her aunt did not believe her.

She was doomed.

Berd tented her nose with her hands as she lay in bed, silent, unable to feel, unable to think beyond the fact that everything had gone wrong.

An hour later, Rose stumbled into the bedroom without knocking, her eyes red with crying. "I told them you weren't, but they didn't believe me. I'm sorry my lady, I'm sorry, but they've sacked me for telling the truth."

Berd pushed herself into a sitting position as she stared at the weepy Rose. She wanted to say 'I could have told you that telling the truth would make things worse.' Instead she said, "What do you mean?"

"Why, my lady, they say you're mad."

Berd allowed her chin to drop to her chest. She had been expecting this. The sight of her panicking in the library, the conversation she had just had with her aunt. Things could not get worse.

Rose's face caved in. "They're going to cart you away to Bedlam, my lady."

The words bore into Berd.

Bethlem Royal Hospital for the insane.

She had heard horror stories of guards being paid to take tens of thousands of members of the public through for an afternoon's idle entertainment and what they did to the inmates. Of experiments. Chains. Of ending up a gibbering, drooling fool… Maybe the stories were merely rumours, and the asylum was really the only place possible where the mentally ill were healed, but she had no desire to go within to discover the truth. Once in, there was no chance of escape.

She squeezed her eyes shut.

Breathe. Breathe. Breathe.

She clenched her hands into fists.

Have to deal with this. Have to take control. Have to make things right.

Rose's sniffling grated on her, but it gave her focus.

She would deal with one thing at a time, starting with Rose.

Berd's eyes snapped open. "Calm down," she ordered.

Rose gawked at her mistress, but obediently stopped her whimpering.

The gesture helped. Berd rolled her eyes, though inwardly she wanted to hug her silly maid. She had not expected such demonstrations of affection from Rose and was touched. "Anyone would think it was *you* going to the madhouse. Now sit and compose yourself."

Rose complied, eyes dark and hopeful. Her maid's implicit trust boosted her confidence. "Good. Now be quiet while I think." Berd wrapped her arms round her knees and rocked.

She had tried appealing to James. That hadn't worked. She had tried explaining to Aunt Agatha. That hadn't worked either.

The only person left who could help her was Charles.

Berd stopped rocking. She had to know if he wanted her. Perhaps James had lied. There was but one way to find out.

"Rose!" Berd flung the duvet off.

Her maid jumped up. "Yes, my lady?"

Berd threw on her dressing gown and strode to her writing desk. "I need to send a message. I need someone…trustworthy."

"Henry," said Rose without hesitation.

Berd cocked her head at the closed door. "Isn't he outside?"

"He was replaced an hour ago. Stephen is outside now."

Berd nodded. She sat at her desk and wrote. The letter contained one sentence.

I need to speak with you.

She sealed the letter and then handed it to Rose. "Get Henry to deliver this to Mr Fotheringay."

Rose started. "Now? My lady?"

It was 8 p.m.

"Yes. And Rose. Very. Important. Tell Henry to wait, do you understand? Tell him to wait until he gets a reply. He is not to leave until he gets a reply."

Rose's eyes narrowed, but then she nodded.

"Good." Berd handed her a pound note. She knew it was vastly more than she needed to pay the footman, but she also knew that Henry could lose his job if caught. The amount signalled the urgency. And the risk.

Rose hesitated, pocketed the money, curtsied and was off.

After an hour, Rose was back, breathing heavily as if she had been running. She handed over a sealed letter freshly edged with black and sealed with black wax. Black denoted that Charles was in mourning for his father.

Berd sliced the envelope open. Even the creamy paper inside was edged black. It read:

I do not wish to speak with you.

She felt herself collapse inwardly.

So it was true.

James hadn't lied. But she had not spent the last hour idle. She grabbed another sheet of paper. This time she wrote one word. All her hopes hinged on that word.

When she handed the second letter to Rose, she repeated her instructions but as she went to give her a second note, Rose shook her head.

"It will be Hen… Hen…" Rose blushed furiously. "Henry's pleasure, my lady. And oh, here's the other." She fumbled in her pocket, pulled the money out, but then as she went to return it, could not look Berd in the face.

Berd had never seen Rose so embarrassed before, not even when they were at the auction house. When Rose began to twist and worry a section of her skirt, the truth rapidly became obvious.

"Why, Rose! You're in love—"

Rose gave a horrified squeak. "Miss, please!"

Berd clasped her hand over her mouth, but there was no need to utter another word. The expression on Rose's face was proof enough.

Rose was in love with Henry.

So that was the reason her maid had coloured so beautifully when Berd had pushed Rose out the door and accidentally into his arms. And that was why, Berd bit her tongue, Rose was so upset to leave her employ. It wasn't her. It was Henry. Rose didn't want to leave Henry. It was Henry, Rose was pining for. That was the real reason the silly girl was distraught. Only…

The situation was impossible.

Marriage was the supposed ultimate goal for every woman. For in marriage, a man received a housekeeper and a companion, while a woman received a household and children.

Unless that woman was a maid.

Female servants were deemed the one exception to the rule: able by way of their career to be supported by and to minister to men. Thus they were never expected to marry.

As the daughter of an earl, I had money enough and rank enough to defy convention. Or at least I did.

"Oh, Rose, I'm so sorry." Berd grasped Rose's cold hands and squeezed.

Rose hesitated then squeezed back, but it was limp. "It's all right, my lady."

Rose must have been expecting simply to work beside Henry for the rest of her life for Berd doubted a footman's wage would be able to support a wife.

How bitter life is for some of us. Though I had thought to fight for emancipation, I never realised all its subtle forms.

Berd shook her head. That made two of them. Two silly love-sick girls who in their own way were fighting for the men they loved. Their union had to be their strength.

This time Rose was gone for two hours. When she returned, she handed Berd the envelope.

Not bothering with the letter opener, Berd ripped it. The letter contained only one word:

Come.

Chapter 21

G INE.

Gine had been the single word Berd had written.

Berd stared at the letter. *I'm right. I'm right!*

It wasn't Charles in the mansion. It was Gine.

A ghost now walked the streets.

Any joy at the confirmation was swamped the next second by profound terror, for she knew what she was letting herself in for. And this time there would be no Charles…

The ceiling seemed to swirl above her head. The green peacock pattern seemed to lift off the wallpaper and to dance as ghostly effigies before her. Together with the charred fumes from the burning candle wicks, she grew so overwrought with dizziness that she staggered backwards and had to clutch at the back of a chair to steady herself.

The shock passed. Her heart started again. There was the smooth, cool feel of rosewood beneath her fingers. The room cleared. Perspiration dampened her brow, chilling her so that she shivered.

Berd wiped her clammy forehead. The only way it was possible for Gine to exist outside the Engine was if something had happened to Charles.

It was only a guess. An educated guess no doubt, based on the few facts at her disposal. Berd had gambled and won this round. She had done it. It was what she wanted. She glanced at the message once more.

Come

Four letters that opened a door for her into the unknown. As if to confirm the invitation was real, she smoothed the pad of her thumb over the tail of the 'e' and watched as the black India ink smeared over the creamy surface of the paper. Still fresh.

A horror was in that mansion. She was merely going into the lion's den so that the lion could eat her.

The room chilled.

But it was only way she could get to Charles.

I haven't won yet.

She was stuck in her aunt's house. And under James's control. She looked up to see Rose's eyes glistening with hopeful tears.

Act as if you have won.

"Thank-you Rose. And thank Henry for me. Tell him he has performed his task splendidly. One last thing. Ask him one question."

"Yes, my lady?"

"Ask Henry what he noticed in the house."

Rose knotted her brows together as if the words did not make sense.

Berd was sure they didn't, but then Rose had never met Gine. Lucky girl.

"Is there anything in particular you mean?"

"No. Just that. Ask him what he noticed when he was in the house."

Rose gaped, bobbed and was gone. When she returned, she stood before Berd, clenching and unclenching her fingers as if trying to rid herself of some unseen dirt. "Henry said... Henry said that he was only allowed in the entry hall."

Berd nodded. That much she expected.

"So he didn't actually see much of the house. I mean it was a grand house and all seeing as it's also in Mayfair. Lots of pictures on the walls. Statuary. I believe Mr Fotheringay's family are in banking and they had connections with the East India Company and—"

"Rose! What did Henry notice?"

Rose flinched. "Nothing."

"Nothing?" Berd stilled, not believing her ears.

Rose trembled, absorbed in the polished sheen of her black boots. "Well...he didn't see much, but he...umm...he..."

"What did he notice, Rose?"

"He heard a humming," the words fell out.

It was the answer Berd expected. But the tension did not ease out of her, if anything it tightened as if a key had been turned and locked it into place. She remembered the infernal hum within the Engine. In her ears it now buzzed louder and louder...

No! Berd shook herself mentally. *Stop it. You have to fight Gine and win.*

She smiled at Rose, pretending to be well-pleased. "Good girl."

Rose beamed.

"Go get my brother. Tell him I wish to speak with him."

Rose scrambled for the door, forgetting to bob in her haste.

Breathe. Breathe. Fear was seeping into Berd, touching her bones with cold. She fought her terror as she settled herself briskly at her desk, attempting to look as business-like as possible for when her brother arrived. James was the prelude to Gine.

Minutes later a knock rattled her door.

She straightened and composed herself. "Come in, James."

If anything, James's demeanour was contrite as he entered her bedroom, even slightly embarrassed. She decided that he was probably feeling guilty about his earlier behaviour, his decision to commit her to an asylum.

It didn't matter; Berd steeled herself. She was playing the game of her life and the risks were hefty. One wrong roll. One mistake and she would pay with everything. "James."

"Berd." James eyed her guardedly as he stood in the middle of her circular turquoise carpet.

Berd waved at the chaise longue; this was her room after all, but he shook his head and remained standing.

"If you are worried, don't be. I won't repeat my behaviour in the library."

James's brows shot up as if he wasn't expecting this level of honesty from her. "Well, I, um, well that's good to know. It's late. You wished a word with me?"

"One word," she said mischievously then handed him the letter.

James's brows creased in perplexity as he read it.

"Fotheringay *is* a man of one word. However, did you get him to—" He raised the letter to his view again, "And today's date, too, to communicate with you?"

"I wish to speak with him."

"Berd! How many times do I have to tell you that he does not—"

"The letter in your hand says otherwise."

James shook the letter. "How do I know this is legitimate?"

She gave a coy smile. "We can always go and ask."

James dug one fist into his hip as he scowled at her.

"What have you got to lose?" she challenged him. Besides a sister and her trust in you? "Or are you so keen to commit me to the asylum already?"

"How on earth did you—" Then he slammed the letter against his thigh. "Rose. Those blasted servants know everything." He shoved the letter back at her. "If I concede, and we go, and Fotheringay decides he does not wish to speak with you—"

"Then I am at your disposal and will do whatever you wish. Without a whimper. Wales. But no Harold. And no madhouse."

James screwed his mouth up as he studied a corner of the ceiling.

Berd held her breath as she waited. She did not think that James wanted the shame of committing her. She was not mad and she was sure that by observing her, he was aware.

So, she had said a few unwise words to her aunt. He knew she would never repeat them. She waited.

James pounded his fist again as he snapped out of his thoughts. "Agreed. And if Fotheringay turns us away at the door you will come quietly away."

Berd almost melted with relief. "Thank-you."

He bowed. "Tomorrow then. At eleven."

"James, no, please. We need to go now. Immediately."

"It's almost midnight. We go tomorrow or not at all. Good-night." James pressed his lips into a determined line. "You said you would obey. Obey me now."

Before she could respond, he bowed and was out the door.

Fool! Berd bit back the remark as a lump fisted in her throat. It had been a victory of sorts.

Tomorrow.

Tomorrow was too late. Only James didn't know that. She had to go now or who knew what Gine would do to Charles. The guess that it was Gine in the mansion had been her last hope.

Somehow Gine had sucked Charles back into the Engine when she had left the stables. For if there was one thing of which she was sure, it was that Charles would never have betrayed her.

Berd paced the length of her bedroom. No doubt Gine had already concocted some dastardly plan. She needed to be prepared when she confronted him. But by now she had been in her room a very long time. A room in which all doors and windows were kept shut and where the sole light came from burning candles. She felt herself descend into the inevitable headache brought on by a lack of oxygen.

Minutes later, Rose bustled in. "Would you like me to turn over your bed, my lady?"

Absorbed in her dilemma, Berd waved vaguely in the direction of her brass bed.

Rose set to work and with Hilary's help, she began to turn over and to shake the feather mattress.

Too late did Berd realise she had made the wrong decision. She had never been present when her bed was turned to see what needed to be done. The resulting commotion made it impossible for her to concentrate. She longed to send Rose away, but then there would be no one to run her errands, be her eyes with what was happening outside. No, she needed Rose close at hand, so she gritted her teeth and waited.

The bed was remade with fresh linen. And the door soon closed behind Hilary. But then as if it were her maid's intention to further pique her, Rose started to tidy up. That in itself was not too bad.

Until Rose began to hum. Her off-key pitch further needled into Berd's head.

Berd raised a finger to her lips.

Rose nodded, picked up a sampler and started to sew.

Berd had just pressed cold fingers to her hot temples when Rose spoke.

"I hope you don't mind me saying this, my lady, but after seeing the state of your clothing when you got back, I think I can believe anything. We burnt them all." Then she clapped her hands. "Oh, but your rendezvous with Mr Fotheringay is so romantic."

It was all Berd could do to stop herself from snapping. Somehow she managed to grate out, "What do you mean?"

"I mean, when you speak with Mr Fotheringay tomorrow, well of course he'll propose," Rose explained boldly.

Rose could be such a dunderhead. Pain made Berd

perverse. That, and the idea of marrying Gine. "Don't you know anything, Rose? Even if Mr Fotheringay proposes for the second time, it doesn't mean I'll accept."

"But…but didn't you speak to his lordship? I heard his lordship order the carriage. Isn't everything set to right again?"

So Rose had overheard James give the order. That was how she knew what was going on. And if Rose had eavesdropped, she would certainly not be alone. It was further proof the servants had been listening not just during this climactic period, but throughout her entire life.

Nothing she did was private.

The thought that even here in the real world, she had been spied on sickened her. It was too close to being back in the Engine with Gine spying on her. "We are going to visit Mr Fotheringay. That is all. And even that I cannot guarantee as it depends on whether his lordship changes his mind. Or if Mr Fotheringay changes his."

A man's prerogative.

She snorted.

"Oh!" Rose's eyes welled with tears and she collapsed sobbing onto the chair at the writing desk.

Berd's mood altered instantly. The last thing she wanted was to upset Rose. "Why, Rose? What's wrong?"

Her maid's face was buried in her skirt. "I thought, I thought everything was going to be all right."

So the earlier confidence was a sham. "Rose, it's not that simple. I wish it were."

Rose's words were muffled, growing more and more

high-pitched. "I understand, my lady. Truly I do."

"Is it Henry?"

At the beloved name, the held back wail finally erupted. "It's nothing, my lady. Truly, it's nothing."

"It can't be nothing. You've been in tears twice now. What's wrong?"

Rose shook her head vehemently.

By now Berd was prepared to strangle her maid. She did not have time for this. Charles's life was in the balance. "Yes!" she demanded. "Tell me."

"Why? You don't really care."

Berd blinked, stunned. "What?"

"It's true, isn't it? You care, in a way. But I feel as if you care for me only as if for a pet."

"I… I…" Berd stammered, unsure as to how she had got herself into this mess. This was one detour she hadn't seen coming.

"Oh, my lady. I'm sorry. I know you do care. And in fact many consider me lucky because you even care that much."

But the irony was that Rose was right; most employers did not care for their servants. Berd was in a way unusual. She cared, but not deeply enough. Exactly like James.

She could only stare at Rose. At the truth revealed. Feeling as if her chest had been sliced open and her shallow heart exposed.

"You see, it's true. It doesn't matter now. I was fired this morning. I thought that after you had words with his lordship that things had been put to right. But I was wrong. And now you're upset. And I'm being perfectly stupid, but I've had enough. I've borne and I've borne and I can bear no more." Rose sobbed.

The problem was that Berd did understand her maid. She may not have understood what it was like to lose a job, but she did understand the universal language of being powerless over her own fate. And of having been in love and to lose the one she loved.

Pain brought kinship.

Berd schooled her voice to gentleness, determined to learn. "No, I won't be. I was upset, but I promise I'll listen."

Rose raised her tear-stained face to Berd, two spots of colour clear in her cheeks.

"Yes, I'm sure. Now what is wrong?" Berd insisted.

Rose cocked her head dubiously. "Well, you see, it's to do with my lady."

"Me?" Berd was totally mystified.

"It's just that you're *the sign*. I think that if Mr Fotheringay proposes tomorrow and you accept, then everything would be all right between me and Henry."

"Heavens! Are you using me like a crystal ball? Rose!"

"Oh, no, my lady. Much more than that."

"Explain."

Rose blew nosily into a handkerchief. "Well, I mean, everyone wants to be you, my lady. We all have dreams and such like, but to be you, the daughter of an earl! So we dream. We watch you as you go about your life. When you went to your first ball, why after the event I held your gown up against myself to see how it would look. I didn't try it on, honest, my lady. Well, just the sleeves. And I smoothed the bodice against my breast. But I had a wash that day, my lady, I did. So you needn't worry about any fleas jumping onto your dress. And then I unpinned that beautiful violet silk, sponged it, pressed it and oh so carefully put it away… Oh! Oh, what have I done?"

Horrified, Rose held up her hands, realisation showing on her face that not only had she admitted her guilt, but that she had also gone through the motion of holding and outlining the gown against herself. She blushed strawberry-red and looked so woebegone and repentant that any repulsion Berd had initially felt on someone handling and donning her clothing in such a familiar fashion vanished. She had no heart to reprimand her maid.

So in a way James was right. Not only did servants know every intimate detail of employers, they tried in their own vicarious fashion to live it.

It was another glimpse into a shadowy world Berd had always known existed; an alternate world where men and women lived who served; a world she was hoping to replace by servants of metal and electricity.

Two worlds.

A world for those who served.

And a world for those who were served.

And those two worlds were presently colliding.

The computer was Gine's world. He, the servant. Now she understood what he wished to accomplish. What he was attempting to do through Charles.

To be Charles…

The servant wanting to become the master, Gine had found a way to switch places with Charles, take over his life. The ultimate coup for a service, the ultimate dream realised.

If that was true then she understood why he had

summoned her. It couldn't be simply to talk. There was something more nefarious to his plan.

Soon she would find out how far Gine would go to keep his secret.

Chapter 22

THE FOOTMAN SHUT the carriage door. James thumped his walking stick twice on the ceiling and at the signal, the carriage rolled away and they drove through fog that changed colour from the ghost of mud to the dilation of yellow peas-pudding.

Berd settled herself on the seat opposite her brother. Her nostrils flared slightly at the hint of nicotine lingering in the enclosed space. She suspected that James had been smoking early. That along with the faint lines around his eyes alerted her to the fact he was worried. He was not the only one.

If she had her way, James, for his own safety, should not be accompanying her. It was, however, an impossibility to persuade him otherwise. She was a female and according to the rules of society, not allowed out unchaperoned.

Unprotected. The reality was that it was up to her to protect him.

She smoothed the folds of her peacock-green pelisse, hearing the comforting swish and rustle of the brilliant aquamarine silk beneath. If only she had the answers under her fingertips. She knew it had to be Gine at the Fotheringay mansion. Yet James was expecting to meet Charles, a human, not a lethal engine.

Somehow she had to warn her disbelieving brother about Gine and about doppelgangers. James needed to be prepared, for that was their best chance of leaving the mansion alive.

I have lost my love; I do not wish to lose my brother also.

A hole had been cut into her heart and all hope fallen out, leaving her hollow and empty and aching. And now horror had crept in.

"Fotheringay is a fool," James announced. "Who in their right mind would turn down marriage to the daughter and sister of an earl?"

So James thought her anxious as to whether Charles would declare his intentions. It annoyed her that all men thought marriage the ultimate goal of every woman. "I see. My worth is to be calculated solely by my relationship to the men in my family. What about our mother? After all, she did reach her majority and she did bear two children. Or is she just to be seen as a child her whole life because she is female?"

At the mention of their late parents, James anger lessened. His young face paled, adding to his vulnerability. "I did not expect to play the role of mother and father."

That was true. Had their parents been alive, it would have been their father's task to check a future spouse's finances and prospects. Just as it would have been their mother's task to check everything else. Now the dual roles fell heavily upon her brother, who was also her guardian despite there being barely five years between them.

James coughed into a fist. Dressed in his dove-coloured morning coat his fair face appeared far too youthful for such heavy responsibility.

"Thank-you for agreeing to this, James," said Berd, her tone softening as she loved him even more.

He was her brother. In his own way, he cared for her. Hence, she had to tell him that their visit was not to persuade Charles to marry her in order to stave off her ruin, but to engineer a murder. Specifically, a death.

"I am glad you did not suggest Aunt Agatha," she said, after muddling about the idea in her head for some time.

He raised a brow in inquiry. "Did you wish her present?"

"No, but that's because I do not know what to expect."

"What *are* you expecting?"

To die. To be trapped once more inside the Engine.

Berd gave a sardonic laugh. All her dreams of being the world's first computer programmer had come to naught.

"I started this journey hoping it would save lives," she mused. "Now, no matter what path I tread, I will be scorned. If Charles does not marry me, I will be scorned for I am ruined. If Charles does marry me, I will be scorned for marrying beneath myself. How wonderful then, that I have never cared for public opinion."

James polished the silver top of his cane with his thumb then examined it intently as if for defects.

"Somehow I have the feeling you mean something else."

Well-done, mon frère. Maybe I can't tell you directly, but I can drop little hints.

Berd smiled what she hoped was a mysterious smile. "Tell me, what did Mr Fotheringay tell you about our kidnapping?"

"Nothing much. Simply that he had been kidnapped first. Then you four days ago."

"Did he mention the identity of the kidnapper?" She held her breath.

James turned to her smugly. "Does it matter?"

Cowards. She let her breath out and baited her brother again. "So you and Mr Fotheringay decided to *bury* the details."

James tapped a finger knowingly against the side of his nose. "Fotheringay will speak to the police about his kidnapping. He agreed that we did not need to involve the police any further with what happened to you."

Clever. That way no one except her immediate family and the servants would know about her disappearance. Of course servants would talk, but if there was nothing in the newspapers and the police kept mum, it would be hard for any blackmailer to prove anything especially if Charles married her…

She sighed. *Where are you Charles?*

It made no sense to her that Gine, who no doubt was pretending to be Charles, would agree to keep quiet. His current behaviour had been to avoid her. Yet, his actions appeared to be protecting her. Then she gasped.

Cads! "The Engine! You bargained to protect my reputation in return for the Engine."

James shrugged, but would not meet her gaze. "Why splash it about the papers? The Police Commissioner is a great friend of his late father's. Actually, Fotheringay and I have half a dozen mutual friends, so the circles we move about aren't too disparate. You may even have met him before this. I just regret the fact you have led a rather circumspect life."

How ironic that James was decrying her lack of choice of a life partner. "Women in my position generally do, don't they?"

The higher born a woman, the more secluded and shielded her life was, but Berd regretted her accusation when James huffed.

"Not when they're out supposedly enjoying their first season. Not when they're supposed to be going to balls. To parties, to—"

"Messing about with engines?" She added innocently. "It was rather interesting how Mr Fotheringay and I met, don't you think? How no one noticed any abductor and how there was no ransom demanded after a year."

James mumbled something that did not sound complimentary.

She toasted him with her parasol. "Might make abduction popular. How to meet your future spouse. Try abduction. But you needn't worry about finding Mr Fotheringay…" She bit her tongue for she had almost said 'don't worry about finding Mr Fotheringay at all.'

"Foppish, frivolous or slovenly, but you may find him eccentric," she finished.

James glanced heavenward and with an

exaggerated groan continued, "Fotheringay's family owns two banks. His income easily surpasses mine, so I have no worries he can provide for you. Fotheringay's New Money, however. Two mayors, but still New Money." He grimaced.

Berd pictured Charles's family barely sneaking across the imaginary line the nobility had drawn in the sand in terms of what was acceptable. Bankers' families were amongst the few that were. Money was what made the upward progression more acceptable, but no one ever admitted to it.

All that money, however, would make it very easy for Gine to escape.

She teased, "What a sordid thought! Are you worried the *beau monde* will think you've sold me off for money?"

James ignored her and droned on, "He is well-known down at the Royal Society. In fact, there is talk about his invention changing the world…"

James was deliberately not taking the bait at all.

She knew she should be telling James about Gine. About what she planned to do when they met, only she herself had no idea.

"And that interests you?" she asked when he stopped for breath.

"It does if it can lead to a peerage from the Queen."

A barony? Somehow she couldn't see Charles accepting a life peerage. She didn't think rank mattered to him. In fact, if she could hazard a guess, she would have thought he'd prefer if she had no rank at all. Gine, on the other hand, would deem it too lowly. If she knew him, he wouldn't stop until he became emperor of the whole world.

"I see. How nice to know you're not upset if I marry someone without a title."

James glared down his nose at her. "Do you or do you not love him!"

Touche! Her eyes misted. And it was her turn to avoid his gaze.

"Good!" He slapped his gloves smartly against his thigh as the carriage drew to a halt on the Fotheringay driveway. "I believe we're arrived."

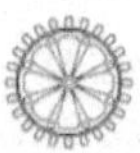

A dark semi-circle of trees blocked the view of the Fotheringay mansion from the street. Like a ghastly grin, they formed the loose curve of the lower lip, with the mansion itself the straight upper lip. And from within, that hum. It entered Berd's bones as she sat in the carriage, pulling on kid gloves.

The door opened, and she was immediately blanketed in static. Every movement she made crackled. Her lungs were twin bellows with a hole in each side.

They were in their own little world of Egyptian darkness. Neither breeze nor bird rippled the sky. All that was left of the sun in the mantle of slate-grey was a dim depression, as though some giant fingernail had scratched it out.

It reminded Berd too much of the sky in the Engine. By now the taste of metal was strong under her tongue.

"Are you sure about this?" Concern was etched on James's face as he held out his arm.

"Yes. Please."

"Courage," James muttered as he helped her out of the carriage.

She nodded. Thinking and acting as if she had won had got her here. Now she had to think like a programmer. Even though she would never be the world's first programmer, she was still a programmer. For what was Gine after all but a program? Well, that was the theory. In practice Gine could and would run circles around her.

The air seemed to vibrate with electricity and the driveway appeared to give under her tread like rubber. She heard neither echo nor footstep. She rubbed her arms to halt the invisible ants crawling up and down. If only she could stamp her feet or jump. Anything! Just to be rid of the nervousness. She might not be back in the Engine, but she was back on Gine's territory. Though she was closing in on him physically, he was closing in on her mentally.

They stood on the front step.

"I do not fancy this at all. Is that sound emitted from that dratted Engine? It would drive a man to suicide. Can Fotheringay stop it? I—"

"James, please."

James huffed then rapped on the door with the end of his silver-tipped cane. They waited.

By now her breath was coming in little gasps. She expected Gine to peel himself off a wall. Or even the front door. Exactly like in the Engine.

James squeezed her hand in reassurance, and she loved him all the more for it.

Then the door opened. The doorman appeared.

Berd started. Her nerves were so on edge she had expected Gine to grab her. This was far too normal. She grinned embarrassedly at James as she composed herself.

James did not respond to her faux pas. His face remained impassive as he handed over their ivory calling cards. "For Mr Fotheringay," he muttered dismissively.

The doorman placed them on a silver salver then bowed and held the door open for them. He said nothing, but he was most definitely breathing.

Berd's heart was in her throat as she stepped over the threshold.

James, there's something I must tell you…

It was no warmer inside the massive mansion. The entry hall was as large as a ballroom with the ceiling at least two storeys above their heads. Their boots seemed to crunch, echoing on the white marble floor, giving Berd the distinct impression they were treading upon the frosty ground of a cemetery on a wintry twilight. She half-expected the dreary scent of raw earth and lilies-of-the-valley. Instead her senses were cloyed with the odour of damp, mildew, dust and decay.

Beside her James sneezed then hacked as if a broken wind-up horse was within his chest, and he could not get rid of it. His asthma. She laid her hand on his shoulder, and he managed to nod while waving her on as his coughing fit eased.

Her heart panged at what she was causing James to undergo. But it was too blasted late to turn back. They were in the Fotheringay mansion.

At first glance all seemed normal. Houses in London tended to have partially shuttered windows and to have curtains drawn across in order to keep out the ubiquitous soot and dirt. This added to the oppressive deadness of the air within, but the windows in the Fotheringay mansion were fully shuttered and the curtains let no light in for the inhabitants who were mourning the recent death of the late Robert Fotheringay, Charles's father.

Even the grandfather clock to their right had been stopped and when Berd saw what looked like a huge mirror over the mantelpiece covered, she was sorely tempted to say the threat did not lie in that direction. It was not the ghost of the late Mr Fotheringay returning that the inhabitants of this mansion had to fear.

But in the stiff yellow radiance from the seven candles on the mantelpiece, what soon became obvious was that the paintings hanging on the wainscoted walls, like the enormous chandeliers above, were covered in dust and cobwebs. Even as she stared, a spider dropped from nowhere. Had she not taken a hurried step towards James, it would have landed in—

She snapped her mouth shut.

It was then she noticed the slightly whiter spots on the marble which marked the spaces where objects had once stood.

The statuary was missing.

Lines and gouge marks showed the direction where they had been dragged from their resting places deeper into the house…

Suddenly, watery blue eyes swum before her while a woman's crackly voice played in her mind, 'Do you wish the company of the dead in your house.'

This was a house where the dead or something worse walked. As if to confirm her suspicion, further up the passageway were open doorways, yawning like the entrances of charnel houses and beyond, from what little she could see, indistinct shapes draped in Hollands.

She repressed a shiver.

The doorman bowed. "Please wait here, my lord and lady while I inform Mr Fotheringay."

As the doorman moved to close the door, Berd turned to James. "James, there's something I must tell you—"

The thud of the front door closing interrupted her. The echo seemed to signify that she and James were sealed off from the rest of the world. Of course, that wasn't true, but it was another sound, a sound that partly died out when the door was shut that alarmed her. For when the door closed, the hum lessened by half.

Her heart skipped a beat. Then it did a triple tattoo as the implication of what this meant became clear. Her attention changed direction. She forgot about the dusty, cobwebby interior, the missing statuary, her enraged brother and that it was her last chance to warn him.

And for a split second, she even forgot Gine.

For in the door closing, one thing and only one thing became very obvious.

The Engine was not inside the house.

For the hum had dimmed.

Blast you, Henry!

This turn of events did not make sense. She assumed the Engine would be close by Gine in order for him to protect it.

And Henry had confirmed the Engine was in the house.

No, Henry had lied —

No, she had simply asked the wrong question.

That was all. She had asked Rose to ask Henry what he had noticed in the house and standing in the foyer even Berd would have had to answer that the most obvious thing was the humming. Henry or Rose had probably decided not to mention the neglect in case he appeared insolent.

Berd now knew that she should have asked him whether the humming was louder in the house or outside because then she would have known where to start looking for the Engine. She wouldn't have been surprised if Henry had been confused with her questions.

If only she had come to the mansion last night. The delay had cost her; it allowed Gine to concoct his plans. She had not known the Engine and Gine could be separated by distance.

In one sense, Gine was the giant and the Engine the heart he had hidden away. If she destroyed the heart, she killed the giant, Gine, but Charles was in the heart. And she would kill him, too.

Now she had the dilemma of either searching for the Engine or for Gine. Already Gine was one up on her for he had split her concentration.

Divide the enemy and conquer.

Great move. Only it wasn't hers.

In order to win she had to emulate him. To think. Fast. And to work with what she was given.

She needed to find the Engine. But Berd knew that while she stood guard over the Engine, she was allowing Gine to escape. He didn't need to come near the Engine. The heartless giant didn't need to. But being in the Engine's vicinity meant the Engine could swallow her up again.

It made more sense to find Gine. Only how could she get him to release Charles? She had hoped the Engine would provide some leverage. But if the Engine could swallow her, Gine would do far worse.

She had no doubt the Engine and Gine each, in their own way, was dangerous. She felt as if not one, but two tigers were circling.

Then somewhere upstairs a door shut. Footsteps pattered, rapidly approaching. There was no time to figure out the mystery of the Engine's location because the doorman had reappeared.

And he was followed by two men.

Berd exhaled heavily, stunned as all three descended the shadowy staircase towards them. And though she couldn't see who the two men were, it was clear there were two.

Without a doubt one of them had to be Gine, but if one of them was Gine then who was the other?

Unless there was now two of Gine.

Her analogy of two tigers was correct. And they were closing in.

Chapter 23

TWO MEN FOLLOWED the doorman down the red carpeted stairs, their expensive velvet suits and bearing garnered them as men of repute. At the bottom of the staircase their features became clear, as did their silvery-grey hair, loose jowls and the 'bow-windows' around their waistlines.

Neither was Charles nor Gine.

Disappointment tainted with relief flooded through Berd, but the tension did not ebb fully. These men were either doppelgangers or human decoys attempting to delay her while Gine hid himself and the Engine.

Her heart thumped anxiously. She itched to wing away to search for Gine and the Engine, but knew she had to stay and find out if one of these men was Gine in disguise.

The doorman made himself scarce.

In the shadows of the foyer it was hard to tell if the two men were breathing, but what unnerved Berd more was the fact they were examining her with avid interest. Not James. Just her.

Under their gaze, she seemed to shrink to the size of a tiny spider while the wainscoted walls seemed to loom monstrously over her like the accursed walls of Luxor.

I'm in a cage. A trap. A pit. If I do not escape I will be forever imprisoned.

Every instinct told her to turn and flee as the men approached. Only her love for Charles caused her to breathe deeply and stand her ground.

Spiders can climb. I will get out of this. I just have to learn to climb.

The two men drew near and bowed.

"Your Lordship. Lady Elizabeth," greeted the older man, his eyes brown and hard as walnuts. He stunk of pipe weed and powder.

This close, she saw the rise and fall of their chests, the dead roses in their cheeks and the black crepe armbands.

The older man continued, "Forgive our news, but Mr Fotheringay has taken ill and regrets being unable to meet with you. In his absence, we are empowered to handle his affairs."

It had to be a ploy, Gine pretending to be Charles. Pretending to be ill. "Liar! Where's Gine?" she demanded.

"Elizabeth!" James hissed, mortified at her impropriety.

Blast! They were playing at manners when Charles's life was in danger. Angered by the delay, she stabbed the steel tip of her parasol on the floor. The percussive ding barely had a chance to reach the walls before it was swallowed in the hum. Silenced as effectively as full immersion in water.

Even in this slight rebellion, she was ineffective.

The two gentlemen exchanged a brief smile.

Her stomach turned. They had not questioned her as to who Gine was, which could only mean that they had to be in the know.

The tension in the air tightened.

Berd knew she needed to get to the heart of the matter: to find Charles. Gine would not be stupid enough to allow anyone in the room with such knowledge. Therefore, she had to go to Gine.

She had to find him.

The doorman had come from upstairs and so had the two men. Obviously someone from upstairs was giving orders. That had to be Gine. And as for where exactly he was, the neglect of the house demonstrated there was no female in residence. That ruled out the morning room, which meant Gine was in the drawing room.

All Berd had to do was make her way up without attracting suspicion. She appealed to her sole ally. "James, I need—"

Without taking his gaze off the two men, James held one hand up, halting her; his rebuke as effective as if he had spoken audibly.

Though every fibre of her being longed to run up the stairs, she knew it wouldn't take much to make him leave. Only the thought of Charles forced her sheepishly to hunch her shoulders.

James narrowed his gaze at the two men. "And you are?"

"Mr Fotheringay's barristers. Messrs Abbey and Masters, Esquire, respectively, Queen's counsel, from the firm Brooke, Abbey and Masters." The older man indicated himself and then his partner.

Engaging silks was a turn Berd did not expect, and one of London's oldest and most distinguished legal firms, no less. A rival to the firm the Lovelaces used. But this was in a way what James had come prepared for. Suddenly, leaving didn't seem like such a bad idea. She had to find Gine and rescue Charles before she found herself engaged to and then married to an engine.

Her spirits brightened as she saw her chances unexpectedly improve when James came inadvertently to her rescue. He bristled as if deeply wounded by the change in plans. "This is highly irregular. Could not Mr Fotheringay have informed us before we set off?"

By being his usual annoying self, James was helping her while totally oblivious to the fact he was doing so. Though her marriage to Charles was James's objective, he would make the process as difficult as possible. She had always assumed her brother acted in this manner to fulfil a sense of his own importance—who he was. It was nice to see even earls suffered from self-doubt.

Things continued to improve. After their initial interest in her the attention of both barristers was now focused solidly on her brother. She was not about to question why especially when it allowed her to take a stride towards the stairs.

As Mr Abbey answered, she gripped her parasol tighter, hugged her reticule to her chest and gleefully took another step.

"We apologise profusely, your lordship, but the onset of the illness was rather sudden. Mr Fotheringay had hoped to be here to meet with you. Thankfully, he had already arranged for us to be present. Perhaps we could retire to the drawing room to discuss matters."

Berd had just taken two more steps when she caught the words 'drawing room.' She stiffened, stung by the fact that she had gone down the wrong path, literally and metaphorically. If these men were trying to get her and James to the drawing room, then it meant that Gine was not in there. No wonder they weren't paying her attention. She was already going in the direction they wanted. How foolish!

"We can then draw up the necessary contracts," suggested the slightly younger gent helpfully, Mr Masters, as he waved at the stairs.

She backtracked to where her brother stood. This was twice the lawyers wanted them upstairs. Gine was definitely not upstairs. She consoled herself that at least she was right about marriage. "James…"

But James was lost in his world of self. He wasn't just the lord of the manor, but the king in his castle. He never even noticed her. "Couldn't Mr Fotheringay have handled this properly? This won't do at all. He should have declared his intentions to me and then I would have arranged for our lawyers to meet."

All three men were so engrossed in their conversation that Berd gripped her skirts, prepared to make a dash into one of the doors on the ground floor. She was lifting one foot, when she heard Mr Abbey say.

"I was under the impression that Mr Fotheringay had."

"He most certainly has *not!*"

Her foot came down awkwardly. The ensuing silence made it worse. For now it was obvious to everyone that she was attempting to move away. Grinning shamefacedly, she turned in time to hear Mr

Abbey say, "Why, yes. I believe Mr Fotheringay had specifically made a request to you that Lady Elizabeth keep her distance from him."

Though the words had been spoken with a gentle air, they still hurt. What stung even more was that again she was wrong. Completely wrong. It was not marriage either. Gine wanted to make sure he never saw her again. Only *he* would have the audacity to invite her to his home so he could sue her. And hire two silks no less to effect this.

Gine was trouncing her.

Even James floundered. "Distance? I was under the impression we were here to discuss marriage."

"Marriage?" Mr Abbey started, then thumped himself on the chest as if that was the only way he could comprehend the word.

The conversation was turning rancid. Soon James would insist they leave. She was prepared to run for it when James demanded, "How on earth did all this happen?"

She should have seen this coming.

As if in answer to his question, both lawyers turned to her. James followed suit.

But Berd had other things on her mind. So what did it matter if all this chaos and confusion was truly her fault! She had to make her move before it was too late.

She sprung for the nearest door. "Gine! Where are you? What have you done with Charles?" Her cries echoed about the void of the foyer.

Behind her she heard Mr Master's triumphant cry. "You see, my lord. This is what this matter is all about."

Even before Berd was half-way across the entry hall, James had raced after her and caught up.

"Berd," he muttered as he took her arm. "We are leaving now."

"No, James, please!" She yanked several times in an attempt to break free, but James simply wrapped his other arm around her waist, increased his grip and slowly forced her back towards the entrance door.

Berd twisted, but it was futile. No doubt Gine was watching all of this. Once again she was physically helpless, and hot tears prickled at the back of her eyes.

"No! James! No, please," she cried as James hauled her towards the front door.

She elbowed him, but James's response was to hoist her off the ground. A thin moan escaped her lips as he balanced her on his shoulders. She hammered the air with her parasol, wishing she could hit him with it.

Mr Abbey nodded as if in agreement at James's action. "Here I have a letter from Lady Elizabeth demanding to see Mr Fotheringay after he expressly requested all ties be broken off."

As they passed him, he held up the letter she had written last night.

Berd collapsed inwardly. They were goading her, but two could play at this. She would goad Gine out.

"Please James, you're *hurting* me!"

Despite her dramatic appeal to her brother's better nature, James never halted as he marched towards the door.

Blast him! Berd wielded her parasol high like a sword then swung it viciously, managing to lance the steel tip across Mr Abbey's sleeve.

He gave a horrified gasp at the thin white line across the black velvet then stared at her as if she were a harridan from hell.

"Gine? Who the devil is Gine?" snapped James, his temper out now. "How many men are you involved with?"

"I'm trying to save Charles!"

Masters held aloft her last letter with the word 'Gine' on it. "Here's where Lady Berd accused Mr Fotheringay of being an engine."

So that's why they never questioned her as to who Gine was. She swung at Masters, but he ducked and she missed. As if to taunt her failure, he followed after her while holding up her letter.

To her annoyance, he was out of reach. She ignored the buffoon as she cast her glance around the numerous doorways along the entry hall. Not a shadow had moved. "Please, James, I love him."

James groaned. "Gine?"

Mr Masters held another letter up. "This was sent one year ago when Lady Elizabeth demanded to be allowed to purchase the property of Mr Fotheringay's late father: an engine."

Each letter impaled her heart. The parasol shook as her hand wavered.

James must have felt her despair for he whispered, "A little cottage in Wales. Please, please."

And even Masters dropped his guard. More importantly, he was back in range. Berd sliced the air with her parasol, tearing the letter in half.

"No! You don't understand. I have to save him. I love him —" Berd suddenly screamed and jerked in agony. Every inch of her tingled as though a live wire trailed across her bare skin. The humming tripled, blasting in her ears. She couldn't see it, but she knew the moment the doorman must have opened the door.

A misshapen slab of cold light streamed over her shoulders, etching and greying each of the lawyer's faces, as though condemning them to stone. With each step, she felt as though she and James descended into a grave. Her nostrils flared at the odour of newly-turned earth. In every corner of the entry hall, shadows bulked as if inhabited. She was sure she heard the eager gnashing of teeth. Every hair on the back of her neck stood on end.

She flung her parasol out in a final do-or-die attempt. And in her dazed state thought she saw starlight gleam a trail along the arc her arm had cast. Then the shadow tip of her parasol touched the uneasy shadow outline of the door.

For a second, light and dark were linked…

"Charles!" she screamed as James crossed the threshold. Though why she called his name she had no idea for she was convinced it was Gine in the mansion. Perhaps it was because deep down, she knew that if he could, Charles would rescue her.

He always had.

As James carried her out into the open she ripped her hat off and flung it at Masters. It smacked with a thud into his gobsmacked face. Let him sue her if he wished, but she was going to go out fighting.

Gine, you are not going to win!

Her cry, however, did not go unanswered. She was about to hurl her reticule at Abbey when a clear voice rang out as if from the vault of heaven. "Please. Unhand her."

As though God commanded, the commotion halted.

A figure had emerged from the upstairs balcony.

Before Berd could determine the figure's identity,

James swung round to see who was speaking. The world spun. When she finally oriented herself, she found that he had re-entered the mansion. She twisted and looked up.

Time froze.

Sound vanished.

Too far away to see the figure's eyes, yet they held her. Too far away to see if he was breathing, yet she knew instinctively who it was.

Charles.

Charles, not Gine.

As if the sun had come out to shine on that dreary foyer, her world brightened to a blazing intensity. In that same moment she believed it possible to fly from James's shoulder into Charles's arms, but then as if the sun was a Lucifer match, its light extinguished as swiftly. The sun snapped out. Black filled the void. Cold burned her heart.

She slumped defeated, unable to believe that not only for the third time today was she wrong, but that her hope was dead.

For she had reasoned it to be Gine and not Charles who was master of Fotheringay mansion as that was the only way she could understand why Charles had reneged on his proposal and why he had never wanted to see her again.

His betrayal had been agonisingly painful. But again she had been completely wrong. She had thought Charles would never betray her, but if it was him in the mansion and not Gine then it appeared he had.

In one cataclysmic event, her world ended.

Chapter 24

"WHY?" THE WORD heaved with meaning, barely audible even to Berd.

Then everyone began speaking.

"Good God, Fotheringay! I'm suing every bone in your body. You'll be hearing from my lawyers," James howled.

"Please no," she begged her brother as he slid her onto her feet.

The shock of seeing Charles made her cling to James for support. Her flimsy green parasol became deadweight in her hand. Then she realised that Charles's gaze had been fixed the whole time on a point behind her.

It puzzled Berd as to why he was acting this way. But programmers loved puzzles.

Mr Abbey hurried up to Charles. "Sir, our advice is for you to retire. We have everything under control—"

"Messrs Abbey and Masters, thank-you kind sirs, but I shall handle it from here on."

Charles strode, ramrod straight, looking as if he

were prepared to encounter the Indian mutineers as well as the Zulus all at the same time. The echoes of a martial fife seemed to haunt the air. Charles's right arm was clamped to his side as though he favoured it. He halted in the hazy oblong of light cast by the open door, his face sickly-white, his brow wet with perspiration.

"Sir, we must insist you follow our advice. Remember in whose company you are." Mr Abbey glanced at James and then cleared his throat. "Two witnesses should be sufficient to assure the court no wrong doing took place. No conversation was—"

"Thank-you." Charles's tone was harder, more insistent.

Cleanly shaven, he no longer smelt of paraffin but of eau de cologne and fresh white carnations. Gone were the shoulder-length locks she had ached to run her fingers through. His jet hair was freshly cut and he was wearing a morning suit that seemed more suitable for Gine. Charles had changed so radically on the outside that she wondered if he had changed also, on the inside.

His blue eyes finally met hers. But all they showed was a deep battle being waged within. If she had felt pain, he appeared to have suffered thrice what she had undergone. She steeled herself for what she would have to do.

Charles turned to James. "Sir, could I have a private moment alone with your sister, please?"

The words had been spoken politely. But in this request, Charles had erred for he had neglected to bow. Fatal. Especially at this point in time.

Berd had not expected Charles to bow to her for

they had, while in the Engine, come to a comfortable understanding. And he had been her intended…

But here was James. Her brother. And an earl. And like most earls full of his own importance. If Charles had forgotten etiquette, James had not. In fact, after they had been treated so ill, James's pride now became a rallying point. Standing beside her brother, she sensed James's hackles rise in anger at the insult. She predicted James's answer even before he spluttered and turned away.

Charles's lack of decorum was not lost upon his legal representation either. The lawyers regarded him, nodding their heads like pigeons, scattering hints like crumbs. "Please, sir, we beg you regard our advice—"

"Thank-you," Charles's tone was harsher as he dismissed them.

Mr Abbey swallowed as if he had a small pebble in his throat then turned apologetically to James. "My lord, I beg you remember how unwell Mr Fotheringay is." Then they bowed and departed.

Even before the lawyers were out the door, James stepped between Berd and Charles. "What the devil is going on?"

"James, please," she hissed, hoping it would not end in fisticuffs or a duel. Not yet anyway. Right now she wanted to handle this her way. Besides, if Charles still wanted her for a wife there was no better time than the present to show him what he was in for, if he married her.

At James's question, the slightest hint of a smile passed over Charles's face. "Only the devil knows."

With such an unexpected answer, James opened his

mouth then shut it, thoroughly confused at Charles's response.

Berd suspected illness the reason for all the pain he had put her through in the last couple of days. She had so many questions, but the most important 'how to ask the one she loved why he was pretending he had stopped loving her' could not be phrased aloud. She doubted he would even answer if she did.

They stood quizzing silently into each other's eyes, unanswered questions raging to and fro before James threw his hand in the air.

"Blast it! Blast it! And poppycock! I don't need to hear any more. I'll be outside the door. You have full five minutes. Make good use of it." Then he glared at Charles as if to warn him he would have his guts for sausages for any wrong doing before stomping out.

She tilted her chin at Charles. "I can see from whom Gine learnt so much."

At her attack, Charles's brows twitched then he was cold stone once more. "You shouldn't have come."

"You invited me," she accused.

His eyes were the frozen blue of the tundra. "I wanted you to know, it wasn't Gine but me. I, who was doing all of this to you."

Her heart wrenched.

Gine had torn her in two; Charles was doing the exact same thing. Only Gine had been kinder —

Gine kinder than Charles? But it made sense.

Charles was the master. The creator. Gine had learnt from him.

She gasped as the lay of the land became blindingly clear. Armed with this valuable knowledge she could now orientate herself. She no longer needed a guide.

She knew the land.

She had thought to win the battle with Gine by thinking like a programmer, by thinking logically.

However, instead of fighting the program, she was fighting the programmer. But though the enemy had changed, she could still win. She tapped one finger against her lower lip, pretending she was musing aloud and that Charles wasn't right in front of her. Sure she was irking him. Glad she was irking him. "You have never lied to me. I believe you're not lying to me now."

Surprise flickered in his eyes before he answered, "Correct."

"Good," she said, thankful she knew him well enough. He wasn't lying. He still loved her. He was Charles. Her knight in shining armour. He had come, albeit reluctantly, to her rescue when she had called. He always had. He always would, if he could, which made it clear he was sacrificing himself for her right now.

Good thing he was in such a sacrificial mood, because it made her plan easier. Time to put it in action.

"James!" she screamed as though Charles was attacking her.

Even before she heard James scramble for the door, she swung her parasol, aiming for Charles's left arm, the uninjured arm. She was surprised to see him raise instead his right arm, using it to shield himself from her blow.

Her parasol slammed into his wrist. The ring of metal resonating across the room as it promptly broke in two, gave her the answer, even as her brother hurtled towards her.

Metal! Charles had a metal arm. That was not possible unless he was wearing armour like a knight. Or because of the energy! But gauntlets could not fit inside leather gloves. And she had not thought it possible that Charles could use the energy to change his appearance.

When Charles flushed in agonised embarrassment, she knew something was seriously wrong. He wrenched her parasol away from her, as she reached out and grasped hold tightly of his arm as a beige object blurred past her.

She released Charles's arm just as James flung himself on him. When the two men rolled together on the ground, there was nothing else for it, but to turn and run, to use the time, the distraction, she had so painfully engineered in order to delve deeper into the mansion. She raced past the stairs, past the open doors, her trail of breadcrumbs the lines and gouge marks of the statuary.

But now she knew! She had seen the shame sinking in Charles's eyes. Only she had not believed such a thing possible.

The hideous truth had been under her fingertips. For in her grip she had felt not the bulky joints of armour, but the smooth, feel of his arm. Instead of muscle, she had grasped steel.

Charles was turning to metal.

The horror of his fate threatened to engulf her. She stumbled for half-a-dozen steps before her footsteps steadied.

One thought carried her through.

Find the Engine.

Find it even if it meant being swallowed up once more.

When the floors changed from marble to linoleum, she knew she was at the back of the house, in the section where the servants lived and where the kitchens and scullery lay. No one came to stop her though.

She could not tell if James and Charles still fought, for with each step she took, the hum increased in intensity.

Deeper, darker and more intense.

Pray James kept Charles occupied long enough for her to find the Engine. She should have guessed what was happening as soon as she had seen Charles. She had always thought it Gine who was the clever one.

But it was Charles who had programmed him.

Charles.

It wasn't Gine alone who came up with the reasons for attracting and distracting her. He had simply been made in his creator's image. At the time, Charles had meant it physically, but of course it passed on to being mentally like him as well.

One of the reasons as to why Charles had not wanted to marry her was clear now. However, knowing Charles, there would not be one reason but three. She had learnt the hard way from Gine.

Berd stumbled upon the door that led out to the back garden, turned the knob and pushed the door open—

Sound blasted in her face, frizzing her hair as the stink of scorching traced fingers against her brow. Her teeth vibrated in her mouth and there was a warm wetness trailing from her nose to her lips. Blood.

Dotted about the overgrown lawn of the Fotheringay back garden was not merely the statuary but also furniture. All arranged in some sort of pattern. As she made her way past the statues she understood the cipher. A simple pattern: concentric circles. The centre was the door of the stables and the inner circles of the circle were mostly empty…

She deciphered the message. The hidden code. She was proven right when as she strode towards the door, a statue-Pan playing his hornpipes-blinked out of sight.

Charles was using the statues and furniture to gauge the range of Gine's power as Gine grew in ability.

The stable doors opened.

She gritted her teeth and continued forward as waves of sleepiness overcame her. Everything around her blurred…

Charles. I love Charles.

Charles, who was turning to steel.

Pain in her chest intensified. It was all her fault.

Chapter 25

I AM NOT leaving. I love you, Charles.

Heat flowed through Berd's body, steaming her alive as waves of sleepiness overcame her.

It must all have been a dream.

A hint of lavender teased her nostrils and she sneezed. Lavender…so painfully familiar…lavender and the room in the book stack. Hope trickled through her and she shook her head, fighting sleepiness.

If she was dreaming then maybe she had never returned home, maybe Charles still carried her…

She shivered and forced her eyes open. "Charles?"

She was back! Back in the book stack. Back in the little blue room. Back in Charles's arms!

She wept as she snuggled against his steel chest. It was akin to embracing a rock, except now she knew why. Even the chrysanthemum in his buttonhole was frozen. Charles must have been at the end of his strength when he carried her. Gine had pumped Charles full of energy and something had gone wrong…

The agony in her chest tightened. She ran her fingers through his jet hair then over his poor frozen face. Snow-white crystals had formed like miniature diamonds on the tips of his lashes and brows. She remembered how in some other life her strangled cry had echoed about the room as cold water swelled up and enveloped her.

Only now there was no water. The panels in the walls were back in place. The door of the elevator was closed and faint white light, as if from hidden daybreak, poured from the cornices of the room.

She massaged her throat, trying to understand what had happened and her palm slid over brocade instead of silk. She stared down at peacock green in place of mauve. Gone were her torn and ripped blouse and pants. Like Charles, they were both attired in the same garments they wore at the Fotheringay mansion. Even his hair was clipped… Either she had really returned or this was this some trick of Gine's.

"Charles, please, please, come back to me."

His skin was ice-blue. His lips blistered and peeled. She knew that if she kissed him she would likely tear her lips on the jagged surface.

She closed her eyes and pressed her mouth onto his. His lips had the texture of frozen custard skin…

Still she hung on, unsure if this was what she was supposed to be doing. In all the fairy tales she had read, it had always been the prince who did the kissing.

The air grew heavy with the sound of rushing water. Its song pressed upon ears. After a minute, she drew back, unable to feel her lips. If only she knew how to kiss.

Then terrified that drawing back might mean losing

him, she pressed down again harder, trying to fill the contours of his lips with hers, banish his cold with her warmth. Unmoving, she waited. Oh, why had she always refused to kiss him before!

She kissed him, again and again and again. The sound of her empty kisses echoed about the room, reminders of failure. Finally, in exhaustion, she pulled back. Or tried to. She was stuck.

Kissing Charles was like kissing a frozen lamppost in the depth of winter. She tried to force her tongue through, to wet enough of the surface so she could escape.

Slowly, ever so slowly her lips began to pull away only…

His moved. His lips moved!

She felt the butterfly flicker of lashes against her cheeks as his eyes opened. So close she was cross-eyed. And then it was no longer her unmoving lips, but his and hers, both moving.

All she heard was water as it pattered down the walls around her. She knew now she could pull apart only she didn't.

She was finally kissing him. And he was kissing her back.

Charles's pupils widened and narrowed and as he focused and saw her, actually saw her, he came back to life with a jerk, his body swayed, collapsed and then they were on the ground, laughing.

"I'm sorry, I'm sorry," they both cried out as they tried to grasp onto and support the other.

Even as they stared at one another, each was leaning forward again only before their lips met, the ground shuddered as if twenty cannons had fired close by.

"What's happening?" Berd called out as Charles yanked her up.

With the elevator door shut, it was impossible to see outside. As soon as she was on her feet, he called out, "Wait here," then released her and hurtled alone towards the elevator.

The sod was going to leave her behind! She raced after him.

Charles turned his head, saw she had followed and groaned. "Please." Worry shone in his eyes.

"No!"

The book stack rattled. She lost her footing. Charles caught her before she fell, but this time instead of demanding she remain, he pulled her inside the elevator as the door slid open.

She was sure they had destroyed the stack's energy source. "How is this possibl—"

"Down!" he hissed, dragging her onto the floor.

Outside the landscape had darkened as if dusk, and neither golden sky nor green-enamelled ground could be seen. They were suspended in a calm cylinder of ginger-scented air. But something had caused the stack to shake.

A mile away, sparks of red light glistened to the left.

"He's started." Charles's voice was grim as he stabbed the button with the number '24' on it.

The door closed. No need to explain who 'he' was. Or 'it'.

Thunder boomed in her ears. The stack rattled, the glass walls shook. Blue bursts followed to the right. She cupped her ears to stop the pain, squeezed her stomach tight as her whole body shook with the next waves of sound.

They were the target.

Once she had suspected Gine of injuring her so she would be forced to partake of the energy. Now she wouldn't put it past him to injure Charles, just so he could pump him full of energy. While Charles had programmed Gine to always save his life, Gine was under no obligation not to kill her.

Between each explosion, a heavy silence pressed like a weight on her chest: a silence more terrifying than the explosions. She had thought at first that it was the explosions she had to fear, but quickly learnt otherwise. It was in that gap of silence, in that interval when she had no knowledge as to whether she would be hit the next second; of being alive or dead; of where the next impact would occur; of the end of onslaught. It was in that long moment she learnt who she was.

Nothing. For all her pride and accomplishments, her wealth and intelligence, in the end she was simply a sack of bones.

Silence, the great leveller, was more frightening than sound.

"Are you all right?" Charles demanded as the ground rocked violently. Something titanic, hidden inside, was erupting.

Her head ducked up. "How's the elevator working?"

Charles pushed her head down protectively. "Why wouldn't it be working?"

"I thought we destroyed this book stack."

"Gine has a lot of energy at his disposal. He's been repairing himself."

Repairing himself.

Thanks to the energy she had brought in with her,

Gine now had a physical form. He had his own two hands. And he could enter the stack. This explained why all the panels were intact. But a machine that could repair itself meant that Gine was becoming more and more invincible by the minute. She had to find out how and from where this energy was coming.

By now it was so bright that she would have believed Charles if he told her they were nearing the sun. Even on the ride there was evidence of Gine's growing power. The elevator reached the top in less than a minute.

The low-ceilinged, dome-shaped room they entered was walled in steel panels, riveted together and lit by hidden lights secreted in the cornices. In the centre rose a copper chair, fronted by a quarter-circle panel filled with controls and what looked suspiciously like a steering wheel. The stink of paraffin and motor oil filled her nostrils.

Charles settled himself in the chair and flicked switches. Banks of ruby lights flashed as the stack's engine restarted. Part of the walls and the roof slid open, giving them a view of half a circumference. Cold air caused her skin to tighten, goose pimpling her arms and legs. It was either that or fear.

Showers of green, blue and red light bloomed, brightening the sky as the explosions tore the air apart. Gigantic dying flowers. Their touch poison. Their scent gunpowder. Even in all this danger, her breath caught at their ethereal beauty.

Thunder exploded, ripping the sky in shock waves, blowing the locks of her hair off her shoulders. Mist peppered her face. She shivered, feeling she was a wishbone wrestled between the hands of giants.

She was actually in battle.

Even when she was on the last carriage on the train she had been indoors. Here she was exposed to the elements, several stories high, and a target.

"Berd!" Charles swivelled to face her. "When the stack starts up, talking will be difficult. I want to apologise. I know I promised not to kiss—"

"No! I wanted to, just as much as you did." She blushed at her admission.

He gave her a tiny, proud smile then pumped a pedal. "Ready?" he called out.

She barely heard him over the roaring of the stack. She nodded and gripped onto the back of his chair.

"Hang on." He released a lever and the book stack rattled, shook and staggered forward. Headlights lit up the ground in front of them like twin tallow eyes in the dark.

"Beats walking," he laughed into her ears. "At least I did something right."

He was blaming himself for Gine. "How can you see?"

He pushed on into the darkness for a while before he answered. "Can't. Half-speed. London fog. Helped." As if the memory cheered him, he halted and gave her a lofty grin.

It reminded her once more of the god she had first met. She grinned back.

"Watch," he instructed as the stack ploughed on again.

It appeared that he was expecting to give her a chance to operate the stack. Charles never explained where they were going. He didn't need to, because there was but one logical target. Gine was becoming too powerful, therefore he had to be destroyed, and the only way to do so was to strike at his heart and brain. Its soul.

The Mill.

The stack's headlight caught on some object that glimmered back, not like polished glass but a dull brown. Charles swung the headlights in a 180-degree arc, searching.

A line of about twenty copper book stacks blockaded their path, resembling naval vessels in formation as they prepared for battle, but otherwise the enamel-green landscape was clear.

She gritted her teeth and tightened her grip on the back of his steel chair. She didn't have to wait long to find out how would Charles handle the situation.

Charles pressed his foot to the floor. Their stack sped up.

She gasped. He was going to crash into them! She buried her forehead into the curve of his neck and shoulder as she waited for the impact, held her breath, looking up barely in time to see their stack crashing through the centre of the copper perimeter. Smashing into them broadside.

On impact the shock waves of a hundred cannons firing exploded in her head. Sound vanished as if her ears had popped multiple times. Her mouth opened, but she heard nothing. Everything appeared to freeze. Even heavy bits of metal that had flown up in the air looked inexplicably as light as eiderdown. Then sound flew back into her ears as the world burst, returning, throbbing painfully into life. Metal debris crashed around them, pounding the landscape like cannon balls.

Her ears were ringing. Her balance shot. Then the front half of the stack dipped and reared upwards like a prancing horse, and she was slipping and sliding, fighting desperately not to lose her grip. For if she did, there was nothing to keep her on the platform. Charles, at least, had his chair.

The whole stack shook as it righted itself. Clouds of metallic dust pocked the air. On her knees and sobbing now that it was over, she pressed her nose to her sleeve to help her breathe, and prayed their stack did not disintegrate.

It held. But it was far from over. She expected Charles to make a run for it, but with great precision, he did the opposite. He reversed.

He was crazy! "What are you doing!"

Charles was already moving their stack to the left. He smashed their stack into the line which toppled to the ground like dominoes. The shock of each mighty collapse slammed like a hand into her chest and her head jerked back repeatedly. She did not think she could take much more punishment, but as each stack thundered to the ground and promptly burst into violent red-and-yellow flames, her screams of fear turned into whoops of joy. Burning paraffin fumes curtained the air, shimmering rainbow auroras.

Charles did the same manoeuvre to the right. Even better, he kept their stack stable as he learnt swiftly how to handle the one he steered. The ground shook and shuddered as the massive structures slammed into the green enamel. Water from boilers spilled onto the ground. Steam hissed upwards.

But the stacks were down.

Breathless, she watched as he navigated them out of

the danger zone. He manoeuvred to the right, but as he did so, she knew their escape had been too easy. Gine was planning something else. Something more deadly. This attack had merely been a warning: Gine observing how they operated for future record.

You've taught me well, Gine.

Lights from the Mill blazed, a Milky Way of stars about half a mile off when Charles slowed the stack. He turned the motor off for the explosions were now behind them. After the constant shuddering and sound, the silence screamed in her ears.

When he pulled her onto his lap, she saw his cheek was gashed and bleeding. She raised her hand to touch his face, but he caught it and pressed it to his lips. His eyes closed for a second and a muscle in his jaw twitched. Then he opened his eyes and gazed into her face, studying every detail of her features. He gently touched the scabs on her bruised lips.

"How I have hurt you. You should hate me. Not have come back," he whispered, pained.

"I had to." She could not look at him, suddenly unaccountably shy.

But even as he pressed a kiss upon her forehead, the ground shook. Something or some things large were heading their way. Yes, Gine had other plans.

But this may be hers and Charles's last moment together. She did not want to rush it. His skin was flushed from the activity of the drive, but chilled thanks to the frigid air. She pressed her lips to his temple where the hair was damp around the hairline and under the sweat, she smelt metal. That explained the liberal application of eau de cologne. She bit her lower lip, held back the tears.

As if he sensed her grief, he wrapped his arms around her. Though it was obvious they were still in danger, his whole focus was on her. His voice was sunshine. "Why?"

"B—because you weren't in that other world."

Charles groaned. "Gine is not going to let us out again."

"He did once—"

"Only because he thought I was dying."

It was true then; Charles really had been dying. She stared down at the ground. "Because of me."

"No. No! Of course not." He embraced her tighter. As if in imitation the walls of the stack creaked. A rivet popped out. The stack could not hold up much longer.

It had been her fault. "It was the water. A short-circuit—"

"It doesn't matter."

"So what do we do now?" She felt him hold his breath then release it slowly.

He spoke carefully. "I want to take you to the Faraday—"

"No!" So that's why he had stopped the stack.

"Please, my darling. You have no idea the dilemma I underwent last night. How much I wanted to see you again. I lost you then. Back there I lost you a second time. I cannot—"

"You did what you did because you love me."

He swore softly, but when he looked into her face, his sapphire eyes were gentle. "You should have remained at your aunt's."

He had sent her away for her own safety. "I can help you. Let me help you."

"You have no idea how strong Gine has become."

"I saw the circles of statuary," she answered stubbornly.

The rumblings were louder now.

The walls shuddered.

He cupped her cheeks. "He's capable of more than just pulling in things that are connected to him, do you understand?"

She nodded. The statue of Pan, though it wasn't in the room with them, she had no doubt it was somewhere in the Engine. As were the other objects Gine had sucked in.

Charles searched her face, his voice strained. "He's been pulling in more people. That's how he got so strong. Only he's turned them into energy. He pulled in all the men that were sent for the Engine."

Gine had swallowed all those people and turned them into energy. And possibly Charles's servants. The house had seemed rather bare. She pressed her hand into her stomach to stop from throwing up.

"Maybe this will convince you I am wrong for you." He tugged at the fingers of his gloves.

"Nothing will." But already she was scared.

She longed to stop him, to tell him that no matter what she would always love him, but the words froze on her tongue as the gloves slid off for underneath his hand was full metal: stainless steel. He flexed his fingers and then tap-tapped the tips together. The clicks she heard reminded of some hideous clockwork apparition. Only this was alive. Living. Charles had become his own mons…

No, she had to believe Charles was in there.

Nausea rose in her. Before she could stop herself she had shuddered and gagged. She pressed her cold fingers against her mouth as she fought the horror coursing through her body.

At her reaction, he smiled grimly. By now the shaking was so loud he had to yell. "So is my chest. Now do you understand?"

Her heart wrenched. "I love you," she squeezed the words out.

He closed his eyes then opened them and in their clear reflection she saw his heart breaking. "You have no idea how long I have waited to hear you say those words, but you cannot mean it. You must not for your own sake. Do you not know I am half machine?"

He was trying to tell her that to survive he would have to continue imbibing energy.

He would become fully machine. An engine.

The explosions were tiny pinpricks. The ground continued to shake. Or maybe it was only her.

"It—it doesn't matter. I still love you. It's—it's…" She reached out and placed her hand on his chest. She could feel no heartbeat. Charles's chest neither rose nor fell. It was as cold as steel.

He watched quietly.

"It's what's inside," she whispered.

"What's inside? I have no heart. Why else am I able to hurt you again and again."

"Then don't make me leave you. You suffered. So did I. Don't make me suffer any more! I can help you."

With precise movements, he pulled on his glove. He did not look at her.

"You are planning to destroy Gine."

He said nothing as he buttoned up his glove, his movements deft.

Beast! He was not going to give her any clues, but

she persisted. "Before you do that you need to program Gine to save you and me. Use an AND GATE."

He halted and narrowed an eye at her. "An AND GATE?"

She could tell he was impressed but trying not to show it. "Yes, when you destroy Gine, you are hoping Gine will remove me from the Engine as my life will be in danger. But you can't guarantee that will happen."

"I see."

"If you use an AND GATE to instruct Gine to save me AND you, and hardwire that instruction in the Mill or use an operation card or whatever it is that you do. Insert that within the Mill rather than in a stack, then we will be saved." She tried not to gloat in her smile.

"What about self-preservation?"

She blinked. "What?"

"Self-preservation. It's what any animal uses to protect itself when in danger. Gine foresees a threat in me so he removes the threat."

"You are his master. He cannot—"

"Bite the hand that…" Charles rubbed his chin tiredly. "What living creature would not kill in order to live?"

Berd closed her eyes. She had not thought this possible, but the American War of Independence…the French Revolution. In history, even kings had lost their heads…

"I don't want Gine to see you as a threat and remove you, but if you are with me the likelihood is greater."

No, surely Gine would obey his programming. Charles had instructed Gine to do everything in his power to keep him alive. Hopefully that instruction was still intact in a stack that was not one of the wrecks burning on the plains behind them.

She snapped open her eyes. It was clear now what she had to do. "Then I perish alongside you. I entered the Engine willingly. I will do what it takes. Besides, what if he doesn't? Do you want me trapped inside the Engine forever?"

"Or you'll what? No, don't tell me. After all only you were foolish enough to re-enter the Engine." He slammed one fist into the steering wheel. "Well, what if we are trapped? Would you still love me if you could never leave the Engine? If I am all there is?"

Trapped inside the Engine… She had entered the Engine in an attempt to win Charles back to her. She had won, in a way. Only she had placed him in danger. She had to get him out. But he was still trying to push her away. Gine had removed Charles from the Engine when he was close to dying. Charles's plan to save them was to come close to dying once more, but Gine would not fall for such a trick again. Gine was smarter than that, but she doubted she could get Charles to see that.

Only one thing to do: Reprogram Gine.

Instruct him to save both of them and to remove them from the Engine immediately.

She would make her way back to the Mill. "You win. I'll wait here," she lied. If she failed then at least she had divided Gine's attention….

Divide and conquer.

Great plan of Gine's, but he didn't have a monopoly on it. She could use it, too.

She could be bait.

Chapter 26

ERD SNATCHED A kiss from Charles's lips and before he could respond, flew out to the elevator.

"Berd!" he called. Though he had begged her to leave, anguish aged his face. She prayed he did not guess what she was about to undertake.

"Go!" she demanded as she inhaled the tantalising taste of ginger. From now on, she would always associate ginger with grief. "Go! Don't wait for me."

Charles clenched the steering wheel, nodded. His eyes were bright with unshed tears, his face pale and distant as the moon as he prepared to dance with Death once more.

She had never loved him more.

She pressed the 'G' button. When she looked back the door had already shut. Gone. This time she was leaving him. The ride was swift and when the door opened, she stumbled out. The hum was louder here on ground level. Noisier than before. She shivered. The dizzying fresh smell of pine made her blink rapidly, but to her surprise she was dry-eyed and excited.

Clear of the stack, she turned around and waved. The top of the stack was a speck. She couldn't see Charles but assumed he had seen her for in less than a minute the stack had rumbled back into motion and was lurching away to meet the other book stacks.

The attacking army of book stacks.

Hundreds of monstrous shadow crabs were scuttling forward on that ghoulish landscape. Pincerless. Amber sparks trailed the ground, the reek of copper and scorching melded with the smell of burnt pine.

She turned away, not wishing to see the battle. She was also running out of time. If Charles failed, there would be no need to reprogram Gine. Charles had mentioned that he had instructed Gine to do whatever it had to do to save Charles's life.

She had to find where Charles had placed that instruction.

If he had told her, she could not recall. The way she understood it, each computer engine basically performed one program. To change programs generally required modifying each engine itself or else inserting fresh cards via the punch reader until Charles came along with his novel ideas of storing past programs in secondary storage. Great innovation only it complicated matters, because it meant that the line of code to save his life could be anywhere.

She doubted Charles would have been stupid enough to place it in a stack. It would mean uploading the program each time to run it. The instruction was too important. Charles would have to have placed it in the Mill. She did not think she needed to find the original instruction. Surely all she needed was to insert a new instruction: Save hers AND Charles's lives.

Then add one more: get them out.

But if it was really that simple Charles would have done so a long time ago. What must have happened was that once Charles had started to execute the program, he was unable to halt its execution. Programs generally executed until the engine ran out of energy or the program finished or there was an error, but this Engine running out of energy meant the end of Charles. And the program never finished because Gine was constantly learning. Correcting any errors.

Engines never allowed the addition of new instructions or the modification of current instructions until the program finished executing. Yet Charles had been able to add that extra instruction. She chewed her lip as she pondered how he had done so. Charles's intelligence was making life complicated. The only conclusion she could come to was that after he added that command something must have happened to stop him modifying the program.

Berd stepped onto moist ground that glowed seaweed green. She had almost reached the waterfall. Ahead the thick ribbon of fluorescent blue burned in the darkness like Jacob's ladder. The waterfall's sapphire light lit up the sides of the cliff face: a taper shining before a masque on a black-and-windless night. Not so long ago she had imagined angels dancing in the air, now silvered outlines of dead men floated in their place, the cold spray of the waterfall their salivary kisses pressed upon her brow. If the water had laughed before, now it wept.

Then the ground leapt like a blanket, shaken as if spread out. She tumbled forward a couple of times before she rolled to a stop.

Giant drops of boiling water seared the ground. Steam jetted into the air where they landed. A book stack must have collapsed!

Berd screamed as one of the monster drops landed on her arm and scorching pain wracked her body. Clenching her teeth, she fought for control as bits of broken metal thudded, smashing the ground around her. She curled her body, cowered, and when the deluge lessened, pushed to her feet, relieved to hear the battle still raged behind her—Charles was alive.

She scrambled forward, hugging her injured arm to her side, refusing to look behind. Smooth as a pane of glass, the waterfall was a window to another world: a vista that burned and boiled with a slow azure fire. Silver shimmered up from its depths, rising as the throbbing veins of insect wings carried the metamorphosing dead to new life.

Berd's wound, swollen from shoulder to elbow, chafed with every movement. Excruciating pain, made her eye the energy with hope, for she knew that energy would not just ease the pain but eradicate it, completely.

As if the waterfall knew, the air before Berd thinned, quickening her progress while currents pushed, eddying at her from behind.

Forward. Forward. Hurry. Hurry. Voices in her head called.

She had to look behind the pane. She had to find out. She had to. Any indecision dissolved into clouds, dissipating like cirrus on a stiff breeze. No conflict. No pain. No Charles. Not even Gine. Only beauty and love and peace. She was about to step behind the veil when a hand rested upon hers, frail as a baby's breath. She looked up into familiar eyes: James.

Berd's scream broke the trance.

"James!"

No, not him! Not her brother!

Her mind had been so much on Charles, that when she neared the Engine she had not thought through the consequences of her disappearance. What tortured her most was that Gine had not turned James into some tangible life-form, like he had done her and Charles.

James was still dressed in his dove-coloured morning suit. He lifted a finger to his lips. His eyes were hollow, yet she could see the self-same determination in them when he jumped on Charles. The door of the Faraday car opened as he led her towards it. She urged him in, but he shook his head. Charles had mentioned that Gine could not enter. But for some reason, neither could James.

She sat and the door shut. Bending forward, she covered her face in her hands. In the silence of the Faraday car, the ghost memories of the two men she loved most in the world hovered around her.

I was a fool to think I could win Charles and defeat Gine.

She had murdered her brother and caused her love to close with death. If only she had retired to that cottage in Wales, for then she would have hurt no one.

The first time she had ridden in this car she had been in love with Charles. Only she had fought it, sacrificing everything to escape the Engine even to the point of sacrificing him. Now she was sacrificing everything for that love.

Gine was dangerous. He had shown that time and time again. This time he had almost succeeded in getting her into the energy, and if it were not for James…

She pressed her fingertips to her temples. She had to defeat Gine, or she had damned them all.

Around her the velvet silence fell like a heavy curtain. She had no idea if the car was going and presumed it was, not that she had any way to stop or to start it, if it failed. Or open it. Charles's plan was for her to remain inside while he fought off the other book stacks. He had reasoned that inside the car, she would be out of Gine's reach. Yet if she was out of reach, Gine would not be able to transport her out of the Engine.

In a way, it was the perfect trap.

She shook her head. Charles rarely made mistakes. It was simply further evidence that he was worried and exhausted. It didn't matter anyway; she was not planning on remaining in the Faraday car. She was going to the Mill. If she failed because Gine culled her, at the very least, she had bought Charles time.

Her right arm throbbed. A sticky substance oozed down the length of her arm as her blister ruptured, plastering her silk sleeve to her pelisse. She wiped her forehead with her good hand then pushed the pain out of her mind.

Countless times, she had focussed on a problem and the hours had flown by. Countless times, she had gone into the stables at breakfast only to come out at supper time. She would open the stable door, and stagger out to find her dinner on a tray by the door, stone cold. Or half-eaten by the neighbour's calico cats. Countless times…

She had been hungry then. Not for food. Only for a solution. So many times she had gone to bed, angry with herself because she had not found an answer, only to find that as soon as she had placed her head on her pillow, the solution had arrived. She had gotten dressed and gone back down again in the freezing cold.

Numerous were the episodes when she had forgotten everything else except for the joy of what she was doing. This frame of mind was what she had to achieve. Be so single-minded and focused in order to reprogram Gine.

The door opened.

Outside the trees gleamed with an eerie slickness as blue light nestled like beetles in their cracks, crawling out when she neared. She stumbled on, the glare of the Mill calling her, trying desperately to ignore the pain from her right arm.

Light and the hum grew as she travelled forward.

The landscape changed, becoming a paper cut-out of black and white. Heat from the Mill beat like a furnace, and she smelled charring metal as her cheeks grew uncomfortably hot.

What worried her most was the intense light. Brilliant beams, as if the sun was low on the horizon, sliced into her eyes, obliterating her vision. She moved forward only with great difficulty, shielding her eyes with her fingers, constantly walking into metal trees. Her pelisse and hands were scored and cut.

She had thought the Mill a single tower rising from amongst the trees, but it had grown into towers of cast iron and glass, ten times the height of the Crystal Palace in Penge. Gold and black imprints of its image rose on the back of her lids when she closed them, showing her a dazzling structure more in keeping with the Hagia Sophia of long ago Constantinople.

Holy wisdom.

Silver balls of lightning burst from within, tailing off in dazzling streams that veined tantalisingly across the surface of the glass walls. But closeness caused the pain in her right arm to flare even more.

Finally, her heart pounding savagely, Berd stood before the glass walls of the Mill, squinting behind the shield of her clasped fingers, tasting browning metal in her lungs. She had just reached out one hand to touch the surface, when she heard her name called.

"Berd!" A familiar voice shouted.

She whipped in the direction of the caller, some distance away to the right, at first eager and then confused. The voice had sounded like Charles. Her heart skipped a beat. No, it was more likely Gine pretending to be Charles in order to stop her from entering. Charles may have improved his driving greatly, but there had been hundreds of book stacks.

Frantic, she turned, intending to search for a door when a shadow lunged at her.

She screamed and jumped back. For one split second, the intense white light of the Mill was cut off by the figure's body, before it slammed against the inner walls of the Mill. She stared, unable to look away, as the figure was wracked with electricity, mouth open, head tilted back.

But only as it sprawled to the ground did she realise that the figure was inside. Inside the Mill!

How did it get within so swiftly?

She would have sworn the earlier voice had been some distance away. And it had called from the right. But something had lunged for her from the left...

She had heard neither its horrific screams nor smelt the burning of its charred limbs because it was within the glass confines. Had it not been, it would have grabbed her. Yet she had heard it earlier. The only conclusion she could come to, was that it was not the same figure who had cried out.

Common sense deemed the figure inside to be Gine, but if it was Gine then it made no sense for him to leap at her if contact with the Mill's glass walls caused such a heinous incident. Gine would know not to touch the walls. But then so would Charles. The difference would be that Charles would leap at the walls if it would save her life.

The figure behind the glass walls…the figure with the sky-blue eyes. For one incredible second, she had thought she was staring into the face of Charles. But she had left him back in the stack…unless Gine had trapped Charles, placing him inside the Mill. Anything was possible with Gine.

All thought of escape or even of reprogramming vanished. Immediately, it was far more important to find out who the figure inside the Mill was because then she would know the identity of the figure on the right. And know whom she kissed in the book stack; whom she had pledged her love to…

Lightning scored the skies overhead and the trees around her seemed to jump up. Thunder cracked a second later.

The Engine was under attack.

"Berd!" The figure to her right reached her.

Berd swung around a tree, keeping it between her and the figure as she tried to determine if the figure was Charles or Gine. She tried to stare into his eyes, but like her, he was squinting through the fingers of one hand as he shielded himself from the heinous glare of the Mill. She could not tell.

"Come! Hurry." He reached forward to grasp her arm only she ducked out of the way.

"What the hell!" he sputtered. "The Engine is being attacked. We need to get out!"

She felt stupid as she shouted, "Who are you?" The truth was that she had no way of determining if he was telling a lie.

The figure cursed loudly and vehemently. "Don't be daft, princess. We don't have time for games. We need to leave before the Engine blows up. Come on!" Again he reached to grasp her arm.

Instead, she kept up a two-step round the metal trees, constantly out of reach but where she could see the figure on the right, which certainly looked like Charles.

But then both figures did.

As she agonised over the identity of the two figures, the left figure, the one behind the glass walls, crashed against the glass again. It was thrown backwards in an explosion of white hot sparks.

"Who is that?" She pointed one shaking finger at it.

The right figure stiffened. "Can you not even tell us apart now?" The edge of his voice trembled with disbelief.

If the right figure really was Charles then she was insulting him by confusing him with Gine. She was risking their lives because she hesitated. But she had to be sure.

Again Gine had tricked her. He had made her focus on something else other than her objective: reprogramming.

And time was running out.

Gine was good. No, Gine was brilliant. A pity he was not on her side.

"I need to know. I need to know who you are. If you are truly Charles then I apologise. But I need to know," she insisted. "That figure has been throwing itself at the glass walls, almost electrocuting itself in the process. Why is it doing that?" Unless it was Charles trying to protect her from Gine.

Lightning flashed across the sky.

The figure on the right spoke through gritted teeth. "It is hard to destroy stacks without destroying some of the Engine's memory. It probably can't remember how to get out."

"Charles has never lied to me."

Thunder boomed overhead. The leaves of the metal trees shook as if in a strong wind and she winced as some fluttered perilously close to her. The tang of motor oil glistened on the air.

He sighed heavily. "I am Charles, and I'm not lying. Now please, please, please *come*, before that thing breaks through."

She was almost convinced. "But how did you get up so fast?"

He tilted his head to the heaven, rolling his eyes, such a Charles-like expression that she longed to believe. "I parked the stack near the top of the plateau."

"But how did you know I was here? You're Gine."

"I'm Charles —"

The glass walls of the Mill cracked. The figure on the left was almost through.

The figure on the right grabbed her round the waist. She whimpered when he brushed against her right arm but turned and ran with him.

"Can it…can it break through?"

"Yes, now run! Run for your life because he will be fast."

"But who is it?" cried Berd as she picked up the hem of her skirts and ran.

"It is all that remains of Charles. But I wouldn't stop to speak to him. His sole objective is to cull you."

The glass wall crumbled just as something inside her disintegrated.

A bone-chilling roar filled the air and Berd knew the creature had fixed its gaze on her: the figure on the left. The creature who had once been Charles. Her love. Which could only mean she was holding Gine's hand. Her enemy.

As if he sensed her repugnance, Gine whipped his hand out of hers. Then he shoved her hard between the shoulder blades.

"What are you doing?"

"Run! Run! Run! I'll hold him off as long as I can!"

All Berd could do was to run and keep running, or it could catch her.

She longed to know how Charles could have changed so much. Or how could Gine call himself Charles. But the selfish question that burned in her mind was if she would reach the Faraday car in time.

Chapter 27

THE DOOR OF the Faraday car cracked shut as soon as Berd entered. She slumped to the ground, too exhausted to clamber onto the seat and dug her fingers into her sides to stop the air, keening in and out of her lungs, from cutting like sheets of metal. Her injured right arm dragged like the chain of an anchor.

Her agonised breathing echoed in the enclosed space. When she lifted her head from the floor, she found she was shivering. Nothing was making sense. She had entered the Engine to find out why Charles had refused to love her, hoping to win him back, but instead, things had gone horribly wrong.

Charles, her love, was trying to kill her. Gine, her tormentor, was risking life and limb to save her, and she had no idea how all this had happened. Gine's lie, saying he was Charles, made her far from grateful to him. But if he was speaking the truth then it meant that Charles was doomed.

Too soon the door opened.

She peered out. She was down on the glass-green

plains, where the wind blew the odour of burnt pine, motor oil and paraffin from the wrecks of half-a-dozen blazing book stacks onto her face. She remembered seeing hundreds. No doubt Gine was waiting for when she was at her lowest to unleash them. She didn't need to look at the blood-seared sky to know she was in hell.

Where are you, Charles?

The landscape shook. Lightning scored its nails into the skies. She scrambled out, rubbing her eyes and nose. A book stack, still intact, leaned next to the cliff. That had to be the original book stack. It was her only hope, though where she would go, she had no idea. Maybe the platform Charles had mentioned so long ago…

She slammed into the elevator as thunder crackled. Cool ginger-scented air of the elevator fanned against her, drying the tears she was trying to hold back as she rode it up. Then the door opened, and she stumbled out. She was settling herself in the empty seat when she heard a cry.

"Wait!"

She looked up and across the empty space to see Gine on the top of the plateau, hobbling towards the stack, towards her.

Gine, who had lied to her. Gine, who had called himself Charles. Gine: who was supposed to have Charles inside him. In the sepia light, his clothes appeared torn, his face a mess of bruises. If he expected sympathy from her he had come to the wrong person.

Then she saw Charles, or what was left of him, a heap on the ground. No, not a heap, it was rising. His torso, his husk, as stiff as a tree trunk, a hollow tree, for all his substance was gone. She could not deal with either Charles or Gine now.

The Charles-creature was Gine's problem. He had tricked her. And now if he expected her to wait for him he was mistaken. She gave one short, scornful laugh then turned to the controls as she tried to figure out how to work this thing.

Thankfully, she had the experience of driving her autocar, and she had watched Charles — No, Gine — earlier. She flicked switches. Her face heated at the memory of his deception.

Hurry, hurry. Hurry before Gine reached her. The stack swung away when Gine was six feet away from the edge of the plateau.

Good. She clenched her teeth and rotated the stack a hundred and eighty degrees.

"Berd, please."

She would be a fool to turn around; Gine had tried to kill her. The term he preferred was: cull.

And he had done something to Charles.

But if Charles is really inside Gine…

Blast! Blast! Blast!

She turned the stack to face Gine. There was but twelve feet of air between them. And the Charles-creature was closing.

Gine was standing, arms loose by his side. "Please." His face was at peace as if he did not expect her to take him. But it made no sense why he would need her help. He was in charge of this place. She had seen him melt into the surroundings, into solid steel walls on numerous occasions.

Gine's chest heaved with the effort of speaking. "I can't kill him, do you understand? I can't kill him. But he can kill me."

Leaving Gine was murder.

Berd told herself she was a fool, but she moved the stack to close half the distance. "Jump!"

No one said she had to make it easy for him.

Gine leapt, sprawling face-down in a heap onto the copper platform. So he wasn't really that helpless. But she could not make out what he was playing at. She didn't wait to see if he was all right, but turned the stack and moved away from the cliff. Away from Charles…

She pressed her trembling lips into a straight line as the stack swayed and staggered like a drunken camel. Behind her she heard Gine's shouts, the slam of his body as he attempted desperately not to fall off the polished platform.

She spread her lips in a mirthless smile. It was her turn to monopolise the chair. When she felt they had travelled enough distance to be safe, she halted the stack, but did not extinguish its engine. Then she swivelled the chair to face Gine.

The platform was empty.

She gasped. He must have fallen off! She shot up from her seat just as she saw his knuckles whiten against the edge of the platform. He hauled himself back up, his face red with the exertion in the dirty brown light.

"How could you?" she screamed at him, throwing all her anger and frustration into her words.

He shook his fist and shouted back, but she couldn't hear him over the rattle of the engine and the storm. Lightning scattered silver streaks across the sky as she switched the engine off. As the stack quivered to a stop, Gine pushed himself into a sitting position. His chest heaved from the effort as if he were actually breathing.

Thunder shook the air.

"I cried out countless times for you to stop! Where did you learn to drive, if one could even call that driving?"

She raised a delicate finger. "Not one word about women drivers. Or over the edge you go." She flicked the air to demonstrate.

His face whitened. But she was in control. "How could you trick me like this?" she demanded.

"Trick you? What do you mean? I saved your life."

"I meant the kiss."

His scowl promptly vanished, replaced by a grin that showed how much he had enjoyed it. "I opened my eyes to find you kissing me."

She spoke through clenched teeth, "I thought you were Charles. I thought I was kissing him."

He arched a brow. "I am Charles. You were kissing him. Me."

She stilled. "What do you mean?" Her voice was tight.

"I explained it to you before." Gine tilted his head back, indicating the walls of the plateau two miles away.

'I?' He must mean Charles. Charles had made mention about how he and Gine were merging each time he partook of the energy. Only right now Gine seemed to alternate into being Gine one minute and Charles the next. Then she remembered she had seen such confusion in him before. After their ride in the hot air balloon and in the elevator, Charles had appeared as if fighting some bitter internal battle. Gine had been trying to take him over back then. And even that once in the book stack when he almost crushed her hand.

"Earlier you said you were Charles. That is the only reason I turned back. Then you called that—it—whatever remains of Charles. Who is the creature? Explain what you mean or I'll throw you back." She placed a finger on a switch.

Gine scrambled to his feet.

"Stay. Where. You. Are," she ordered.

He shrugged and dropped obediently. "Very well. Charles told you about the line of code."

Her heart almost stopped. Surely he did not mean that line of code!

"Charles programmed me to always save his life."

Perspiration dampened her body and she sank back onto the chair.

"What I did, I did because of my programming. If a program performs a bad line of code, is that program bad? Remember, I have no choice in the matter. If I tell you, promise you won't throw me off?"

She wet her lips. "I promise. Go on."

"He made me always do what I had to, to save his life. But how could I accomplish this task, if he were not in the Engine?"

She nodded. So that was why Gine had refused to allow Charles to leave the Engine, because Gine required Charles to be in the Engine in order to protect him. That also explained why Gine stopped Charles from reprogramming him. Gine was trying to protect Charles from himself. Unfortunately, it made perfect sense.

"When you entered the Engine the situation changed. Radically. Suddenly, he wasn't so much interested in saving his life…" He gave her an awkward smile.

"But mine. So when I asked him not to partake of the energy, I was in one sense killing him."

"That's why I wanted to remove you from the Engine."

"Why didn't you?"

He smiled sarcastically as lightning flashed. "There is more than one way of dying."

As if on cue thunder crashed. Ozone tainted the air.

She half-closed her eyes, her lashes fluttered from the weight of the truth. Now she understood. If Gine had removed her, he would have broken Charles's heart. That's why Gine had sent the second swarm of bits. He confirmed what she had suspected. That he had been trying to keep Charles alive.

"I would have succeeded if you hadn't been around. Then when you asked him to find a way to stop the book stack, the room filled with water."

Lightning flooded the air with light, swirling dizzily above her head like water. She felt as if she were back in the stack once more, unable to breathe, drowning.

"You had no choice but to pump him full of energy. Only there was a short circuit." Her voice was dead flat when she spoke.

He sighed. "He kept attempting to sacrifice himself for you. Trust me. It was hard to fulfil that command. But I did in the end."

His words chilled her. "You let me and Charles out."

"I had to because he was dying. I pumped him full of energy or else he would have succumbed. But after you left the stable with your brother, Charles discovered he was…" He rubbed his knuckles against his nose.

"Part Engine. Not just mentally but also physically."

Gine gave a little laugh. "You make it sound like a horrible thing."

She ignored his quip. "So when Charles discovered he was part Engine…"

"He decided two things: The first was that he would destroy me. The second was that he couldn't marry you."

So now she knew the first reason why Charles would not marry her. But she needed to find out the second, and the third. She pressed a hand against her stomach.

"I tried to save his life and then later my own. Then you re-entered the Engine. My instructions said nothing about letting him back in. I tried to keep him out, but he kept on wanting to get back in, because he was trying to get to you. He hurt himself badly the first time he got in. I knew he would hurt himself as badly the second time. So badly I would have no choice but to inject him with more energy."

Gine had tried to keep Charles out or Charles would have become an engine. But thanks to Charles's stubbornness he didn't succeed and Charles had become an engine. All along Gine had been trying to save Charles. He was a better friend to Charles than she had been to him. "But I didn't get pumped…"

Gine nodded slowly. "I admit statistically I have only a population size of two. I had to pump you full of energy. You see your muscles were paralysed. Your heart went into spasms. Basically, I had to force you to breathe or else you would have suffocated. As you have not had much energy in you, you survived the process the second time better than he did."

Than he did…

Lightning blazed, tearing the sky apart, exposing the truth on Gine's face. Thunder rumbled, rocking the whole landscape. She kneaded her stomach to stop the nausea rising. The electrical storm overhead was nothing to the storm inside.

"Each time I pumped Charles full of energy, he was turning into an engine. A program. As he lay dying, I did the logical thing. He loved you. His love was killing him so I switched it. Only because of the short-circuit it went rather badly. He doesn't just hate you now…"

Cold fingers clutched her throat. "He wants to cull me."

Cull. Kill.

Lightning leapt across the sky. Thunder followed. Then the landscape went black, except for the orange fires from the wrecked book stacks that at two miles off resembled dying embers. The turquoise waterfall thinned to a blue thread. The Mill, a milky way of silver stars, glimmered in inky blackness casting little useable light.

Her world was ending. Because she was dangerous for Charles, Gine tried to remove her from the equation. It was the logical solution.

A flag. A switch. A toggle.

Just like that and Charles's love for her was gone.

"You saved my life when the lightning struck." Berd's voice was raw. "You saved my life again in the stack. Back there you saved my life again. But you were never programmed to do so." She stared into Gine's face. "You saved my life countless times though I was bad for Charles."

"Yes, bad. Bad. Very bad." Gine absent-mindedly brushed non-existent long hair off his face. After a couple of flicks, when his fingers contacted only with air, he looked up and gave her a sheepish smile. For some reason, she could see him more clearly now. Her eyes were getting used to the darkness.

It seemed normal to speak in the gaps between the thunder and lightning, to feel the shadowed presence during the blackness that was Charles…

"Why do you always save me?" she persisted.

"Why do I always save you?" Gine gave a bad-tempered snort. "Utter stupidity. Figure out why, and you'll know precisely what is going on."

"But that's, that's not possible, is it?"

His answer was a tight-lipped smile.

"No, it can't be. It's only because there's a part of him in you." Berd nodded, desperate to agree with her answer. Yes, Charles had explained it all to her. He had merged with the Engine. Parts or all of him were now part of it. She looked down at her chest. Then his. Gine's own had been cold.

Gine rose from the floor and strode over to her. He picked up her hand and placed it on his chest.

Beneath her palm she could feel the thump of his heartbeat even through his lemon satin waistcoat. The thunder in the sky seemed to have settled in his chest. He was turning into Charles just as Charles was turning into an engine.

"Yes," he said shortly. His lower lip quivered as if he were trying to hold back some emotion. Under his long black lashes, his shining eyes were iridescent blue. They watched her every move. Just like Charles used to…

It was madness to think an engine was in love with her. Really in love with her. At first she had thought it was because a part of Charles was in Gine, but looking into his face now…

She snatched her hand back. "You murdered James!"

"Did I?" He cocked his head, looking so much like Charles, especially now his eyes were the same colour. Standing this close, she could smell him. That familiar boyish scent. The taint of metal was gone. He was living, breathing, and waiting for her to say the word.

When she breathed out, he breathed in.

She itched to slap him. "What do you mean? Of course you did. I saw him!"

"He never entered the Faraday car."

"You sucked in James."

"I created an illusion of James."

She glared at him. "I don't believe you."

"If I hadn't done so, you'd have entered the waterfall. Then you would have been turned into an engine, too."

There was only one reason, she could think of as to why he had stopped her. "You're mad."

Gine flinched. His face hardened. "Am I? Madder than he? I could have let you die so many times."

It was true.

The blackness of the night flitted inside her. She raised her chin as lightning tore across the sky, wanting to be sure he saw her face clearly, saw the hatred, and tasted her revenge. "I cannot love a murderer. Charles isn't a murderer. You are. You're the murderer. You killed all the workmen. Sucked them up into the Engine to turn them into energy. Used them."

His face cracked. The skin thinned, pressing against the outline of the bones. For a moment, he bore a haunted, gaunt expression then he covered his face with his hands.

Thunder rumbled. She had finished him.

"You're right. I am. Man is made in God's image. Gine is made in my image. I have created a monster. Therefore I must be a monster."

His voice was the same. His body was the same. Only something, something inside had changed. Something else had taken over.

"No!" she gasped, aghast at what she had done. Gine must have morphed fully into Charles now. And she had unjustly accused Charles of multiple atrocities. She tried to take it back though she knew it was too late. "No. You are not a monster."

He never heard her.

Charles's voice was perfectly calm. "Soon I will be responsible for your death. Already I am responsible for the deaths of so many."

"I love you…"

"How can you love a monster?"

"You can't blame yourself for what Gine did."

"I programmed him. I put those thoughts in him. I made him do what he did."

"You aren't a monster. You love me. Monsters don't love."

"Frankenstein's Monster loved."

Frankenstein's Monster did love. And when his love was rejected the Monster turned bad. She had rejected Gine's love. She stared open-mouthed at Charles.

"Monsters kill. Gine is me, don't you understand. I am becoming Gine just as much as he is becoming me."

She grasped his hand and clutched it to her heart. "Then go away from Gine! Come with me."

"I created him. I should have stopped him. I didn't and it's too late."

That was it. That was the second and the third reasons. Charles would not marry her for three reasons: because he was turning into a monster; because he had wanted to keep her away from him to stop her from coming into Gine's reach, and the third reason was now clearer than ever—Charles was addicted to the energy.

Even as she opened her mouth to deny the truth, the sky glimmered blue. Electrifyingly blue. Waterfall energy blue. The iridescent blue of Charles's eyes.

What a fool I was to never before have noticed the connection!

What had been the waterfall elongated, stretching like molten toffee. Then taller. Wider. Two branches shot out to the left and right. Arms.

Her heart pounded. "What's happening?"

"He's entered the waterfall," he said dully.

A figure wavered in the blueness. The Charles-creature was growing. She shook her head, refusing to believe her eyes.

"He's absorbing all the energy." Even as Charles/Gine spoke, he grasped hold of her arm, attempting to lever her out of her chair.

The gall! "No!" She slapped his hold off. "I'm driving!"

"You can't drive!"

Beast! She screwed up her face and started up the Engine.

He glared at her. "We have five minutes if we're lucky, before he gets here."

Gine/Charles was planning to run...

It was then she noticed his silver eyes. The energy was affecting him, too. But if Gine had Charles in him then Charles would have Gine in him, too...

She jumped up. "You want to drive? Then drive!"

He eyed her suspiciously as he plunked himself down in her place. She kept her mind blank, smiled demurely, moved around and then gripped onto the back of his steel chair.

If Charles/Gine thought he had won, he was in for a shock.

As he swivelled the stack in the opposite direction to the Mill, she shouted. "No!"

He looked up startled. His bewilderment allowed her to reach over his shoulder, grab the wheel and swing it. The stack pivoted in the direction of the Mill before he seized the wheel. She clung on. Neither would let go. They glared at each other across the wheel.

Then he threw one hand into the air. "You call me mad? That's suicide!"

As if to prove him right, the plain was instantly populated with stacks popping out of the ground. She had no doubt the Charles-creature was controlling them. Charles had won this world but lost his soul.

She pointed remorselessly in the direction of the Mill. "We're not making a run for it."

"I can't kill him."

"I can't kill him either. But the last thing I want is

for him to be loose in the real world." She swallowed hard. "This way, he doesn't get out."

Gine slowed the engine.

She stomped on his right foot, forcing the pedal down. The stack sped up again.

"I see," he spat. "This is why you didn't mind me driving. Can I make mention this is my foot you're squashing. I'll have you know it isn't metal."

"You're lucky I haven't clapped hands over your eyes." She removed her foot, endeavouring to look as stern as possible, but inside she was smiling.

She had found Gine's weak spot. And she had proven it when she had startled him as she seized the wheel. Driving apparently took a lot of effort and while Gine drove, he wasn't able to read her brain to see what she was thinking. It gave her time to plan at least for now, when there was only one Mill. Imagine what Gine would be like with two Mills or more. Heaven forbid.

Berd had deduced that the Engine had been reading her mind the whole time. It was the only logical explanation as to how he was always one step ahead of her.

After all, they were all energy.

"Keep going," she ordered.

He kept going, though his lips moved.

No doubt he was calling her names. As she was doing the exact same thing to him, she ignored him. Fair's fair.

She was asking him to destroy the Mill. This time it was for real. Earlier because Gine had headed the stack in the Mill's direction, she had assumed wrongly the destruction of the Mill was his objective, but he had never mentioned anything about doing so. *Then* it had been a ploy. *Now* she was making it clear she was prepared to destroy the Mill.

The time for bluffing was over.

She had expected after his earlier tactics for the other stacks to dodge and manoeuvre out of the way, but the only stack dodging and manoeuvring was theirs. If a stack stepped into their path, he simply went around. It made their course circuitous rather than straight, taking them longer to get to their objective.

"Ram them!"

"I can't," Gine fumed.

"Why?"

"Instructions to remove us from the Engine are in one of them."

He had to be jesting. "What about earlier?"

"I removed the memory from those stacks I downed. There are no more spares."

She could have strangled him. Gine had tricked her once more.

The ground jumped up. A couple of book stacks to their right toppled over. At first she thought Gine had done something clever. But the ground was actually shaking.

The monstrous Charles-creature had started to walk.

Time had run out.

Each time one of its massive legs landed, the plains shook. It was coming for them. At its speed, they had less than a minute. And they were still a mile off from the Mill.

Two more stacks toppled to their left.

"Ram them! Forget the instructions," she screamed.

Their stack swayed recklessly as he stepped them over the wrecks.

The sky was lighter. Half a mile away, she could see the Mill. Pure white light sparked continuously, neurons passing data from one end to the other, an invisible weaver weaving an invisible garment from an invisible pattern on an invisible loom. When she and Charles died no doubt their energy would be part of that invisible material.

The Charles-creature roared.

Berd screamed as every object glowed luminescent as it blew apart. Each individual particle shimmered. Then they all came back together again. The stacks jerked and rumbled forward. Only their stack remained motionless.

What new game was Charles/Gine playing at now? "Keep going!" she screamed.

He pumped the pedal madly. "Can't! The stack's done for. He's removed the energy. Run! Run for it!" Gine jumped to his feet, grabbed her and they raced for the elevator.

The air sizzled, crackling and crinkling as if electric blue ants marched up and down invisible lines. The edges of the platform shrunk as if eaten by termites as the Charles-creature bent down.

Her hair blew wild across her face. As the elevator door closed, she saw the Charles-creature's fingers touch the chair where they had been sitting seconds ago. It burned into metallic sawdust. That sizzling end was what was in store for them.

As she stared at Gine his face glowed azure, as if he were some animistic god. His fingers were fused into the control panel. Though the Engine was breaking up, he was causing the elevator to work.

"You're the Engine. Seize control back!" she demanded.

"I can't. It's too late. That's the last of it."

Couldn't or he wouldn't? "Don't be absurd! Why not?"

He could only stare at her. He pulled his fingers out and his face returned to his normal colour. The door slid open. They were on the plains again.

"Run," he growled.

He must be joking. "No," she cried out. "I'm not going."

Gine clenched his fists in frustration. "Do you want to die here?" He pushed her out of the elevator.

He was serious. But she was, too.

She stared at him as it dawned on her what was happening. Gine was deliberately removing the 'Engine' from him. That was her only conclusion. But if he removed the Engine then all he would be left with was…and then she understood.

He was.

Gine was the Engine, or had been. He had been the servant in this place and then the master, only as he grew, became more Charles-like, he understood that being master was not what he wanted. He had learnt from Charles.

Power wasn't everything. Life wasn't everything. Love was.

Her voice broke as she spoke. "I once left Charles. I'm not doing it again."

His hands dropped to his sides.

She stared into his eyes. "Who are you?"

Walls of copper sulphate blue slid down around them. His face contorted as if in pain.

Tears filled her eyes. "Who are you? Really. Deep down."

Frustration cloaked his face. He gritted his teeth and glared at her. "You should have run…"

The walls began closing in.

"You said you loved me."

He glanced away though there was nowhere to look, for the walls were almost touching them.

"If you are Charles, then know that I love you."

His face tightened. He tilted his chin defiantly at her. Everything around her sparkled as if turning to stardust. She could barely hear herself speak. Bubbles were popping in her ears as her molecules dissembled.

"But if you are not Charles then be Charles. Be Charles and I will love you."

As his face disintegrated, he laughed. "You knew we weren't going to make the Mill. You knew. You tricked me. Did you accomplish your objective?"

She nodded. Her insides were melting.

"Ah, but you wore green," he muttered as he stared into her eyes. "You wore green." Then he smiled and all that was left were his blue eyes. And she was blinded.

Chapter 28

"**B**ERD!"

Berd blinked. Walls rose around her as she lay prone on the ground. Only they appeared to be made of wood. Oak. She was in a building of some sort. She opened her mouth to answer, but managed a croak. The odours of roasting wood and scorched metal billowed over her. Her nostrils flared. She gulped for air. She had been breathing in smoke that scorched her throat. But smoke meant fire…

Danger.

She pushed herself up. The world swirled dizzily, and she collapsed, nauseous, unable to move. Not just her throat hurt, but every inch of her. She did not remember ever aching so much. She cleared her throat in order to shout, to say where she was, but again managed only a guttural whimper.

The voice cried again, "Berd!" from somewhere outside the building, more urgently this time. James!

Help me!

Beside her a figure rose, coughing to his feet.

"Charles," she whimpered. Please, let it be true that they were really back.

Charles turned, his blue eyes, red-rimmed, focused, then he smiled and his arms slid around her. His strength engulfed her. They were back! Back! Back in the Fotheringay stables. Gine had kept his word and returned them.

"Come on." Charles's voice burred; he tightened his embrace. Somehow the room appeared to float. No, it was not the room. It was the Engine in the middle of the room that created the illusion: the Engine that with its copper platters and dazzling towering carriage spires, still resembled a miniature city of steel and gold. The air around it wavered, mimicking currents in a fast-moving stream. The strong odour of burning metal emanated, thrumming from it, the heat licking the walls of the room and blackening the wood. But the scent was dissipating, each pulse weaker. The hum dimmed. The Engine was dying. Gine was dying.

Together they staggered out the door. Before they were through, hands seized her.

"Berd!"

James! She could not remember ever being so glad to see him before. She threw one arm around him, but the other remained possessively around Charles's waist. She would never let him go… She gasped. Her right arm no longer hurt. Gine had healed it. She had a lot to be thankful to him for.

Her brother glared at Charles but made no move to impede his progress. The three of them stumbled forward. When they reached the safety of the kitchen door, they turned to observe the stables. The whole wooden building shimmered and throbbed with a strange white radiance as if a star had descended to earth. The surrounding grass shimmered as if soaked in melted glass. Scents of cinnamon toast and peach jam rippled the air.

"What happened?" James wiped his brow. He sported a black eye she assumed was courtesy of Charles. Their feud was forgotten as he handed a steel flask to Charles.

Charles hesitated, but then took it and held it up in a toast of truce. "Thank-you."

Gruffly, James nodded before turning to her. His tone was noticeably gentler, as he said, "I'll get you water, Berd."

She barely heard him for she was reaching out one hand for Charles's cheek. The cut was gone. Charles bent his head as she tilted hers upwards. Their lips had almost touched when they heard James clear his throat.

"Your water."

They jumped back. Berd's heart was still thumping wildly, but it was the flask of brandy she reached for.

Charles's said nothing, only grinned as James's mouth dropped open. He handed the flask over to Berd.

As Berd drank, she heard James snap his mouth shut. But neither of them said anything as she had her drink and then handed the flask back to James.

Even after his drink, Charles's chest heaved as if he had run two marathons. He wiped his mouth with the back of his hand. "I take it, Lovelace, that the Engine didn't swallow you up." The corners of Charles's eyes crinkled.

James replaced the flask in his pocket before speaking. His eyes bore the look of a man who had seen strange things and was still trying to work them out. He spoke as if he had been planning for a while what he was about to say, "I saw you go through into nothingness. Then I ploughed into some kind of wall. I pushed against it, but couldn't get through. I threw sticks, anything I could lay my hands on, at it. Couldn't believe my eyes, when the ruddy things also disappeared." He shook himself as if he still couldn't quite believe it. "I called, but no one answered. I walked around the stables and tried various other entrances but none would let me in so then I returned to where I saw you last and kept calling."

"James, you didn't, shouldn't have tried to get in." Berd's voice was high. If he but knew how close he had come to being lost forever.

He kicked at the grass. "Poppycock! You were inside." Then his shoulders drooped. "I'm sorry, Berd. You did try to tell me, and I refused to believe you. But what happened? How did you escape?"

Charles leaned back against the building. "I'm afraid you'll have to ask your sister that question."

"Berd?" James lifted his head, eyes bright.

"The world's *first* programmer. My program got stuck in an endless loop. She got us out of that loop and out of the Engine."

At Charles's admission, a grin spread over her face.

Berd knew she had done it. But men had somehow always downplayed her achievements, if they had ever admitted to them in the first place. But to have Charles undeniably confess to James that she had done it, well!

"Oh!" she squealed, her delight increasing when he nodded, his iridescent blue eyes shining with pride.

And if Charles hadn't caught hold of her hand, she would have danced about the grass.

She had done it!

She was the world's first programmer!

Men would have to start taking women seriously. The computer was now a viable tool. Lives could be saved. But importantly…

Grandmother, I have vindicated you!

If Charles didn't know before, he should know now that this was all the wedding present—

Wedding? No, he hadn't even asked her. Well, at least not in this world.

If James wasn't here, she would have thrown her arms around Charles. As if James knew what was in her mind, he annoyingly, played the part of the big brother to perfection. He studied her blushing face for a long moment then turned to Charles, sizing him up. "I'm glad you think so, Fotheringay, especially if you become a member of our family as you weren't marching to that drummer a while ago."

She gasped. She had wanted to have the issue of her marriage settled, but James had thrown her to Charles like a bone to a dog. Berd wanted to hide her head in shame.

But if there was any shame in being engaged to her, Charles didn't appear to think so. He pressed her hand to his lips as if this was the opportunity he had craved for so long, and James had presented it to him on a silver salver. "I intend to rectify this immediately, if you will allow me? And can I offer my humble apologies for—"

James waved the apology away. "A drink at your club and we'll call it quits. And yes. I'll get my lawyers to call on yours tomorrow." He narrowed his eyes meaningfully at her. "Unless you have any objections?"

Her future been settled. Just like that! But when James asked grumpily, "So how did you escape?" for the umpteenth time and both she and Charles answered, "The Engine," together, like a newly-wedded couple, she knew it was too late to argue. She blushed furiously and delightedly as the blood rushed up her throat.

"I was going to give you a sporting chance to get away, Fotheringay. Five minutes should do the trick, but I can see it's too late." James chuckled, as he gazed proudly at her. "But how did you escape?" he insisted plaintively once more.

She had to put him out of his misery. Even though she had been through it all, it was hard to put into words what had happened. Gine coming alive, fighting to stay alive and then sacrificing it all…

"I reprogrammed the computer."

It was the truth. The simple truth. And for now it would suffice.

"Do you want all the technical detail?" She arched one brow innocently.

James winced and held his palm up.

In the end, Gine had become human. That was why Gine had never wanted her to turn into an engine. He wanted her to fall freely in love with him.

Many people fell in love with their inventions: the late Charles Babbage with his Difference Engine and then later with his Analytical Engine. No doubt, the late Mr Fotheringay and Charles were also in their own way in love with their engine.

And then she, too, fell in love. She, who knew so

little of romantic love, that she could not recognise it at first.

She had insisted she would love Charles when he turned totally into an engine. And that she would willingly remain in the engine with him. In the end, it was the essence of Charles she had fallen in love with, whatever vessel it was in. But if that was the case then…

"We have to go back," she said quietly.

"Are you sure?" Charles's voice was soft, but there was no anger in it, only acceptance. As if he had come to the same conclusion she had. Gine would always be a part of them and if they lost him, they lost a vital part of themselves.

She bit her lip then answered. "Yes. I love you, but I love him, too. Does that upset you?"

Charles's grin only broadened. 'No' he mouthed then laughed.

Beside them, James was frowning, perturbed. "Berd…"

"It's all right, James. We'll be back. We just need to get something very important."

"Come, if you wish," Charles offered with a mischievous twinkle in his eye.

"What? I mean, what's inside?" James coughed into his fist before staring at the green grass.

Furniture and statuary still dotted the grounds in concentric circles, the inner circle the emptiest. It wasn't safe, but who wanted to live in a safe world.

Charles cocked his head knowingly at her, as he replied, "A world where every woman is a princess."

"Or every man a prince." Berd reached out and squeezed his hand.

They walked towards the stable. As if the Engine knew they were returning, the light softened, glistening gold like the morning sun on a newborn winter's day. It was welcoming them back.

Berd's heart beat faster, but it was with joy and anticipation. She was becoming whole once more.

As Charles reached out to grasp the door, it swung open.

A man staggered out. He was dressed in workman's clothes. Four men followed. They took little notice of the three wide-eyed young people, and instead acted as if they were in a dream. They staggered off.

James gaped, dumbfounded. "Who, who…"

"The workmen I sent to retrieve the Engine," muttered Charles. Then he chuckled. "Gine's obviously found a new power source."

"How?" she asked, but Charles could only shrug delightedly.

One couldn't be upset with ingenuity.

And after a while Berd laughed with him, too. So the workmen were back. If she ever wanted further proof of Gine's heart, this was it.

Only James knotted his brows, even more deeply puzzled.

Charles gripped James's shoulder. "You ask what is in the stable. In truth, I am proud to say, a part of me."

"Interesting bag of tricks you got in there." James rubbed his hands.

Tricks? Berd wanted to smile. No, not now, not today. Two thousand years ago tricks may have fooled the ancients in Alexandria, but in the end, it was simply due to a man named Heron who was gifted in mechanics. He had used his inventions as tricks in the temples to pretend to the worshippers that their gods were real, but what Charles had invented was real.

The computer.

Had poor Heron realised the implication of his steam ball and invented the steam engine, perhaps the industrial revolution would have occurred then. And perhaps, the computer would also have been invented. She was glad it had not. This was her chance, her moment. And not just for her.

But for all womankind.

And especially, you, too, Grandmother.

"No, no tricks," said Berd. She gripped Charles's hand tightly in her right and James's in her left. Her heart beat faster as she answered, "What's inside is the future. Our future."

The End

Author's Notes

1. In the Bible, Abraham attempted to sacrifice his son Isaac, but the sacrifice was halted by God.

2. *Frankenstein* by Mary Shelley (1797-1851) was published in 1818 (Lackington, Hughes, Harding, Mavor & Jones).

3. Nobility was never placed in asylums. For the purpose of the novel, and in order to dramatize Berd's situation, artistic licence was taken.

4. *The Strange Case of Dr Jekyll and Mr Hyde* by Robert Louis Stevenson (1850-1894) was published in 1886 (Longmans, Green & Co.) so theoretically Berd should not have been aware of the novel.

5. *Alice's Adventures in Wonderland* by Lewis Carroll (1832-1898) was published in 1865 (MacMillan)

Dear Reader

I FIRST LEARNT of Ada Lovelace – the world's first programmer – while at university where I was studying to be a programmer. I thought her fortunate to have worked with Charles Babbage, the inventor of the Difference and the Analytical Engines. It wasn't until years later while researching for THE GHOST ENGINE that I delved more deeply into her history and discovered the horrible truth.

Ada never tested any of her programs because the Difference Engine was never built, but most disconcerting was not only the fact she died young, but the way she perished. The irony was that the computer as we know it, a device so ubiquitous and necessary today, the invention that is forever linked to her name, didn't exist until around the time of the Second World War (depending on which text you read).

In January 2015, I was privileged to visit the Computer History Museum in California and see the 'Difference Engine No 2' in operation. According to popular theory, Charles Babbage had never been able to build either full-scale model of the Difference or the Analytical Engines due to the primitive metal-working techniques of his day.

However, this theory was challenged when in 1979, Australian Allan Bromley took a year's sabbatical leave from the University of Sydney to study Babbage's papers (see Wikipedia – Allan Bromley). Notebooks containing six thousand pages, along with three hundred machine drawings and several hundred notations from Babbage, convinced Bromley that even with the technology in Babbage's day, it was possible to build the 'Difference Engine No 2'.

Thanks to Bromley and the Science Museum in London, Babbage's 'Difference Engine No 2' was finally built between 1989 and 1991, just in time for the 200th anniversary of Babbage's birth set to be celebrated in 2001.

Nathan Myhrvold commissioned the construction of a second 'Difference Engine No 2' and it was this engine I saw in the Computer History Museum.

Today, computers are essential in our lives. Yet during the 19th century, computers were only a dream. Had that dream become reality, it may have saved countless lives, including Ada's.

Ada died young. Of cancer. In great agony, she had asked her physician if she could request a second opinion. The physician's answer was as I stated in THE GHOST ENGINE, that should Ada do so, he would wash his hands of her. Somehow Ada's pain made its way into my novel, and Berd, my plucky protagonist was by her own means going to rectify this terrible injustice.

Although Ada never tested her programs she never gave up. Despite ill health, she persisted, corresponding with Charles Babbage. Her thoughts preserved in her diary allow us insight into her brilliance. Imagine what she would have done had the Difference Engine or even the Analytical Engine been invented. Or she had lived longer…

Thank you for reading THE GHOST ENGINE.

I hope you have been as moved as I have by the courage of Ada.

Theresa Fuller
November 2017

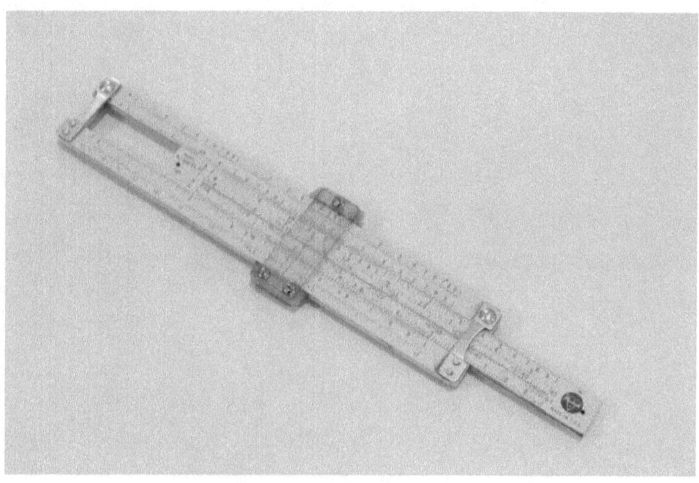

One of the late Allan Bromley's slide rules.
From author's private collection.